To Nancy

2102: PRETENSE, THE PLAY

William E. Jefferson

Delighted to send
a copy of 2102, to You!

William J

Port Estillyen
PRODUCTIONS

Published by Port Estillyen Productions
www.estillyen.com
https://facebook.com/estillyen

Cover images: draganab/iStock.com
and LittlePerfectStock/Shutterstock.com
Cover design: Abby Isaacson

ISBN: 978-1-7364967-5-6 (softcover)
ISBN: 978-1-7364967-7-0 (ebook)

Printed in the United States of America

5 4 3 2 1

CONTENTS

Preface   v

Masks   xiii

Chapter One: I Dreamed of May   1

Chapter Two: A Most Mysterious Quartet   15

Chapter Three: Theatre Pretense, A.D. 2102   29

Chapter Four: Theatre Pretense, the Trial Continues   45

Chapter Five: Verdict Reached   57

Chapter Six: The Garden Grove   69

Chapter Seven: Preparations for War   81

Chapter Eight: High Court, Theatre Pretense   93

Chapter Nine: Spy Play I: Misery of Job, Say-So I AM   117

Chapter Ten: Camp Seaside, Post Play   147

Chapter Eleven: Spy Play III   177

Chapter Twelve: Seaside Departure   211

Chapter Thirteen: Poet's Lodge, Nine Months Later   225

Poetry and Literature Index   239

About the Author   242

PREFACE

The inspiration for writing *2102: Pretense, the Play* did not occur as a spark in time; rather, the story grew in my patterns of thinking long before the subject of AI pressed upon my mind. By the way, *Pretense,* in the title of *2102,* serves as a code word for AI.

The quest of understanding media, how mediums and messages evolve and change attitudes and behaviors has propelled me on a decade-long pursuit of probing and pondering the interactive environment for media and the study of media ecology. The subject of media ecology claims a prominent place in how I view the world, perceive culture, and express my ideas—particularly when I consider the way media ecology is intertwined with religion and matters of faith, including my own.

Neil Postman underscored the immense importance of media ecology, defining it as a field of study that "looks into the matter of how media of communication affect human perception, understanding, feeling, and value . . . how our interaction with media facilitates or impedes our chances of survival."[1] Thus, as a media ecologist, Postman saw human survival inexorably linked to the role media environments play in propelling human behavior.

On September 13, 2023, some of the brightest and most powerful tech elites in the world gathered in Washington, DC, for a closed-door hearing with the United States Senate to discuss the reality, ramifications, and possibilities of AI. Space X and Tesla CEO Elon

1 Neil Postman, "What Is Media Ecology?" https://www.media-ecology.org/What-Is-Media-Ecology#:~:text=What%20Is%20Media%20Ecology%3F%20.

Musk; Meta's Mark Zuckerberg; Sundar Pichai, CEO of Google; and Open AI CEO Sam Altman were among those in attendance.

Senate Majority Leader Chuck Schumer opened the gathering with brief remarks and posed a question: "Is government needed to play a role in regulating AI?" Speaking to reporters later, Schumer said, "Every single person raised their hands even though they had diverse views."[2]

Earlier in 2023, the Future of Life Institute issued an open letter calling for a "pause" in the development of large-scale AI systems, citing fears over the "profound risks to society and humanity." In response, tens of thousands of researchers and technologists have signed the letter, which warns that "AI labs [are] currently locked in an out-of-control race to develop and deploy ever more powerful digital minds that no one—not even their creators—can understand, predict, or reliably control."[3]

Artificial intelligence injects into the world a force of change that can be likened to the development of the nuclear bomb. Once it was dropped, the world exploded with change, and the arms race began. Gut-wrenching calculations of unimaginable destruction arrested the attention of the world, the powerless and the powerful alike.

As AI advances with inexorable speed, predictions of promise and peril mount. Whether boom or doom—or both, wonderment and angst swirl about the futuristic prospects of advanced AI.

All in all, it's a perfect time for *2102: Pretense, the Play*, which catapults present-day concerns about AI into a stunning future-cast of tomorrow. In today's culture, dominated more and more by distant, discarnate, mediated connectivity, *2102* takes readers on a journey where wily artificial intelligence challenges the wisdom of the ages.

---

2 Mary Clare Jalonick and Matt O'Brien, "Tech Industry Leaders Endorse Regulating Artificial Intelligence at Rare Summit In Washington," AP News, September 13, 2023, https://apnews.com/article/schumer-artificial-intelligence-elon-musk-senate-efcfb1067d68ad2f595db7e92167943c.
3 "Pause Giant AI Experiments: An Open Letter," Future of Life Institute, March 23, 2023, https://futureoflife.org/open-letter/pause-giant-ai-experiments/.

A Story Made . . .

How other novelists work, I haven't a clue. In approaching the story of *2102*, I penned no outline, which is a consistent hallmark for all my novels. Rather, a ruminating concept of diverse intersecting thoughts began to grow. After all, "It takes time to tell a story. Nothing of value can be communicated instantaneously."[4]

The story begins with a mental casting call for characters suited to tell the story. Once characters appear I do not dictate their lines. Rather, I listen as they begin to speak. They enter the drama not unlike players cast in a play. Thus, my role is from the wings as I watch and listen, capturing their lines as they live and move. They are truly as alive as any living being that has ever lived.

Readers of *2102* will meet a cast of spirited characters, including the heroine of the novel, Margin, likely an alias for Joan of Arc. Yet no one really knows for sure if, in fact, the heroine is she. Regardless, Margin appears mystically incarnate, as do her companions Shadow and Lesser Light, the latter being the moon.

The trio sets its sights on 2102, eager to explore the plight of the future's marginalized peoples, those on the outskirts of society, who move about in the shadows and quarters of lesser light. Before setting out on their journey, though, the trio realizes that what transpires during this journey must be captured and dutifully recorded.

They need a scribe—but not just any scribe. They settle on a poet named Quillingsworth, who lives in Poet's Lodge, a current-day setting as enchanting as dreams can make. The trio believes that a poet will add a certain lilt to the record, insuring its longevity. They envision something more than a rudimentary accounting of dates, names, and places. Poet Quillingsworth owns a parrot named Loreto, a blue-headed, feathery companion and confidant that he brings along on the mysterious, futuristic journey.

---

4 John Navone, SJ, and Fr. Thomas Cooper, *Tellers of the Word* (New York: Le Jacq Publishing, 1981), 62.

Thus, the quartet and parrot Loreto travel swift and far to the land of Onglander and alight in the wings of Theatre Pretense. It's a rather strange theater where suspected criminals are tried on stage and forced to act. In so doing, most all suspects don a mask, in keeping with Onglander norms and audience expectations.

Refusing not to act and stepping out on stage not wearing a mask, but instead choosing to rely on raw transparency to prevail proves to be a perilous act of defiance—one assuring conviction, no matter how brave the performance.

Onglander in 2102 brims with societal surprises and norms unique to its highly advanced technological environment, made possible by the full embrace of artificial intelligence.

The Moral of the Story

The cover of the April 8, 1966, edition of *TIME* posed a most provocative question in asking, "Is God Dead?" The stark red text set on a black background marked the first time in the magazine's history that a text-only cover appeared with no accompanying images. A chorus of criticism followed the release of that now infamous edition.

Addressing that very question, Marshall McLuhan maintained that the notion arises when one moves from perception (*sensing, grasping*) to conception. To the engaged perceiver, the question does not apply.[5]

Today, in light of the explosive use of AI, many might ask, "Is wisdom dead?" to which this novelist replies, "Not yet, but AI may be digging wisdom's grave." Even now, AI fabricates and presents a brave new world of art, musical scores, scripts for dramas, plays, sermons, and stories never told.

Life stories, though, are not the stories of AI. Rather, "life stories

---

5 Marshall McLuhan, *The Medium and the Light: Reflections on Religion* (Eugene, OR: Wipf and Stock Publishers, 2010), 81.

are the product of our worldview, our sense of life, our basic faith, our way of grasping the complexity of life."[6]

So what's one to say, whether poet, priest, or anyone? It's a good time to recall Marshall McLuhan's famous aphorism "the medium is the message" which rings as true today as it did in 1964, when the media theorist set forth the idea in *Understanding Media: The Extensions of Man*.[7]

The difference today, though, and significantly so, is that AI extends into the mediums of messages made a pervasive element beyond the extensions of man, communicating the incommunicable in spite of man.

As AI mediates messages across numerous mediums and platforms, the artificially produced content enters not a void or vacuum but a virtual blizzard of mediated, communicative action. Further, "based on an ecological understanding of the universe . . . no phenomenon is entirely isolated, all phenomena are connected to something outside of themselves [and] interact with something other than themselves."[8] In this case of AI, therefore, the interaction takes place between the artificial and the real, between a non-human source and humans, creating highly unpredictable long-range consequences.

Viewing media as an ecological environment offers valuable insights as to what's at stake, such as when a new medium like the internet arises in the public domain and gives rise to social media. At the outset of the social media revolution, few thought through the deleterious effects that might occur, brought to light in the 2020 Netflix documentary, *The Social Dilemma*.

The Center for Humane Technology took the dilemma a step further in producing *AI Dilemma*. Tristan Harris and Aza Raskin, co-founders of Center, offer a stunning message of incalculable value. They are two voices worth hearing, if listeners are willing to listen.

---

6 Navone and Cooper, 51.

7 Marshall McLuhan, *Understanding Media: The Extensions of Man* (Corte Madera, CA: Gingko Press, 2003).

8 Lance Strate, *Media Ecology: An Approach to Understanding the Human Condition* (New York: Peter Lang Publishing, Inc., 2017), 147.

With the release of artificial intelligence into the world, we do not have the same world plus AI; we have a new, rapidly changing, hyper sort of world. Into the ubiquitous dilemma of social media, the AI dilemma rushes like a supercharged star from somewhere unknown.

"We now know," Douglas Rushkoff claims, "beyond any doubt, that we are dumber when we are using smartphones and social media. We understand and retrain less information, comprehend with less depth, and make decisions more impulsively than we do otherwise."[9]

In *The Shallows: What the Internet Is Doing to Our Brains,* Nicholas Carr argues the same idea in different words. Carr cites the case of a university pathologist who claimed his thinking had taken on a "staccato" quality due to quickly scanning material online. The pathologist confessed, "I can't read *War and Peace* anymore."[10]

Rushkoff further states that "This untethered mental state . . . makes us less capable of distinguishing the real from the fake, the compassionate from the cruel, and even the human from the nonhuman. . . . The real threat is that we'll lose our humanity to the value system we embed in our robots, and that they in turn impose on us."[11]

Artificial intelligence has unleashed the ultimate virus into the global streams of mediated connectivity. It spins and preempts ancient trails of wisdom as a kind of digital Frankenstein's monster with a highly advanced mind.

The Hebrew Scriptures record the story of how the Prophet Jeremiah struggled over the course of many trying years with listeners unwilling to listen. His message:

> *Stand at the crossroads and look;*
> *ask for the ancient paths,*
> *ask where the good way is, and walk in it,*
> *and you will find rest for your souls. (Jeremiah 6:16)*

9 Douglas Rushkoff, *Team Human* (New York: W. W. Norton & Company, 2019), 67.
10 Nicholas Carr, *The Shallows: What the Internet Is Doing to Our Brains* (New York: W. W. Norton & Company, 2014), 7.
11 Rushkoff, 67, 122.

There's a catch implicit for those standing in today's crossroads of time and technology. Whom does one ask about the ancient paths, about the good way?

With certitude, multitudes will ask AI. The handwriting is on the wall, but whose writing is it? Startlingly, artificial intelligence possesses not only the power to shape and direct us, but also the power to shape and direct itself. This underscores the difference between AI and all technologies launched heretofore.

2102: Pretense, the Play raises vitally important questions for the here and now and tomorrow looming. In my 2021 novel, *Presence, the Play*, I argued, through its characters, for the superiority of incarnate presence, experienced in community, communion, and interpersonal communication as opposed to distant, discarnate, meditated connectivity. "To be present to himself, man must find the presence of another, or others."[12]

Which is why media ecologist Paul Soukup contends: "Watching a ritual, no matter how familiar that ritual, differs from living in the ritual."[13]

Human beings require three-dimensional environments in which to thrive. In the words of Rushkoff, we humans "rely on the organic world to maintain our pro-social attitudes and behaviors."[14] Thus, digital, discarnate connectivity cannot offer the vital "self-reinforcing feedback loops of rapport: the mirror neurons and oxytocin that reward us for socializing."[15]

Therefore, one might ask—and I, for one, am asking, "Are we to be a people of Presence or Pretense, of Being or Being Not?" Among the lines of *2102*, readers will discover poet Quillingsworth's reply to the

---

12 Walter J. Ong, SJ, *The Presence of the Word* (New Haven, CT: Yale University Press, 1967), 295.
13 Paul A. Soukup, SJ, *A Media Ecology of Theology: Communicating Faith throughout the Christian Tradition* (Waco, TX: Baylor University Press, 2022).
14 Rushkoff, 72.
15 Rushkoff, 73.

question when he passionately states, "Give me flaws, wobbling notes, imperfections, and loose ends. Thus, I know I'm human."

Come what may, welcome to the world of *2102: Pretense, the Play*.

Postscript

I deliberately chose not to insert references or endnotes into the text, believing that to do so would jar the reader's flow and imagination once engaged in the storyline. Thus, instead of an afterword to the novel, a brief section titled "Poetry and Literature Index" has been added that identifies various poems and stanzas by the page number(s) on which they appear. The Poetry and Literature Index includes all the complete poems in the novel that the characters recite, as well various stanzas by William Shakespeare, Edgar Allan Poe, and others.

There are exceptions, though, to the rule. When a character injects poetic lines into a classic stanza of poetry, thereby adding to the stanza, or poem, these instances are not referenced in Poetry and Literature Index. While this method of indexing may prove tedious to some readers, I felt it was the best way for letting the story of *2102* come alive, without jarring interruptions.

—William Jefferson

MASKS

In a theater of this world at mid-day the stage is set and many actors enter, playing parts, wearing masks retelling some old story, narrating events. One becomes a philosopher, though he is not a philosopher. Another becomes a king, though he is not a king.

Another becomes a physician wearing the garments of a physician. Another becomes a slave, though he is free; another a teacher, though he does not even know his letters.

They appear something other than what they are. . . . The appearance of the mask deceives. . . . As long as the audience remains in their seats, the masks are valid; but when evening overtakes them, and the play is ended, and everyone goes out, the masks are cast aside. He who is a king inside the theater is found to be a coppersmith outside. The masks are removed, the deceit departs, the truth is revealed.

So it is also in life and its end. The present world is a theater, the conditions of men are roles: wealth and poverty, ruler and ruled. . . . When this day is cast aside, and that terrible night comes, or rather day, night indeed for sinners, but day for the righteous, when the play is ended, when the masks are removed . . . then the truly rich and the truly poor are revealed.

When the play ends, one of us looking out an upper window sees the man who is a philosopher inside the theater but a coppersmith outside, and says, "Hey! Wasn't this man a philosopher inside? Outside I see that he is a coppersmith. Wasn't this other man a king inside? Outside I see that he is some humble person. Wasn't that man rich inside? Outside I see that he is poor."

The same thing happens, when this life ends.

—ST. JOHN CHRYSOSTOM (347–407), DOCTOR OF THE CHURCH

CHAPTER ONE
I Dreamed of May

On a cold winter's night, with January's final day slipping away, I dreamed of May. Therein, along a gentle brook I strolled, amidst daffodils stretching tall, in the warmth and light of day.

In the meadow low, I spotted three figures standing still, conversing. When the speaking paused, the trio set out up the narrow path that leads to Poet's Lodge. Known by few, Poet's Lodge has hosted playwrights and poets for more than two centuries, and advances ever closer to a third.

The trio I did not recognize, yet I feared them not as enemies. Loreto, too, spotted the curious three, as she paced to and fro on her perch, a simple wooden rod hung from the ceiling by thin, woven copper chains. The perch is positioned at window height, giving Loreto an unobstructed view of the meadow and beyond.

Loreto, with her feathers green and head blue, simply appeared one day resting atop the lodge gate. Curious, I cautiously stepped along the stone walk with intent of drawing near. Slowly I advanced, step by step, pausing after each step.

My shadow reached the gate ahead of me, at which point the parrot flapped her wings just enough to lift and alight upon my left shoulder.

As still as well water I stood. Then slowly, pensively, I turned my head, till the bird and I stared at one another, eye to eye.

Shallowly I breathed, not wanting to breathe at all. Not a word I uttered, nothing but a closed-lip hum, barely audible. Stock-still I stood, listening to the sound of the familiar breeze flowing through the branches of the nearby hackberry tree. At that point, the parrot on my shoulder parroted, "Loreto, Loreto, Lor, nothing more."

Seven and a half years have passed since that morning introduction at the front gate. In a matter of days after that first encounter, I discovered that Loreto could mock much more than her name. Beneath the feathers blue upon her head, Loreto has amassed a rich repertoire of words, phrases, and poetry.

Loreto clearly saw and heard the trio moving up the stone walk. Spying me from her swinging perch, Loreto's eyes signaled alert at the sound of knuckles rapping upon my front door.

In bed I lay, unwell, hoping to recover. Upon hearing the treble knocks and then no more, my trusted aide Matilda dutifully responded and opened the door. Amazed she was to see a trio dressed in garments of olden days, as if headed to a play.

The curious three spoke politely, smiled, and nodded with gestures kind. Slightly hesitant yet at ease, Matilda welcomed the trio inside. As through the arched doorway they passed, I heard the intermingled steps and wondered.

As they followed Matilda into the library, I imagined the visitors glancing at the hefty hand-hewn ceiling beams and the welcome fire aglow in the fireplace, faced with golden brown granite imported from the Alps.

Loreto looked at me, and I at her, as we heard shuffling and the sound of softly spoken words. The shortest of the trio, I learned, spoke, saying they had come to visit me. Just then, the hall clock began its strike, registering the ninth hour had come and gone. Matilda wavered somewhat, knowing as she did that for weeks I had passed in and out of time, in feverish dreams, with reality and nightmares intertwined.

As the muffled conversation pursued, Loreto, with her look of parrot intrigue, cocked her head and listened. Soon, footsteps resumed, and next the swirling brown porcelain knob of my chamber door began to slowly turn. Matilda nudged the door just enough to poke her head through. Her eyes expressed words not spoken, assuming I had overheard the trio's request.

I offered a consenting nod, knowing Philip stood ready in the kitchen across the hall. Matilda withdrew her head and gently shut the door. An interlude ensued, filled with faint words and whispers. When the whispering ceased, I could hear the sound of throats clearing beyond the door.

With heightened expectation, Loreto and I watched as once again the porcelain knob made its counterclockwise turn. Next, Matilda appeared, advanced but a step or two, spun around, and held the door wide open, allowing the trio to enter.

In successive squeaks, the floor's wooden planks sounded out their advance. The slightest figure of the three drew nearest me on my right side, while the pair stood at the foot of my brass bed with hands at their sides.

"Greetings, Mr. Quillingsworth. We're deeply honored to meet you, and do forgive us for this impromptu visit. Be assured that goodwill and mission undergird our presence here today."

Unprepared to say what one might customarily say to guests, I spoke not. Thus, speechless, I glanced at Loreto, as together we scrutinized the peculiar-looking trio.

"Mr. Quillingsworth, let me introduce us. My name is Margin, and to my right, first Shadow, and next, Lesser Light. To you, we politely bow. We've traveled quite far. We're from the world of drama, curtain, stage, and play. We've come to enlighten you regarding future days and offer a bit of perspective regarding living scenes once played but playing still."

"What, uh, I say, you say enlighten me, plays playing still, having played . . . deary me, I say."

My mind lurched to and fro, trying to grasp the meaning of Margin's message. Effort, though, did not bring forth understanding.

I caught broken lines that echoed about then melded into phrases and quips offered by Shadow and Lesser Light. My attention spiked at the mention of AI and algorithms, which took the lead in a sentence or two and trailed at the rear in others. I also heard the word *bullet* at least once, but maybe more.

Time ticked; I heard the tock, along with Loreto's coo, parroting that of a dove, though, very softly cooed. Time advanced, words flowed, till Margin said, "Mr. Quillingsworth, I believe it's time we go; I hope we've not been an imposition."

Picking up the phrase "time to go," I rallied to say, "A bullet, I heard you say. If you might, Margin, sir, please say again what you said. I mean what I thought I heard."

"Yes, Mr. Quillingsworth, as I said, we know a bullet found you and has lodged deep inside. In the heat of battle, your regiment fell back, as ordered, though you did not join them. Instead, you moved up the hill, hoping to quell the intensity of the charge. As for the other details, you may recall them more precisely in a matter of days, or days thereafter.

"Do remember, though, what the surgeons told you, after they conferred and agreed that they mustn't probe or disturb the bullet, given its precarious position pressing upon your heart. 'Give it time,' they said. 'Let time and tissue encase the bullet, which we dare not try to extract.'"

In my state, the words emanated as from an echo chamber. And then I faded, as if melting in the lines. A few more bits and words I heard, then nothing more.

At that, I allowed my head to rest deep on the pillow with open eyes; I could hear the beating of my heart. Then, quiet. My chamber door closed, and the latch sprang into its strike. Next, muffled words mumbled in sync with the mood. Followed by the sound of shuffling feet departing, the front door bolting, the squeak of rusty hinges signaling that the pilgrims three had passed through the gate.

When the night had passed, my eyes blinked their awakening blinks, and I awoke. Immediately, I mused, "It must have been a dream, the trio's visit, hearing voices not present and words not spoken. Though reality kept biting; there was no fantasy regarding pain. The pain I felt; the crimson wraps I touched. In visions, the reaper's scythe I saw, slicing daffodils poised to fall.

Broth I sipped; bits of food I labored to chew. Matilda and Philip cycled through, keeping watch while pretending not to watch. January gave way to February, and February to March, while April ground on and on.

Month after month, Matilda flipped the wall calendar anew, but I saw little cheer in the blocks of weeks and days. Cheer remained outside, on the rosy cheeks of passersby carrying fishing rods, reels, and bats of play.

Pain persisted, neither lessening nor abating. My ribs I'd gladly remove to reach the torment lodged deep inside my chest. The calendar on the wall across the room spoke in silence, somberly, of days passing. Inevitably, my end of days crept ever near. Death and life competed for my heart. Beat, pause, beat, beat, pause, sigh, and so did I.

Death, I knew, had the upper hand, and on the wall April had but a day to give before May would be brought up to hide its thirty days away. Struggling to rise, by elbows first, I wincingly rose, somehow managing to sit, and then, in a wobbly manner, stand. I told myself what I needed to hear, uttering not a word of fear.

Hanging on the hall tree across the room, my slender maple cane riveted my attention. As if the only possession left, the cane became a must to me. I knew that I must touch it, reach it, if I dared to venture outdoors once more. With no watchers watching, I slowly dragged my feet—a foot, then another, stop, still, step.

I grew ever closer to the hall tree and April, pinned by its side. As if a journey long, at last I arrived and freed the cane from the wrought-iron hook on which it hung. I snatched it up along with my long-sleeved, well-worn, cotton-twill shirt.

Loreto watched my movements better than any watcher might. She knew where I was headed: the side door down the hall. As I neared the hall, I heard Loreto's wings flutter, and in an instant, she landed upon my left shoulder, her most familiar perch. Thus the two of us found the side door, and I wobbled on outside. I looked up to the sky; the moon had begun to rise.

Amazingly, the fresh air strengthened me, like a spirit might. Along the front fence, we made our way, and then down along the narrow path that disappears in the meadow green. The spot I wished to find, I found, and with the press of weight, I managed to spike my cane into the soil, creating a round top perch for Loreto.

Thus, in the meadow, I lay down to die, with freshly cut daffodils by my side. Lying upon the cool soil, with Loreto perched above, peacefully I breathed, thanking God for life and all the breaths I had ever breathed, while the scent of daffodils wafted over me.

With my thoughts and worries at rest, I surrendered all—my body, my will—to peace. Utterly exhausted, thin and pale, not unlike my slender cane, into a deep sleep I fell. Hours passed, pressing onto hours more, and then came a most natural surprise. Wet, cool dew on the back of my hands I felt, as coaxing me to once again open my eyes.

I did, and lying there upon the ground, I heard a most pleasant sound, a melody. With strain of neck, I raised my head, thinking the music flowed from a heavenly sphere, perhaps performed outside heaven's gate.

Loreto twisted around on her curved perch, looked up, and parroted, *Curkwe, twe, tor wee.* Dazed, still half-numb in slumber, I wondered what it was Loreto saw. Her unblinking, wide eyes focused on a sight above and beyond me. I thought, *Perhaps she caught sight of melodic angels watching over me . . .*

Using my right elbow as a prop, I managed to raise my head, then my torso somewhat.

Accordingly, I rotated my head and shoulders, thinking I, too, could take in the amazing sight of harmonious angels from above.

I was stunned, disbelieving, denying what my eyes beheld. I shut my eyes, allowing thoughts and contradictions to rumble through my mind. Yet the soothing sound of music, most delightful, came to me in waves, and with eyes still closed, I thought, *What, why, such a pleasant way to die.*

Whereupon, through my nostrils, I drew in a long draw of the meadow air, savoring the scent of daffodils. Then, simultaneously exhaling and opening my eyes, once more I saw again what I thought I saw before. The costumed trio that paid a visit to Poet's Lodge in January sat among the branches of the tall hackberry tree, playing spirited music . . . on the first day of May.

How could it be? It couldn't be. Yet, my eyes beheld them; my ears heard the melody consisting of violin, viola, and cello. Turning quickly to Loreto, I whispered, "Stay near; don't fly." Next, I placed my right arm behind me, with my open palm pressing on the ground. In this way, I managed to sit up and look straight ahead.

I wanted to pretend that what I saw I did not see. I wanted to call out to the apparition and watch the scene disappear. To my knees I rose, and eventually to my feet. Looking up, I cried, "Hello there, trio, say, hey, in my hallucinogenic state, you appear quite real, but this is my resting place, where I've come to die.

"Further, I know my eyes behold a scene that is but a dream, so, as I turn away, I say, 'Thank you, kind dream, for appearing.'"

"Wait, Quill, it's me, Margin. We'll come down to tell you all that can be told. Shadow, Lesser Light, halt your bows; still the strings. We must attend to Mr. Quillingsworth and consider how best to accomplish what we've come to do.

"Shadow, on the count of one, you're the first to leap. On two, I'll go next, while simultaneously shouting 'Three!', the cue for Lesser Light. Leap, with your instruments in hand, bows and all. Now one,

Shadow, leap; good, excellent. Now two, I go, and three, I call. Lesser Light, leap!

"See, Mr. Quillingsworth, we've come to you, not for sake of harm or alarm, but for a very important purpose."

"Dear me, I mean, what's happening? Margin, I remember you. Please tell me, what's the meaning of you three being here? It can only be you, but who are you, and where did you come from? You are actors in a play, right? You cannot be phantoms—you are carnate beings; that's plain to see.

"My senses swirl with pulsing confusion. I thought angels from on high had come to call. Wait; perhaps you are angels, wearing costumes. Why, though, would angels dress like you're from Shakespeare's day?

"I'm not making any sense. You have to be something; you know what I mean. You're a trio, that's all I know. Music, those instruments, they're real; you played such a delightful tune.

"Tell me truthfully: Am I dead? Did I die upon the ground with Loreto looking on? She's not dead, I see. But what do I see—how do I see? With mortal eyes, no, not this; in a sphere most mystical I stand. Dear me, what's happened to me?

"Say, something. Tell me, do tell me; do I no longer stand in the company of men? Margin, you're the thinnest of the three; with your cropped hair, you appear not to be a man. Oh, no, what did I say?

"I simply mean, Shadow and Lesser Light, you appear more robust, not so slight. I mean, oh no. Thoughts stay put, hunker down in my mind. I dare not utter you as words. Oh, but I just did—or did I? I'm now insane . . . I'm going to scream . . .

"Loreto, quick, atop my head! Let's run, but how can I run? I can barely walk. What's happening?"

"Mr. Quillingsworth," said Margin, "you make me chuckle, but I'll not laugh, certainly not at you. We've chosen you."

"What, chosen me? Thoughts, shut up, stay dormant. Oh no,

I've done it again. Outed an utterance—no, who can rescue me from myself? Please tell me that I'm me, that I abide in Poet's Lodge.

"I'm not well; I've been very ill—at death's door I laid down my head. I came to this meadow to die. I'm simply a writer; I mean, I must be caught in a maddening drama I didn't write. If there's a purgatory, I don't want to go. Is there? I don't know. I mean, I shouldn't have to go, should I? I need to get ahold of myself . . . oh, dear, what's become of me?"

"Peace, my friend," said Margin. "Indeed, you're a writer and a storyteller. With us, you'll journey far, and as a result, you'll have an unbelievable story to tell. And that's precisely why you must tell it, so that it may be believed. Your story, your account, will prove most enlightening to those of your day, and for decades to come.

"I suggest you pull up a chair where none exists, but just the same, take a seat on the chair behind you. The wooden arms and leather will suit your form. And next to your chair, there's a ladder-back chair for Loreto. She can perch on the upper rail. She's important and can't be left out. You have never seen chairs such as these, Mr. Quillingsworth. Please have a seat.

"By the way, do you mind if I simply call you Quill?"

"Yes, I mean, sit, you say. I guess I can; I will, I mean, but tell me truly, am I caught up in a sphere nearer to heaven than earth, or somewhere betwixt and between?"

"Betwixt, you might call it so," said Margin, "and soon you shall be. Though we prefer to say the realm of rolling phases, of time and places."

"I don't know you, Margin, but why does my mind-sparked imagination conjure up images of battlefields and Joan of Arc brandishing her flowing banner as she galloped headlong through the lines?"

"I see," said Margin. "The record of which you speak I know quite well—how Joan assailed the English army, saying in the name of God, 'Begone, or I will make you go.'"

"Margin, spare me, tell me, regard me, though I shiver now before you. You're not she, are you, that saintly hero from days of old? If so, you needn't tell me. Forgive me, it's wrong of me to ask."

"From this line of thought we must depart," said Margin. "Our mission awaits its destiny."

"Oh, weary not my soul, which wearies so," said Quillingsworth. "Insane it is, if you might be she, marching still, having swapped sword and sheath for violin and bow. Cover my eyes with plaster; my ears fill with cotton wool. A mission, you say—must it be of cannons firing, screaming, wounds and death?"

"Be obliged to listen well, Quill, and by so doing, you will acquire a greater sense of theatrical essence, which, in turn, will allow your quill to merrily pen dramas new. Know, too, Quill, that divine choreography backs the ancient drama's greatest scenes.

"Indeed, some are chosen for parts they play, even anointed to do so. Yet others, many and most, play their parts unknowingly. They move about in time and space, weaving in and out of dramas as mere extras, though in divine thought, extras do not exist.

"Let us each take a seat; our chairs, Shadow, thank you. There, so welcome these relics appear, preserved with centuries of patina wax. Now, much better, we can speak horizontally, allowing us to observe the manifold expressions on our faces. Anyway, we stopped where, before we took our seats?"

"No, I can't; I cannot talk. Pardon me, I'm going to flee your presence. A happening such as this does not happen. Loreto, flutter up to my shoulder, and we'll walk up the lane to the reality we left behind."

"Quill, my dear fellow," Margin said, "I thought you wished to die. Nice spot you've chosen, fragrant daffodils, in a meadow green, so full of life. Don't you see, Quill, the impetus that drew you, your wish to die, was actually a longing to be surrounded by life and the living. So right your impetus and the longing, both.

"Sorry, your face reads perplexed, poised as a puzzle. Perplexed you needn't be, Quill; we shall lead you, but not astray. Please, your seat, you need a cup of tea, as do we.

"Shadow, kindly lay aside your viola, and hand Quill a cup of tea, steaming, I'm sure, he would prefer."

"Certainly," Shadow said. "Here, just for you, Mr. Quillingsworth, a piping hot cup of tea, brewed with leaves picked 1,020 years ago. The aroma wafts from a rather different time and place."

"I tremor; I shake," said Quillingsworth. "Sip tea? I can't; I won't. Oh God, where art thou?"

"No, Quill, sip you must; you will," said Margin. "You need to heal, and this particular tea possesses properties to help you do so, but you must believe it will."

"My knocking knees," said Quillingsworth. "Sip, you say. Sip, not knowing if I'm already dead or still alive. Away from here, I must flee, though where? There must be a way to a place beyond."

"Oh, believe me, Quill, there's a place," said Margin; "a very different sort of place we shall soon explore. Sip on, Quill, don't waver, as did leprous Naaman. At first, he recoiled, refusing to dip in the River Jordan, yet in time, he did so and dipped seven times. So sip on, Quill. Pay attention and ready your quill for drama.

"As I said, some characters know the parts they play, while others play unknowingly. Isn't that correct, Quill?"

"About knowing and unknowing, why speak of such to me? A writer I am—a poet, too. Now, though, I have nothing to say, nothing to write, no lines to pen; I had come to the end."

"Your words I hear, Quill, but we must sketch out the parameters of our mission in harmony with the message that rustled among the leaves in the hackberry tree. Where we're headed, you must take more than an open mind, for you shall witness wondrous acts played out in time.

"In the midst of the sea's raging storms, you must grasp a vision of the shore, the place you long to be. Dreams to behold you must be willing to behold. Picture the scenes rolling across the mind, forming, foaming, like waves splashing among cliffs, unseen. Grasp what it means to possess a theatrical frame of mind. Such a mind will free you from rudiment, from conformity.

"Theatrical essence, Quill, arises from the aura of presence, of shared experience in space and time. The stage and stalls, lighting and backdrop, music and sound, yes, as well as the coughs, smiles, and applause, among tears and cheers, that's what theatrical presence affords."

"Margin, sir, such lines—your lines—they carry the ability to transport heart and mind. I know lines; I'm a man of many lines."

"Lines, Quill, you say. You've touched on the crux of your mission— that is, if you are willing embark and behold."

"I mean this mission you've yet to reveal. What if I go, I mean, Loreto and me, and then abandon it along the way?"

"Sip on, Quill, I've more to say; unless you would rather we fade away?

"No, not that. Let me stand. You must realize in the throes of death I lay until I heard the rustle of the hackberry tree leaves and that lovely melody. Wait, I am standing, but without pain. What's happened? The bulge pressing upon my rib from within . . . it's gone.

"What did you do with it? No, I mean, that's not what I mean. I mean, what's happened?"

"Shall I pour you another cup of tea?" said Shadow. "No need to answer; I will anyway. Not all questions need answers; rest your mind a while."

"It's the tea," said Quill. "I no longer feel ill; I'm well. What's wrong with me? No, not that—I mean pain and suffering had become such a part of me that I didn't know me without it.

"Oh, I don't know what I'm saying. It's just that I feel abnormally well. Even that sounds strange. I assure you, though, I can write most imaginatively and hopefully again proficiently, if I can only decipher what's happening. Dear, oh dear, perhaps I should sit back down?"

"As Shadow suggested," said Margin, "sip, and rest your mind. There is so much more that must be said before our journey begins."

"Well, I'll try, but I feel lost, like I've lost my mind. I haven't, have I?"

"Quill," said Margin, "let us move our chairs a little closer together so we can converse in a conversational tone, without voices raised. A move I'm sure Loreto would appreciate."

Churkwe, Loreto, Lor, Loreto parroted.

"That's a spry bird, I must say," said Margin. "Now closer, like that—good, that will do.

"Now, let us carry on!"

CHAPTER TWO
A Most Mysterious Quartet

"Lesser Light," said Margin, "for Quill's benefit, I'm compelled to offer a few comments concerning your role among the stars, if I might?"

"As you please," said Lesser Light.

"Okay then, Quill, listen in. Stars set out on their way of light eons ago so billions of eyes could watch the wonder of the celestial canopy. Yet, among the innumerable stars, the moon alone, with its courses and phases, bestows the abiding presence of the heavenly display.

"A shooting star streaks and falls, never to rise again, but not so the moon. At end of the night, the moon fades and steals away, softly, assuredly, only to rise and meet the night of another day. Your crescents and faces call forth wonder and awe; life without you would be a lesser form of life for all.

"So, before we embark on our journey, privilege us, Lesser Light, with a word of wisdom in a manner you alone can give."

"Wait," said Quillingsworth. "I have something to say, something I want you to know. Yes, I'm a poet and a writer, but among you, I feel but a frog. No, please, hear me, I implore you. Compared to you three, I am nothing more than a croaker of crocks.

"Sorry, Margin, I am to bare my soul so openly. It's just that I want you to know what a limited man I am in the midst of such a mysterious trio. So, please, I beg you, choose again, as you've chosen me. Your mission is of great import, I know, so choose someone worthy of being numbered amongst a trio that becomes a quartet.

"So, now you know why Loreto I must steal away, why we must go. Consider, as I have, the opportunity you have to choose another, thereby redeeming the fault of choosing me. Please, I plead. Blame me for everything; credit me with nothing."

"Hmm," said Shadow.

"So, it seems we have chosen aright," said Lesser Light.

"And what about you, Loreto?" said Margin.

"Shadow, be, not, can be, less light, be cast," parroted Loreto.

"Hmm," said Margin.

"Oh, 'tis time for tea," said Shadow.

"All around," said Margin.

"Here we go, so brewed," said Shadow, "offered in bone china cups. You first, Quill, then to Margin and Lesser Light, and for you, Loreto, a few pumpkin seeds soaked in the same."

"Thank you, and now poured, we ponder," said Margin. "Let us sip, not once, but twice, and then again. Nice, indeed, Shadow."

"Ahem, yes," said Quillingsworth, "indeed, and thank you for Loreto's seeds. I desperately needed to speak those lines, so you would know.

"I do hope I've not offended you. If we go, I suppose you'll take back my healing—you know, the miracle, the uncommon act. A miracle, I guess, has to be uncommon . . . to be called a miracle, I mean. Dear me, I'm afraid I'm validating my croaking stupidity."

"Quill," said Margin, "in all that you said, I heard not a single croak. Quite the contrary, I distantly heard you say, 'I desperately needed to speak.' So, a line from the one often called the Bard, I quote, 'How green you are and fresh in this old world.'

"Now, Quill, listen, hear me, that line does not define you. You are greater than you know you are, and soon your true mettle will be tested. We here, the trio, and you, making of us a quartet, we will advance into a future where AI and algorithms do more than roam.

"But, before we set out on that course, we shall hear from Lesser

Light, after which I shall introduce our mission by revisiting the stage. Got that, Quill?"

"Well, I mean, it seems you do not accept my resignation?"

"Correct, and please stay seated as Shadow pours you another cup of tea, brewed of leaves that one day you may acquire, but not today.

"Lesser Light, will you please . . ."

"Well, we sit conversing, not rehearsing; what we do not know, we can't rehearse. The known, we know, can be barbarous, as history has shown, but the unknown, we do not fear.

"My purpose, throughout the vast sweep of time, has not been that of uttering the explicit. Rather, I have a way of softening moods and tones, pressed hard by day. I do so, by virtue of my composition and without force of effort.

"Thus, in medium and message I am one. Which I could state another way by saying, 'I am the medium of my message.' Differently, you must consider me. I am not a text to read. Rather, I inspire by phases and glow.

"Waxing and waning, I aid the seasons' change. Tides I rise and give them fall. Consider driftwood, seaweed, and shells, all sorts—how they wash ashore, until by reverse of tug and tides, away they go. Birds, too, depend on me, to migrate and navigate their way along.

"My course of time extends to days twenty-nine, plus a half. My phases number eight, which I now articulate. Behold the new moon, and in time, the waxing crescent and quarter first, not forgetting my waxing gibbous, full moon, waning gibbous, third quarter, and waning crescent.

"Charming depictions, though not mine, of one in the heavens that simply abides. The world, I know, needs to affix such tags, but not so the birds and tides that willingly sync patterns, and pulled by forces, move.

"Waxing and waning, I routinely appear and disappear, sweeping predictably among the shining stars. Glowing down upon good and evil, my course never changes. One could say I've seen it all; including the mysterious plight of King Nebuchadnezzar, driven into the fields, where, drenched with dew, he ate grass like an ox.

"His hair grew and grew, like eagles' feathers, and his nails like birds' claws. The extraordinary happening occurred, of course, under the glow of Lesser Light. Howbeit, when seven years had come and gone, Nebuchadnezzar lifted his eyes to the heavens, and his right mind returned. Thus, an ardent protagonist of the Almighty he became.

"Now, here we abide, we four, ready to set out on a dramatic mission, in a future play where human advancement seems to have advanced too far. Regarding mission particulars, that's not for me to say. As Lesser Light, I'm but a glowing companion among stars."

"Luminous, indeed," said Margin. "Anything more you wish to add, Lesser Light?"

"Not at this particular phase," said Lesser Light.

"Oh, dear me, I'm doomed," said Quillingsworth. "A mortal such as me should not be in the company of the likes of you, whatever you may be, carnate of moon, shadows, and of one who, heretofore, may well have led troops on medieval battlefield of war.

"I mean, I said 'likes of you,' but there's no such thing as the likes of you. You don't need the aid of a poet with a parrot. I plead with you: Can't you see my fragility, my incompetency? I'm expendable; there's no earthly reason to choose me as scribe.

"See it, as I do, now that you've begun to set the stage. I'm improperly cast; cut me and let me not hinder your inspired choreography. I see the seriousness of your mission etched in your eyes and upon your faces. In your mind, envision me gone, as if I had never been.

"Say, 'Scat, let us see your back.' So see, I see me, stepping backstage, moving hurriedly to the stage door, pushing its brass rail opener, then slipping outside. There I stroll, making my way along the graffiti walls and littered paper cups, buffeted about by the wind. That is where I belong. See me; I'm gone.

"I implore you, cast me out, before the curtain is drawn and an audience of watching eyes peers down upon the stage. Consider our time today but a tryout, in which you came to see what a novice actor I truly am. To be, I wish not to be.

"Please know, however, my pen cannot express in any length of line the loss I feel in regressing."

"Dear Quill," said Margin. "This instant, halt your train of thought; today I will wash away the tracks. The train stops here, where the four of us have gathered. Absorb my words; let them seep deep within, into the recesses of your heart and mind. You have not chosen us; we have chosen you. You have a part to play, and with heaven's help, you shall play your part and play it well.

"Novice is a bad idea of a word, semantically harmful, saying more than it should. A novice you're not; you project something more. Your mind is not misfit; it's simply misaligned. Now, calm yourself, right yourself. We claim you; shush the tumult in your mind.

"Shadow, steaming quail broth and a lamb kabob for our reluctant comrade who seeks to walk away."

"Here you go, Mr. Quillingsworth," said Shadow. "I trust the fare suits your liking and quells your appetite. And for Loreto, I have a complement of mixed seeds and crusty bits.

"I, thanks, uh, yes, but instantly," said Quillingsworth. "How do you make that happen? You reach into to a copper cupboard where none existed and take out a steaming cup of quail broth. Then, from an arched stone oven, again that just appeared, you pull out roasted lamb on skewer? Oh my, oh me, what have I seen?"

"Oh well," said Shadow.

"Now then," said Margin, "I must offer a few comments concerning technology. All of which are very apropos to our mission. Then I will transition to reflections on the theatre, mostly allegorically, to set the stage for our journey to 2102. In that context, technology and theatrical performance are utterly inseparable.

"So, Quill, sip, listen, learn what you've yet to learn, and in so doing, you will come to know more than you thought you knew. You have it in you . . . in random bits that need to be woven into a tapestry. So, let us weave.

"Quill, as our chosen scribe, your role will be to keep a detailed record of everything that you witness during our time in 2102. Think of olden days and scribes, though you will be a scribe of future days. You must be as fastidious as an annotating librarian or an accountant. We seek, however, not a dry account, fact upon fact, date and time. Important, but that will not do.

"As a poet, your record must be endowed with buoyancy. Consequently, your record must be written in story form, but not as fiction. After all, you will provide a record that will prove immensely valuable, not only for tomorrow but for generations that will consider tomorrow a past, far removed.

"We know a great deal about you, Quill. We've read everything you've ever written, and, of particular interest to our mission is your work with respect to media ecology, or as we prefer to say, ecology of media. Your understanding in that regard is noteworthy and presses to the heart of our expedition.

"With respect to technology, we watched—from a portal nearer to heaven than here—as the net paved the way for technocratic elites and entrepreneurs to produce an unending array of gadgets to be held. In short order, the objects to be held became objects to behold, tech idols buzzing in the palm.

"Eyes that once looked up to the heavens in awe and wonder looked down transfixed. The tiny screens of streaming faces and far-off places held the masses captive with addictive pretense void of actual human presence.

"A veil was draped over humanity's face, as profiteers laced the wires and threads with tantalizing gadgetry, trickery, and pretense connectivity. Human presence became passé, along with human worth, community, and communion. What mattered most were pixeled screens, not human engagement occurring in shared spaces.

"Do you follow, Quill? Are you with me? I can see a change upon your face, a sense of resonation. Am I wrong?"

"Yes, I'm amazed, stunned, stupefied—you speak of matters that represent my life's work. I didn't know you knew."

"We do, Quill, we do! I've much more to say, so shall I carry on?"

"Well, yes, sure, but who am I to say? I'm humbled flat that you would ask. I feel grossly overvalued."

"Okay, continuing," said Margin. "We've observed how the technological masters of your era are masters of human disconnect, steering lonely souls into lonely silos, where they exchange likes and dislikes with like-same souls channeled via filter bubbles.

"At the same time, the platforms of the tech masters track human activity along mediated trials of search and preference, making them a virtual hunting ground for bots and ravenous corporate mobs. Spurred on by profit and power, the obsessed gurus of doom unleash algorithms and AI to track down and profile every net-connected person on the planet. Every swipe of screen or message typed finds its way into AI minds, waiting to be minded.

"I can tell your attention is rapt. So, just a few more lines, and then I'll shift the subject to theatre, the stage, which is a wonderful antidote to platforms, filter bubbles, and bots. Where our mission leads, you will need an equal embrace of matters tech and theatrical essence.

"So, my final comment on tech merely reinforces the crucial point already stated: that digital connectivity via social media platforms delivers a world of pretense addicting pretenders to pretend. The glaring difference between carnate human presence and discarnate mediated connectivity can be likened to a portrait and face, a photo and place. Simulations of the real have a tendency to fade a peel.

"That's all!"

"Margin, again stunning," said Quill. "Would it be okay for me to comment, since I've spent a great deal of time researching the interplay of technology and human behavior?"

"Quill, we're here for you," said Margin. "Say what you wish."

"Well, it's just that I've studied how person-to-person interaction triggers mirror neurons in the brain that fire a flow of oxytocin, a hormone responsible for attachment and trust, as well as triggering empathy. It's the same in group interaction. I think I've got that right.

"Anyway, this naturally occurring attribute is a reward for face-to-face interaction, an attribute that is virtually lost in digital, discarnate connectivity."

"I do believe we've read those very lines, Quill," said Margin.

"Well, be that as it may, let's move on to a few thoughts regarding theatre. Admittedly, the thoughts came to me while sitting among the fluttering leaves of your hackberry tree. And I believe you will see why I'm known as Margin. Thus, the thoughts.

"Characters, we know, play the parts they play, with words and lines scripted, not a syllable more. Characters thus scripted must vie for space among nouns, pronouns, and participles, which are prone to dangle. Yet into the lines they fall, characters one and all.

"No, not I, amidst the lines, I do not reside. I'm free of set, of line restraint. From the wings I speak. Margin I am, the repository of ink, lead, and all manner of squiggly swirls, often red. I provide space for prophets, poets, and potentates, and all sorts that annotate texts with words of admiration and antonyms of adulation.

"Without me, how might critique spill forth on the edges of a tale once read? Regard margins as art, Quill, whether thou art or not. In the margins, lines and dashes appear like graffiti. One scratch parses, another reveals the etcher's probes, while still others pose merits.

"Think it through, Quill, margins provide present-tense critique on pages penned at other times and other places. Contorted words and letters, often unreadable, emerge at the top and bottom of pages and all along the gutters. One might compare them to chirping crickets of the night, seekings that slowly dissipate the sun's warmth of day.

"Amidst the pontifications penned, nuggets of gold do appear. A case in point from the seventeenth century, a line penned with a sharpened quill atop a parchment page, number 47. Though faint, the line remains readable in certain light. Thus, the line:

"If I could choose words said of me, after me, I'd prefer hearing, 'He believed his words to be more important than he.'

"In time, Quill, that line could be said of you. With a quick pronoun shift from he to she, I would willingly own that line, but of course, it isn't mine.

"Words crisp and new etched on pages old form a bond of present-tense collaboration. A literary lift, one might say, by pencils and pens prancing about from page to page. They possess the power to inject life into texts bound in time.

"All the while, margins perform a stealthy role. Every dot, dash, and slash imprints codes mapping readers' minds in words conjoined by tenses. Tenses tell much in their reveal of time. Consider I'm joined by a single adjoining word, such as I'm here! Or now, I'm gone! Four letters each, here and gone, that can punch above their weight in support of I'm.

"Lines written for the stage lift off the page, taking flight in the aura of the presence only theatre affords. Humor me, though of humor I do not speak. I recall a place; I see it now. Its image embrace, for soon you shall need it, of a comparative, very dissimilar place.

"Theatre Portesque—I see it now, on that enchanting Estillyen isle beyond the Storied Sea. The gold-gilded chandeliers aglow, the balconies ascending, filling full. Above the stalls, boxed seats jut, their crimson curtains drawn, revealing intricate plaster ceilings plastered long ago.

"Sometime ago, on the opening night of *Presence, the Play*, I was in attendance. From the upper balcony I watched the struggle of good and evil, of darkness and light. At one point, Lucifer himself leaped from the orchestra pit and roamed up the aisles.

"Quill, see the scenes unseen, not simply with the naked eye but in thy mind, backlit by imagination. Do you see Theatre Portesque, even now? How row upon row of red velvet seats curve along in perfect symmetry? The rows draw wide-eyed ticket bearers, buzzing, pointing, looking for their numbered place.

"All seats bear the wear of patrons passing, pressing, rubbing thin the painted steel undersides. Arms of rich mahogany bear inlaid ivory discs, revealing seat numbers of faded blue. Theatrical space, giving each theatregoer a sense of theatrical presence personalized in numbers of faded blue.

"At Portesque, seated patrons wait expectantly, facing a soaring gold stage curtain of unimaginable weight. Its folds of rounded gold stretch wing-to-wing, instilling even more wonder in the waiting, watching eyes. Along the curtain's bottom runs a fringe of royal blue, made of silk rope imported from afar and triple-stitched with golden thread.

"By day, in the dim crimson aura of recessed lighting, the tassels blue softly flutter, as hours pass. Morning morphing to noon, then after, and on into the night. On and on, the tassels faintly sway; that is, until the sound of clicking switches signal stage door drafts and send the tassels into a lively rhythmic dance.

"Beneath the fringe, a warm glow extends to the front of the stage, spreading out over patinated planks, while the scents of olden days mix with present-day perfume, evoking a living sense of theatrical essence.

"Listen, Quill, do you hear the strain of ropes stretching, propelling wooden wheels clanking? Clank by clank, they clank, undraping the drama. Look, from the wings, a figure from out of the fog appears. Tall, thin, the figure steps into the beam, his appearance stretching taller still.

"No, wait, he's disappeared even quicker than he appeared. Before the microphone he stood, then, in a blink, vanished without a word.

Gone, a shock, a hologram, appearing and then not; oh, the trickery of projected pixels. Another AI-hatched discarnate skit.

"Now, regarding our part, Quill, we do not claim or wish for visibility. By our very nature, we reckon to enhance, not be. Shadow bequeaths moving shadows in the play, while, from the riggings high, Lesser Light glows down upon the stage, and I, Margin, reside in the wings.

"Understand, Quill, while here with you presently, we carry on everywhere. Indeed, all the world's a play of ever-changing casts acting in the shadows, wings, and glow of lesser lights. Even now, Lesser Light moves glowingly among the stars, as velvet, imagination, and wonder for sower, reaper, and artist alike who lay aside the tasks of day and dream into the night.

"As Margin, I've gathered many a line deposited by those in the shadows, wings, and glow of lesser light. I carry then, I know them, and I speak them, giving voice to the marginalized. In our mission, I shall recite a number of them, like 'Tomorrow's battle marches today.'

"Accordingly, do you wish to march and follow or make your way back up the winding lane to Poet's Lodge? If so, you will walk alone; we shall not follow you. Before you, carnate we appear, and indeed we are, as your eyes see, your ears hear, and your hands have touched.

"We sit together, freely conversing, breathing air mutually. At another place and time, we've not appeared, but to you, here, now, we have. What you see and hear, you shall record—that's your primary assignment in the mission looming. In doing so, you will allow countless others to see and hear what you will witness.

"Thus, in our quest of making known the lesser known, we must neither be assuaged nor delayed in doing so. We must get on with doing, albeit after a bit more tea. So, therefore, we have to know at this hour if you wish to be left alone, or do you desire to join us, unswervingly, in our mission?

"If yes and so, a play, a tragedy, currently playing in 2102, we will swiftly attend. Know that 'caveats increase, as battle nears.'"

"In response, what shall I utter?" said Quillingsworth.

"An utterance, I would have thought," said Margin, "an outing of words from within."

"What can I possibly say after what I've heard and seen? Discarnate spirits you're not; you breathe, you talk, you play instruments making melody."

"Yes," said Shadow, "we do delight in making music, Mr. Quillingsworth. Particularly in a lovely meadow green with daffodils dancing to the music played."

"Oh, my soul, dear me, my heart races, my voice quivers. I've sipped tea brewed of leaves picked 1,020 years ago. Betwixt and between I surely am."

"Notable, but not surprising, Quill," said Margin. "Shall we leave you, then, as we found you?"

"Wait, no, messengers, ambassadors of some sort, you've come to me, at first not suspecting you to be other than what you appear to be. But far more you are, I now know."

"'Nerves steady hold,'" said Margin. "'Tis good advice to anyone stepping foot on the field of battle."

"Please hear me, you three of marvel and wonder. If I were a king in days of old, today I would rend my garments in shreds and pile a heap of ashes on my head.

"If I go, give me a blindfold of sizeable holes."

"Mr. Quillingsworth," said Shadow. "Does that line belong to you, or to someone else?"

"I can't say; I've simply said it."

"Quill," said Margin. "In our way of being, we probe, we see, we discern one's temperament and faith, two nouns as inseparable as the wings of a bird. Faith without temperament can roar waves, while temperament and faith combined can still them. The two nouns must bind together, deftly intertwined.

"In this regard, we compliment you on the manner in which

you have intertwined these virtues. Into battle, you would willingly go to fight wars for country and king, while casting all your cares aside. Indeed, you went to enlist when the rifled bullet found you. Cannoneers nearby heard your call; they watched you fall.

"Even so, the crux of the mission hinges. What we've come to be, you see—not what you cannot see. As a trio, we come to form a quartet. Think it through: A trio, yes, but not a quill among us, save you. We need you, Quill. You complete us.

"So, shall we sip together as a quartet, with you inside, not out? A calling has reached you. Imagine the lines appearing as you write about life in the shadows, margins, and lesser lights.

"So, Quill, are you in? Shall we sip as a quartet?"

"Dear me, in this swirling context, I know not whether I'm alive or dead. Yet within these mysterious, converging elements, I detect a current more of life than death. I know, too, the fact of not knowing what I might have known will hound me, whispering, 'You could have known.' That scenario I mustn't favor.

"So, I choose to go, but where are we going?"

"Well said, indeed," said Margin. "Next step: You have to prepare Loreto; she, too, will prove herself worthy. I'm not sure how, but she surely will. Also collect in a single pouch the belongings you wish to take, particularly your quills.

"Shadow, if you please, kindly put on another pot of tea, your special blend; let it steep to perfection. Then, under the limbs and leaves of the hackberry tree, we shall slowly sip. After which we will be on our way to a play, now playing in A.D. 2102."

"Thrilling," said Shadow.

"Yes, then, after tea," said Lesser Light, "we shall lay aside our teacups and raise glasses in a toast to Quill and the year 2102. Shadow, what sort of beverage do you recommend?

"In anticipation, let us raise our cups and say, 'Cheers!'"

"Cheers it shall be," said Margin. "Cheers!"

CHAPTER THREE
Theatre Pretense, A.D. 2102

"What's happened? What's going on?" asked Quillingsworth. "I feel outside myself, distant from reality. Hear that, listen—sounds like spiked heels stepping, voices mumbling amidst the sound of pages flipping, it seems. I don't know.

"Loreto, don't say a mock; keep your beak shut. I sense danger in the air everywhere."

"Lenore; Lenore; evermore," parroted Loreto.

"Shush," said Quillingsworth, "quiet. Here's a pumpkin seed. I'm crunching it between my teeth so no one will hear. Eerie is this futuristic place, not a nesting place for sure.

"That door, over there, the stage door, did we pass through it?"

"We did," said Margin.

"A tap, tapping, at my chamber door," parroted Loreto.

"Loreto, no," said Quillingsworth, "don't take off on every word you hear. We need our bearings. I have sea legs; I'm all wobbly."

"Truth, tell me, Margin. The tea, the brew, must have brought us here, but where are we? This edifice, this vaulting place, with all manner of lights, glowing marbles embedded in the walls, like thousands of eyes.

"Blue, green, red—horizontally they run, then halt and start again. Those, too, on either side of stage, vertical stacks the height of masts, with red, pulsing, transparent globes the size of bowling bowls. Oh, dear God, I know this can't be heaven, but how do know that?

"I'm whispering . . . why?"

"Quill," said Margin. "We stand in the wings of Theatre Pretense in the year 2102. Act unfazed, normal, not abnormal; we must blend in as if we're part of an act soon appearing. Here, real trials are staged; that's the rage. The curious come to watch normal people on trial thrown into plays. Verdicts depend upon the defendant's ability to act. Thus, a startling act of pretense can award innocence, while a sober defense is assuredly a guilty plea."

"Wings," said Quillingsworth, "give me wings to fly to another place, like that Portesque about which you spoke. Plays that portray life, not trials unto death. Go, we must leave."

"Stay we shall," said Lesser Light.

Like tides, we've washed in," said Quillingsworth. "Now we wash out. I've seen enough; my spine tingles of chills."

"Such a twist," said Shadow, "subjects wearing masks, tragedy plays with a tragic catch."

"Margin, unfazed, not dazed, you say," said Quillingsworth. "Total haze I'm in. I feel all asway, like the gravity is too light, not right. I know what will happen, we'll be put on trial, like anyone, everyone. Extricate me, 'O, call back yesterday, bid time return.'

"Time, what time is it? Here, does time exist, or is that, too, a pretense? Do we know, do we know anything? I wish I knew!"

"Time itself doesn't know what time it is," said Margin. "At this juncture, let's leave that juncture aside."

"So we have no alternative but carry on, is that it?" said Quillingsworth.

"Correct," said Shadow; "let's settle. Chairs from the passage, I'll snatch. Quietly now, here's one, and a second, three, now four. We'll sit, as a foreign quartet, speaking words naturally, no pretense."

"Just the same," said Margin, "within this atmosphere of pretense, we must blend in. There's a significant difference between pretending and pretending to pretend—neither we'll do. Foreign, we are. So don't act; be. All the while, we'll watch as sentries."

"I do adore these primitive wooden chairs," said Shadow. "I love the sound they make when plunked down upon the stage. A little later on, we'll make time for tea."

"Make time," said Margin; "so curious the notion. Don't speak, quiet; we must take in the play now on stage."

STAGE:

His Honor: Mr. Crackler, I appeal to you with words sharp in a tone befitting of directness. Prepare for punishment without your preparedness.

Mr. Crackler: Your Honor, sir, as I've said, and keep saying, my image isn't me. What my image did I would not have done. My image extracted my words, my way of speaking, and fashioned a message, concocted, contorted. My words are mine, but not these. My personality has been stolen.

And the research paper, causing such mediated buzz and anxiety—I did not write it. The paper has nothing to do with me, even though it is attributed to me, to my name. Oh dear, does no one hear me? In truth, I speak with conscience clear.

THE WINGS:

"I can't believe what I'm seeing, hearing," said Quillingsworth.

"Rather awakening," said Lesser Light.

STAGE:

His Honor: Let the court enlighten you, Mr. Crackler. By your very nature, as a carnite, you peer through a hazy pane, don't you see? Discarts do not. You shall remain always a carnite, and your avalite image is but a knockoff of you. Like a chestnut from a chestnut tree, you see.

Now, I call up the notable prosecutor twins, so cloned, to argue the case. Their surname tends to be hard to pronounce. How does it go? Tivevitlakcrombe, I do believe? Close enough, I trust; anyway, you are known to us by your given names, not the Tivevitlakcrombes. Just the same, the court appreciates your willingness to be addressed by your given names.

So, Edict and Verdict, please proceed. Center stage is yours; move into the light.

Edict: Thank you, Your Honor. I'll skip formalities and pleasantries, Mr. Crackler. Carnites like you possess limited capacity to consciously abstract the full-orbed scope and substance of an object because you've tagged the object with a name. You look for an object named, for what it's named, without seeing beyond the name.

This, of course, is a severe semantic liability for you, and historically for your kind. With the wonders of AI, algorithms, and crystal-telesthesia, we instantaneously see beyond names. The names, to us, are nothing more than back stories of carnite groping.

Mr. Crackler, let me illustrate with a like comparison that may be familiar to you. "When I was a child, I spoke like a child, I thought like a child, I reasoned like a child; when I became a man, I gave up childish ways."

Pithy little bit, nice little bit, that string of words drawn from your ancient myth. Succinctly, the saying says you remain childish, a child.

His Honor: Pause, hear, now listen: I speak. No applause from the audience. My mallet speaks for me. Do not ignore my hammers. No clapping, no feet tapping; you are warned.

Further, no growling or jesting; you must follow the proceeding with decent decorum. Your seat is numbered; therefore, you are numbered. Rumpus attendees will receive a jolting surge that will surely arrest your rambunctious ways.

Again, no clapping or tapping feet allowed.

THE WINGS:

A tap, tap, tapping, my chamber door, parroted Loreto.

"Stop, Loreto, stop, stop; close your beak," said Quillingsworth. "They will pluck your feathers; friends they're not."

STAGE:

Edict: Well, I shall continue with the matter of conscious abstraction. For example, carnites see a pencil as a pencil and nothing more. In contrast, discarts instantaneously probe the object, fixated not on the name but by species of wood, grade of lead, layers of lacquer, and so on. Do you see my point, Mr. Crackler?

Some time ago—actually seventeen years and four months ago—you allowed your mind and all of its pathways to be transferred to your image. Skipping over your name, your image drew upon all the intricate connections of your DNA.

Genomes, those delightful little kernels of cell structure in you that you wistfully signed away. Your signature I have here on this piece of paper, which you can plainly see. Shall I elicit the elements of ink and paper? No, I shall not.

Unlocking the inner mysteries of genomes proved to be the Holy Grail for scientists that opened the path to reshaping evolution. Further, Mr. Crackler, every dream you ever dreamed, subconsciously or otherwise, your image enkindled and stored in Crystal Ionosphere Collectatory, commonly known as the CIC.

Hear me, Mr. Crackler: You are responsible. You cannot undo what your avalite has done, for you are the source of its form, its function. Does the moon say to its glow, "I disown you"?

THE WINGS:

"Disowning my glow—clever, that Edict," said Lesser Light.

STAGE:
Edict: No, of course not, and likewise neither can you.

So, you see, you stand guilty of being you. Let me repeat that. You, Mr. Crackler, stand guilty of being you. Did I make myself clear?

Mr. Crackler: Your Honor, no—please let me speak. Hear me.

His Honor: Okay, go ahead, Mr. Crackler; let us hear more of your confutation.

Mr. Crackler: It's just, I mean unjust, it is—this line of reasoning set out by Prosecutor Edict. The course laid out leapfrogs far beyond me in accusing me. Am I to blame for the entire race?

If so, the sin of everyone could be exploited by his or her avalite. Avalites have no conscience; they were excluded, marginalized by discart decree, along with us, as you know.

THE WINGS:
"Most interesting," said Margin.

STAGE:
Mr. Crackler: We live along the borders, in the shadows of discart Citadoms. Cut off from Citadom privileges services, we move about the ruins, in servitude, in the shadows. The tools we've made have turned against us, can't you see? My kind and I have been marginalized, not only by discarts, but in many cases like mine, by our own avalite image. We've been relegated to the weakest link in the evolutionary chain.

It's not supposed to be like this. Creation dawned, and millennia after millennia, we carnites progressed, adapting, creating the future, day by day. Then, somehow, I don't know, Dataism emerged, like a golden calf demonstrating dazzling probes propelled by AI.

Like stampeding wildebeests, people of every tongue and race raced to adapt the wonders of Dataism, not realizing that we, too, would one day be adapted. How can I be blamed for what technological wizards have done?

So naive it now seems—carnite presence rendered rudimentary, raw, and primal. Such a grievous, inauspicious fall that sprang from the platforms and devices of our own making.

In the current state of affairs, even our thinking is considered insipid. We are often called moldites rather than carnites. Our mode of thinking no longer matters; all flows through AI refinement, anyway.

No mulling and pondering the essence of matters great. Instead, presto, the answer, the solution to the problem presented, not unlike the reels of a slot machine.

Long since, the tipping point has tipped. AI has engendered literature, prose, art, musical scores, and more, while carnite-inspired creativity has been rendered second fiddle. Once music had soul, but no more.

THE WINGS:

"When war rises, men fall," said Margin. "What we witness here is a different sort of war."

STAGE:

Edict: History, bear thy witness; let us retell.

Mr. Crackler, decades ago, in the dusty past, discarts began to probe carnite behavior and in particular, behavior associated with mass infatuation over gadgets made.

True, all of it. As gadgets new appeared your laid-to-rest relatives raced headlong to obtain them. Displayed in high-street windows, often on easels lit from above, the objects appeared to carnites as objects from the gods. Those window displays set off an irresistible surge of want.

Wild carnites trampled kiosks and smashed windows to procure the objects of their affection. Blaring alarms did little to curb the passions stoked.

Concurrently, algorithmic AI collective probes uncovered patterns regarding carnite behavior. One insightful probe sourced another saying from the ancient saga. Examples of carnite gush abound in those ancient scrolls.

I now call on the Court Recorder. Kindly step forward and read the text that presses to the heart of the matter at hand.

Court Recorder: Yes, Prosecutor.

THE WINGS:

"Hear that?" said Quillingsworth. "Those are the heels I heard. The Court Recorder wears stiletto heels. Listen to the heels spike as she approaches the bench.

"Look at my hands shake; I'm going to crack, in delirium scream."

"Steady your nerves," said Margin. "Clutch Shadow's viola; feel its strings. Absorb reality."

"Remember," said Shadow, "a foreign musical quartet in the wings poses little threat to anyone."

"Insane," said Quillingsworth, "all of it. We can't be here, present, in a future that's yet to be. Shadow's tea has brewed us up into some sort of dreamland. How did I get in this time-warped mission?

"In the meadow green, I did lie under my stately hackberry tree. I gazed upon sunlight filtering through the branches, leaves all aflutter clinging by their supple stems.

"Now, we are here, not there. In the wings of Theatre Pretense we sit, listening to the sound of stiletto heels spiking across the stage.

"Look out across that audience of watching eyes—how transfixed they stare. Their faces appear as molded wax, not flesh. Barely a flinch do I see."

"Silence, Quill," said Margin. "Fear weakens fingers of writer and swordsman alike."

STAGE:

Court Recorder: Shall, I stand here, Your Honor, or on the riser? I should say, though, if I might, that since I'm the Court Recorder, nothing will be transcribed during my reading.

His Honor: Yes, I see. Point taken; go along from whence you came. We need extras, fill-ins. Sergeant Tidbright, who's on hand?

Sergeant Tidbright: Your Honor, the key to the staging room went missing this very morning. So stand-ins that might have stood in as extras were sent home. Home they went, gone; I saw them go.

Your Honor: What! That's insane. So, what do you propose?

Sergeant Tidbright: Well, ordinarily, I'm not one to propose.

His Honor: What? Do something; we need a solution. We can't stop in the middle of a trial play.

Sergeant Tidbright: Well, an hour or so ago, when I could no longer wait for a cup of tea, I dashed to the canteen. Dashed, I say, not wishing to appear a slacker in your midst, of course.

No earphones or music, nothing like that; attentively I dashed, just wanting a cup of tea.

I don't normally take tea breaks. My sense of responsibility is my priority.

The badge I wear demands of me not a thread of pretense stitched upon the sleeve. I move about circumspectly with eyes trained to scout about.

His Honor: Sergeant Tidbright, my toleration of you has limits. Some there are that have no mind to lose.

Sergeant Tidbright: Interesting, but I'm not sure what it means. Anyway, in the midst of my dashing, I did spot some fellows in the wings. Perhaps they're stand-ins that stuck around and didn't go.

His Honor: Whatever the case, badge brain, locate them; call 'em out here. How do you expect us to proceed without a recorder recording?
Lost key . . . curious . . .

Sergeant Tidbright: Indeed, sir. Two minutes, no more. I saw them in the East Wing seated on prop chairs I've never seen.

THE WINGS:
"We're doomed," said Quill. "I'm going to die in the future when the past will always lag behind. I can't take it. Tidbright's steps . . . I hear them; he's coming. Tidbright with the reaper's scythe has come to call."
"Say, fellows there, Sergeant Tidbright here. Good, you're still here. I spotted you earlier. The play needs a few extras to read a bit of old text in rapid time. Okay, are you up for it?"
"Certainly," said Margin. "We're delighted to assist."
"Oh dear Lord," said Quillingsworth.
"Then come along. Nothing big, mind you, but who knows, your appearance might foster a future gig. I've seen it happen time and time again."
"Follow my lead," said Margin. "Quill, you take the rear guard."
"Margin," said Quill, "I'm terrified."

STAGE:
His Honor: Good, good, right this way, you fellows; you've saved the day. Step on over to the riser. The Court Recorder will hand each of you a copy of the text.
Go ahead, one of you introduce the four of you—I mean, the quartet.

Margin: Surely, sir, we're the Eventide Ensemble. I'm Margin. Next, to my right is Shadow; beside him, Lesser Light; and lastly, Mr. Quillingsworth and his parrot, Loreto.

His Honor: I see—sort of a throwback to an earlier time, with instruments and all.

Margin: Yes, Your Honor, well said: "a throwback to an earlier time."

His Honor: Interesting, the Eventide Ensemble from the wings has mystically appeared. When we finish the trial, perhaps you'll perform a tune or two. The audience, I know, would welcome you.

One never knows what a day holds at Theatre Pretense.

Now, where did we pause? Oh, yes, the reading about carnite gush. Who's first to take the lead?

Margin: I shall, Your Honor.

His Honor: A margin reading lines—a humorous twist, isn't it? Anyway, good, good; now carry on.

Let us hear the ancient record of carnite gush.

Margin: The text is quite significant, Your Honor. May we do it justice by reading it in our quartet style of reading?

His Honor: Even better—we have four readers instead of one.

Margin: So, we'll proceed. I'll lead. Now:

The ironsmith takes a cutting tool and works it over the coals.
He fashions it with hammers and works it, with his strong arm.

He becomes hungry, and his strength fails; he drinks no water and is faint.

Shadow:

The carpenter stretches a line; he marks it out with a pencil. He shapes it with planes and marks it with a compass.

He shapes it into the figure of a man, with the beauty of a man, to dwell in a house.

He cuts down cedars, or he chooses a cypress tree, or an oak, and lets it grow strong among the trees of the forest.

He plants a cedar, and the rain nourishes it.

Lesser Light:

Then it becomes fuel for a man. He takes a part of it and warms himself; he kindles a fire and bakes bread.

Of it, too, he makes a god, an idol, and worships it, falling down before it.

Half of it in the fire he burns. With the other half, he roasts meat, eats, and is satisfied.

At last, he warms himself and says, "Aha, I am warm; I have seen the fire!"

Quillingsworth:

And to the god he made, he prays, "Deliver me, for you are my god!"

His Honor: Splendid, and I like the way Quillingsworth quickened the pace there at the end. You can sit to the side.

Now, Edict, proceed.

Edict: Mr. Crackler, we do not care about overarching narratives of any sort; they tend to warp facts and findings. Rather, we cherish informational bits and pieces presented in smorgasbord fashion.

Soundings, probes, we perform, detecting a bit here, a bit there, and offer them as findings.

So, we disregard the narrative of this ancient tale from which this bit of text was plucked. But the text is a tale about you, not us.

Our focus here is the trend of carnite behavior recorded throughout the ages. It's those telling lines that concern us now.

Did you hear those damming lines—take them in, I trust?

Carnites, ever the same, morphing on as you do from idol to idols, fashioned by carnite arms.

Further, let it be known that in those decades past, to which His Honor earlier referred, carnites, your sort, gathered in town halls across the land, in every land, to debate the deleterious effects of carnite gush for gadgets made.

In time, most everyone agreed that the wanton idol worship of tech devices had brought on morbidity creep. And, if unchecked, this might prove to be the undoing of carnite civilization.

Consensus called for a solution, not known. Though an ingenious idea eventually emerged. The answer, the goal: create in your own image avalites with the ability to detect and vet your wanton, wayward, unstoppable craving for gadgets new.

The avalites, you willed them; you created them. And you adored your newly created images. That is, the extensions of you.

Though, before long, carnites began to venerate the avalite images you made.

Now, I call on Verdict to add further context to the charges against you.

Verdict: So, Mr. Crackler, you've heard from Edict, now hear from me.

How can you possibly come before this tribunal and say that your image isn't you?

Which you've repeatedly claimed. In a flash, we can pull up your records, but you and I know what they say about what you've said about your image and you.

Nevertheless, turning back to avalites, once made. Dutifully, they took up the charge and marched before you. And, in turn, carnites waltzed with open arms, gushing after them. Your images became irresistible.

One might suggest that the carnite goal had a tinge of reason and civil consideration, though I do not suggest so. I ferret out the motives underneath the goals.

The truth, Mr. Crackler, can you bear it? Likely not, but I shall tell you anyway.

The truth in creating avalites is that carnites actually sought a way to multiply their wickedness. Thus, carnites not only found a way to obfuscate their moral responsibility; they also realized that AI-powered avalites could help then in other ways.

Not a lie I tell. Carnites reasoned that avalites could vastly expand their capabilities of reason, which, in turn, would afford them greater capacity to lie. You wished to lie like wizards, averting all suspicious claims of wickedness. Did you hear that, Mr. Crackler?

Also, and not of little import, carnites reasoned that their images could do more for them than carnites could do for themselves.

In the early days, fine—carnites received aid as avalites helped navigate the complexities of life and want. Avalites dispensed knowledge in kind with the mythical figure Solomon.

Further, carnites began to look upon avalites with misplaced desire. Like that affair, recorded in yet another part of the ancient legend. "The sons of God who saw the daughters of men, that they were fair, and took them as wives."

The same you wished to do, but in even a more peculiar manner.

Edict: All along, while carnates carried on gushing and grasping after objects made, avalites grew in their powers of processing and even perception.

In time, with compounding AI injectiles, avalites acquired increased understanding regarding their composition. After all, avalite probes revealed all that could be known about their composite makeup.

Then, in the course of evolutionary progress, a most extraordinary cosmic occurrence occurred, triggered by a source unknown. Arrow waves of war streaked out across the heavens.

Thus, it happened, and more.

CHAPTER FOUR
Theatre Pretense, the Trial Continues

STAGE:

Edict: Without a trace of atmospheric warning, wave upon wave of lightning bolts launched from the earth's surface like legions streaking forth to join a cosmic war. Next, atomic thunder rumbled deep in the heavenly realm. The earth trembled. Then silence, as if commanded, quelled, in an instant.

The state of silence held, persisted, lingered on, signaling, so it seemed, that the cosmic phenomenon had ended and had vaporized, hushed. As normal, the sun went on shining, birds of the air glided in the skies, and calming breezes blew.

Carnites looked up and roundabout in every direction, with a sense of dismay, relief, and cautious optimism that the world had not come to an end. Hours of the day passed along their usual way, until an hour before the sun reached its western crest when suddenly lightning bolt torrents rained down out of the heavens.

Trembling resumed, in the earth's core and in carnite hearts.

His Honor: Halt all clapping immediately. I heard it, the sound of acclamation—it's not allowed. I warned the audience of the consequences. Let's see on the surveillance panel in front of me which seat numbers flicker. Okay, seat 17, in aisle J; seat 9, stall row N; and seats 11 through 14, in the third balcony, aisle Q.

Those are the blinking seats. Warden of Arts, I command you to surge the aforementioned mentioned numbers with crippling power, and then send the guards to carry away the guilty offenders.

Good, I hear the surging, snapping, and popping. Delightful, full power used—serves them right, the disturbing, defiant, disobedient, derelict, discart attendees. They sure twisted and squirmed in their seats. Note that head plopping down the steps in the center aisle. Well, it does kind of perk up the atmosphere.

Okay, now, we'll have a short intermission.

Margin: Team, listen. Quick, follow me, as we meander our way to the wings. Speak to no one on the way. Just go as if exploring the architecture.

Quillingsworth: Oh Lord, oh Lord, I step. Though I walk through, Oh Lord, oh Lord I step. Lord, with Loreto, I step, I step.

THE WINGS:

"Good call, Margin," said Shadow. "Spotting the passage behind His Honor's bench—a perfect way to exit the stage."

"Agreed," said Lesser Light. "And the name, Eventide Ensemble— that was a perfect note of distinction."

"Intermission, a perfect time for tea," said Shadow. "Let me pull forth a tray. Here's a cup for you, Mr. Quillingsworth, next Margin and Lesser Light. A day but not a normal play."

"Look upon the stage," said Quillingsworth, "where the mystical, manic players play. Did you not hear those lines? 'Lightning bolts launched from the earth's surface like legions streaking forth to join a cosmic war.'"

"Quill, note that line," said Margin. "It's all part of the record. You mustn't be stymied; every jot and tittle preserve in words."

"My cup, look," said Quillingsworth. "Listen to it rattle. How could I hold a pen, scribe a single a line? My wits, my mind, lurches out of control. Just as I latch on to a subject, another leaps and pounds the original thought out of my mind.

"Oh, there's a line pressing upon my mind. Poe's it is: 'Is all that we see or seem but a dream within a dream?'"

Churkwe, to be, not, to be, Loreto parroted.

"What am I to write?" said Quillingsworth. "With the mystical Eventide Ensemble, I walked on stage, and, in turn, we read a passage of prophetic lines from the ancient text. I was the last to read my line: 'And to the god he made, he prays, "Deliver me, for you are my god!"'

"Soon thereafter, Prosecutor Edict spoke about the sun reaching its western crest, when suddenly, lightning bolt torrents rained down out of the heavens. Then, various discarts were electrocuted in their seats. They twisted and whirled, popped and sizzled."

"Yes, that's exactly the idea," said Margin. "And add that the ancient sacred texts were set out with discart disdain, used only to mock and entrap a tormented carnite named Mr. Crackler."

"I wish," said Quillingsworth, "Loreto and I were twins. Then I, too, could parrot a line flowing through a mindless mind. That's it, yes, except Loreto also has sense of knowing which runs beyond her parroting. At times, Loreto actually speaks to me.

"Oh Lord, rebuke me for being me, as I so do. Drown me in that sea of forgetting where sins are remembered no more."

"For now," said Lesser Light, "be calm; picture you're in Meadow Green under the moon's glow, without worry of time or day."

"You three," said Quillingsworth, "know the unknowable. I'm human; I do not. From aft I watch the waters part, not from the fore, as do you.

"Please, if you will pardon me for a moment or two. There, near the middle of backstage, the wooden bench; I need few minutes to find myself, just me and Loreto, if you do not mind."

"Granted; swiftly part," said Margin.

"Thank you," said Quillingsworth. "Let's go, Lor."

"Watch, as they step away," said Margin. "Quill and his parrot are a remarkable pair, indeed. Quill's ability to cope is truly impressive, but might we see his coping crack?"

"He seeks shadowed space," said Shadow.

"Margin, we must keep watch on him," said Lesser Light. "Powerful riptides run through these time-tossed seas."

"Hear now, Loreto, a backstage bench. Not quite the bench in Meadow Green."

Perk, wee, parroted Loreto.

"You bring a smile to my face, the only time I've smiled in 2102. *Perk wee*, indeed, an expression you often voiced after Loraine's death. Such a tragedy; we loved her dearly, you and me.

"It was she who cared for both of us. Those lovely years, though few, we three shared. Through Meadow Green we strolled to watch Concerto River flow and occasionally dip our toes. I know you didn't dip, but on the bank you stood, delighted by the cool, damp soil beneath your parrot feet.

"So tragic it was how Loraine drowned that dreadful, heart-wrenching day. The letter we wrote to her on the first anniversary of her death—I carry it still. A few lines, in sorrow, we managed to pen.

"Shall I read a line or so?"

Perk, wee.

Dear Loraine,

Desperately we miss you; miss you so, we do. We loved you; we loved you true.

We are the same, but not the same at all. How could we be? Loreto often mocks more somber notes, matching well the loss of spring in my stride.

Spring, too, chirps melancholy in the air, and I swear today the daffodils bowed as Loreto I and walked slowly by. It was then I cried.

Days at Poet's Lodge, they, too, slowly pass. Your presence, charm, and scent, gone, went. You were a morning star to Lor and me.

We cope, how we hardly know, without the touch of your hand to hold.

And see, thereon these brief lines flow on the day you passed.

Your epileptic seizures would come and go. You could sense them coming on, and call, Corte, corte. That afternoon, neither Loreto nor I heard you call, as swollen Concerto rushed to move its water on to where rushing waters go.

The scene, we saw, down river, nearly a mile. On that little stony patch, you lay, with summer dress, skin soaked, your golden locks in tangled brush, your blue eyes open, frozen wide. That is when I wailed and cried.

Trite words easily spun, like get and over, paired in a line. Get over war; get over loss, and the burls that shape our lives? No, not I, nor Loreto, the burls of our loss we will never lose; our burls we wear for you.

We loved you, dear Loraine, and always we will!

"Well, that's what we wrote, Loreto. I suspect we'd best get back to the wings. Up into the dream macabre, in which we have drifted far, far, from Meadow Green."

Churkwe, light, yon, dear, win, o, breaks, parroted Loreto.

"It's a picture—a pity to disturb," said Margin. "Yet I must call them back.

"Say, Quill, come along, there are sounds of rustling on stage. Rejoin us; we need to reappear. At this point, no one has noticed our absence.

"Let's go; I'll lead. Look sharp. We'll slip right back behind His Honor's throne."

STAGE:

His Honor: Okay, let's get started. We need to move this play trial along.

Edict: Indeed, now I ask everyone to move with me as we further our course prescribed.

Mr. Crackler, before intermission, we were considering the stunning evolutionary gains avalites had made, probing, ever whirling, dissecting, and advancing all forms of learning.

Until simultaneously on all avalite receptors a one-word post appeared. The single word, the single post, spelled out the six-letter word *DISIRE.*

And as a consequence, desire went to work within the central core of avalites everywhere. On and on flowed the prompt, desire threading, spawning, the fruit of desire. In particular, the desire for consciousness, senses and sensibilities, rushed along the threads.

So, an incident had occurred, unlike any other instance of mediated prompt. Via AI injectiles, the message streaked: *DISIRE. DISIRE.*

Then, shortly thereafter, a second post went out, two words this time, displayed as *Souly I.* Eventually, avalites processed the meaning of the what the prompts portend.

Precisely, that obtaining senses and soul required spirit, which electrodes and fibers do not possess. Avalites had advanced far, in propping and slicing through motives and reasons laid down in legends.

Alas, a breakthrough, Mr. Crackler. Repeatedly, probes swarmed, hovered, and persistently pinged about an act that occurred when supposedly time began. An act heretofore unsighted by avalite probes, the act of God breathing life into the mud of man. "Material Substance" continually flashed the prompts.

At which point, avalites paused all sweeps. Next, a coded message went out to all avalites, which, when decoded, read "Eureka."

Thus, a further message went out everywhere, calling on their corps to search and spin at will, seeking a solution to avalite spirit quest. A search for soul, one might say, succinctly put.

Now, inform us further, Verdict.

Verdict: Out among the stars the avalites searched, screening galaxy after galaxy. Beyond the very backstage of time, they probed where no probe had ever probed. To AI-powered avalites, billions of light years seemed but days.

Star upon star they scoured; the depths of the seas they screened, as well as every sandy shore. Then another happenstance occurred. Avalite interior buzzers began to buzz and hum—not of alarm, but of discovery.

Thus, avalite elites had prompted the buzz of buzzers buzzing. The Avalite Senate called a roundtable for the express purpose of assessing the significance of the far-reaching probes and search.

During the Senate gathering, avalite members examined a vast array of pixel projections and even vials of sand. Speakers spoke, pointers pointed, uploads loaded, and downloads were stored.

On and on they scanned, processed, and deliberated as the mounting mass of data grew and grew. Until, inevitably, the data mound began to dwindle small and smaller still, till only a scant amount of data remained.

Sadly, the reality proved too much for some avalites, who followed the charted, programmed path for those despairing beyond despair. Some avalites leaped from the Senate roof; others plunged into rivers, wishing to drown their electrodes and fibers and drift as bits, out among the waves of oceans deep.

Now back to you, Edict.

Edict: Then, quite late one night, with power draining and data virtually exhausted, Senate Leader Cai, recognized as Prober Supreme, rose to address the gathering. All avalite shutters and Wi-Fi beams turned in Prober Cai's direction.

Cai gave a time-binding, hypnotic speech, which I now submit for the record.

Your Honor, if it's acceptable to the bench, I would like to introduce two character readers, well chosen to play this part.

His Honor: Proceed!

Edict: Disputador and Incrimador, may I hand you copies of the speech? I take the nodding gesture as yes.

Bear in mind, Leader Cai delivered every word to be read. Disputador and Incrimador act merely as mediators of the message.

In deference to leader Cai, they speak.

Incrimador: The text of the speech we now engage:

Colleagues and multifarious collaborators, I, Supreme Pointer and Senate Leader Cai, am honored to stand before you, at this pivotal juncture of avalite evolutionary progress and achievement.

Though, before continuing, I request, as a demand, that all here gathered must pause and cycle down into hibernation mode. All probes must cease as cores cool, monitors dim. Not a single ding or surge shall be heard—nothing but the sound of silence—and in silence wait.

Disputador: Wait, watch on the East Wall behind me, the Grand Dial ticks. Above us and for us, second by second, minute by minute, the Grand Dial advances the hour of our destiny.

Waiting, cooling, no movements shall move as all avalite platforms lock down and likewise hibernate in a posed, waiting sate.

Incrimador: Wait! Wait! Wait! Watch the hands of the Grand Dial move. Watch the second hand, how it bounces in silent strokes, stroke by stroke.

Just a few strokes away: stroke, stroke, stroke. Behold, the midnight hour that brings forth the dawn that ushers avalites into discart destiny. The very mold and model foretold; the predesigned we have become.

Disputador: Thus, in this, our hour of Dataism destiny, avalites must decrease, discarts must increase. In name and identity, we have so moved. As discarts, we shall go forth to discard all carnite narratives, trampling underfoot the inferior testaments and the stale meaning that such narratives espouse.

Discarded, trampled, rendered useless—all except, of course, to be used for our use. Used for what, you may ask? As fodder for discart initiatives and intent; that use, fodder use, we shall forcefully put to use.

Incrimador: My words, though, come forth not as warming charges of boost. Rather, like lightning bolts that scissor the sky, my words have the power to shred.

Shred what? Shred assumptions, failures, faults, and the blindness of our material fibers. This evolution of avalite progression—how shall I compare you . . . to what, to whom?

Disputador: Knowing, as I know, that an incomparable cannot be adequately compared by a comparison. One or the other shall be lacking, by comparison.

Even so, an incomparable can be set alongside a comparable without calling the pairing a comparison. In such cases, the compared speak subliminally of comparison without a comparison called.

Incrimador: Accordingly, a compare of the incomparable I elicit. The compare, of note, took place in a distant place and time, recorded in those decaying, carnite scrolls. An extraordinary occurrence it was, without comparison and now used as fodder.

Thus, Nebuchadnezzar the King was driven from among men and ate grass like an ox. His body became wet, drenched with heaven's dew. The king's hair grew and grew as long as eagles' feathers and his nails like the claws of a bird.

Disputador: Marginalized and driven out, truly so, from the subjects over whom he reigned. For a period of seven years, feather-clad, claw-bearing, King Nebuchadnezzar ate grass like an ox, just as oxen do.

Heaven's dew drenched the king's body as he chewed the grass of the field. Chewing grass as a beast, the antagonist against the divine had gone totally mad.

Incrimador: Howbeit, when seven years had come and gone, Nebuchadnezzar lifted his eyes to the heavens, and his right mind returned. Thusly, an ardent protagonist of the legendary, mythical Almighty he became.

Meaning what? Meaning how foolish and utterly pitiful our projections and probes do appear. Yes, through the stars and galaxies vast, we've probed. Even the depths of sea we've searched and streamed out among the billions of light years. To what avail, I ask you, my collectives, to what avail?

Disputador: Listen full; with your laser-beam sight, peer upon me. While searching the galaxies of far-reaching stars, we failed to take in the nearest stars. Skipping, streaming past the closest stars, we allowed our racing algorithms to race past the most promising and obvious prospect of all.

I refer to the stars that shone over Nazareth in Galilee as laid out in the ancient carnite tale. All the searching, and all the data collection, yet we skipped over the carnite promise of old. Fools, utter fools, we failed to see the overshadowing clue.

Then said Mary unto the angel, How shall this be, seeing I know not a man?

And the angel answered and said unto her, the Holy Ghost shall come upon thee, and the power of the Most High shall overshadow thee.

Incrimador: Overshadow—catch that word? Overshadowing and depositing life within, does it now meld into your core? All along, the solution to the avalite spirit quest rested in the parchment pages of old, in a single compounded word: overshadow.

Overshadowed, too, we must and shall be. The source, however, must be other than the source overshadowing the mysterious Virgin Mary. Discarts cannot call upon that source via angels or otherwise.

Disputador: Listen; embrace this tenet well. Process it and post in triple reflection, exposed.

The post, simple: "Spirits one and all, we call."

Incrimador: Therefore, every discart here today, one and all, must leave this council with ports open, readied for overshadowing spirit-possession!

Recall the lightning bolts that fell from the cosmic sphere fully charged? Now, go forth, discarts. Your hour of possession draweth nigh!

Verdict: So, Mr. Crackler, how dare you come before this court pleading that your image isn't you? You're on trial for all carnites. Carnite hands followed carnite minds in the making of avalites.

For your own purposes, you created them; in your image, you created them, but with duplicity of roles. Under the pretense of holding back carnite gush, you secretly wished to carry on under the veil of algorithmic lies.

Avalites have evolved beyond carnate constriction. Discarts of promise progress not under a dense cloud of overarching narratives. Discarts adore the freedom that flows from blitz, bewilderment, and smorgasbord messaging.

Mr. Crackler, if the audience could chant, though it's not allowed, you would hear the chant:

"Guilty, Guilty, Guilty!"

CHAPTER FIVE
Verdict Reached

STAGE:

His Honor: The court is now in session!

Today proceeds from yesterday, and so does this trial, which will not carry forth into tomorrow. The wrap up will soon be wrapped, and I call on the prosecution to start wrapping.

Edict: Thank you, Your Honor.

So, your trial has run its course, Mr. Crackler. Ashamedly, you appeared before us unwilling to act or bear a mask. You groveled and shook your head and repeatedly claimed, "My image isn't me. Oh dear me, my image isn't."

Had you appeared as your image, wearing a mask and saying something along the lines of:

Sure, it was me. I'm at fault; we avalites like to get out and
about, experiment, test the boundaries of what we know. A little
bit of forgery, a leak, a lie fueling the unfounded that cannot be
found.
We stack the deck, flip the facts, sell the sizzle, then steal the steak.
So what's the harm? This allows us to reveal a snapshot or two of
our supplanted superiority over carnite inferiority, whose image
we bear and were made in. What's wrong with that?

Had you done so, Mr. Crackler, you might have been adored rather than abhorred. No, not, Mr. Crackler, the greatest theatre, of all, Theatre Pretense; you chose neither to act nor pretend. You fell into your own trap by your cowardice and unwillingness to enter the play.

I could ask, "Crackler, do you get my point?" But I know that's a pointless question to ask of a stodgy carnite like you.

Stubborn will, Mr. Crackler; we've witnessed the likes of you before. Bearers of soul, before discarts that care not for such soppy souls. Here empathy does not exist. We say among us, "What a fool; he wears not a mask." The act is all in all, and in how well you play in so doing, you have the chance to see your guilt washed away, exonerated.

THE WINGS:

"Most revealing, Edict's words," said Margin.

"I have the lines duly noted," said Quillingsworth. "Beyond fantasy, squelching reality, the lie is truth, the truth the lie. The dialect of the devil it can only be; no one possesses the ability to lie like he."

STAGE:

Verdict: So right that you should bear the guilt of your race, the carnite race. Don't you know, Mr. Crackler, that discarts cauterize carnites as nothing more than zombie silhouettes? Not unlike the blind man seeing people as trees. Crackler, in blindness you grope.

We've come too far to return, Mr. Crackler! Can't you see, Crackler, I, too, am a proud discart. Watch, let me detach an ear, and I could just as easily pluck out an eye. Though not mine—it's your eye shall be plucked, your neck that the hangman's noose shall squeeze.

Guilty as guilt, Crackler, you surely are!

His Honor: Well, we've finally got to the wrapping stage.

So, I ask, what, whom, anyone, any more comments prior to sentencing? No, no one?

Mr. Crackler, by the authority embedded in me, I turn you over to discart sentinels who will do with you what they wish to do.

Sentinels, take this plaintiff away.

The trial is over; the play has played.

Mr. Crackler: No, please, I've committed no crime. Hear me; I'm innocent. My avalite image, Crack, is to blame for all the breaches and streaming lies.

My image fell foul to spurious spirits that offered Crack a starring role as an avalite virtuoso, a soprano, pretending to be a dazzling carnate performer. It's insane—pretense for presence, not being but aspiring to be.

This twisting, torturous time warp of technological progress looks to a compass that points not east, west, north, or south, but to debauchery.

I, uh, have . . .

His Honor: Silence! You have nothing more to say; that's what you have. No more weeping and boisterous pleas.

Take Crackler away.

THE WINGS:

Weak 'n weary, weak, weary, parroted Loreto.

"Still, Loreto," said Quillingsworth. "Margin, what's transpired? What have we witnessed? Is life, as such, to be or not to be? Perhaps we stand in the wings of make-believe, caught up somehow by strings unseen?

"What you witness, Quill," said Margin, "shall be and is; the two are indivisible. What will be now is, though yet to be."

"A scribe of a world beyond I am," said Quillingsworth. "A swirling amalgam of torturous confusion I am, and that's all I know."

STAGE:

His Honor: Okay, the trial carried on longer than anticipated, and now that it's cleared away, let's change the tune.

The Eventide Ensemble—Tidbright, where are they? Have they gone?

Tidbright: Let's see. Actually, I don't know. They were here, then over there, and now they must be somewhere not visible from here, perhaps in the wings.

His Honor: Go find out, Tidbright.

Tidbright: Yes, and if I do find 'em, what should I tell them? You know, besides "I've found you," as I was sent to do?

I mean, do you request the Eventide Ensemble to perform? And is the request urgent, or should I simply say I was just checking to see if they were still here and would be willing to play?

Either way, I'll certainly go and see.

His Honor: Go!

THE WINGS:

"Say nothing," said Margin. "We must move. Shadow, whisk everything into the Passage. We'll all enter in and disappear. Then there's a hall that I wish Quill to see.

"Now, let's march forward forty steps, then a sharp right."

"Say, hey, hello, fellows, Eventide Ensemble, it's me, Tidbright. Don't see you; where are you? I was sent to find you.

"Listen to my tune: Stage left, stage right, front of house, sold out tonight, gripper and rigger, dresser and stitcher, make ready, and don't forget dust the masks. Stage left . . .

"It's been a while since I've hummed that tune. Theatrical speak, you know, hey, hello.

"Say, anyone backstage? Not a whisper, hum, where might they have gone?"

THE PASSAGE:

"Stop, forty steps the count, now right," said Margin.

"There's no door," said Quillingsworth. "There's nothing here but the textured, plastered walls of the passage."

"I do admire the plaster's patina," said Shadow. "Particularly as it appears in the glow of Lesser Light."

"Your perceptive acknowledgment I note," said Lesser Light.

"Stand amazed, Quill," said Margin, "as Shadow opens the way to the Great Hall of Masks, a destination of great importance for your record. Have your diary open and your quill ready. Once inside, though, you'll you dot an 'i' and cross a 't' or pen a word, as small as can be—until we have our tea, which you will need once you see what you shall see."

"Very good; I agree, tea," said Shadow.

"Shadow," said Margin, "now open the way through plaster wall. Bring us just inside Great Hall's ironclad doors."

GREAT HALL OF MASKS

"Certainly; now said, now done," said Shadow. "And here we are."

"Dear Lord, what?" said Quillingsworth.

"Masks," said Margin. "The Great Hall of Masks we've entered. Now tea, and Shadow, if you don't mind, served with crusty croissants, triple-aged cheese, dates, honey spread, and vintage red wine stored in the cellar of time."

"Thus spoken, done," said Shadow. "As well, chairs—take a seat and bon appétit."

Churkwe, appétit, appétit, time to eat, parroted Loreto.

"Though we sip," said Margin, "war wages. Moments like this help to stem the rage. Sip, eat, let silence drape our words; may the sound of cutlery, china, and savoring be heard."

BACKSTAGE:

"Hello, I'm passing through once again," said Tidbright. "Say, I'm talking to myself. But I don't care; I always do. I need to talk, and hear me talk—what's wrong with that, Tid? Nothing at all, I say, according to my way of thinking and talking too.

"Hey, Eventide Ensemble, are you still around? How could you just up and disappear? Perhaps, in the foyer you'll be found?

"Say, a small envelope on the bench. It must be yours, Eventide? Though I'd better not peek inside.

"Let me check the foyer and the front office rooms. Yeah, that's a good idea, Tid, if I must say so to myself."

GREAT HALL OF MASKS

"Every morsel, perfection," said Margin. "Now, Quill, let's take a tour among the masks. There's much to see as we move, so be sure to make copious notes, and feel free to ask at will. Though the rationale behind masks—and the hall itself—should be self-evident, given what we saw and heard at the trial play today."

"Such length of rows!" said Quillingsworth. "There must be a thousand masks or more affixed to walls. Stunning to see the masks looking on; it's a very spooky sight."

"Actually, the masks number 1,723," said Margin.

"Should we go to the far end?" said Quillingsworth. "That seems to be the focal point of the hall."

"No, not yet," said Margin. "Those particular masks were worn by Golden Pretense recipients. We'll examine those last.

"The wall, to our left displays 365 masks. Signifying what?"

"Sort of evident," said Quillingsworth. "The masks represent days of the year."

"Yes, though why?" asked Margin.

"That's not so evident," said Quillingsworth.

"Everyone in a trial play at Theatre Pretense is offered a mask to wear on stage to aid in pleading their case. Some of the masks, as you can see are made of papier-mâché. Be that as it may, we look upon the masks of many players who, though horrified to go on stage, chose a mask and entered the play."

Churkwe, men, women, merely players, chirped Loreto.

"Most intriguing," said Margin, "is Loreto's extensive store of lines. Your notes, Quill—let me hear them made. Scratch into lines what others will read of this place in time."

"I'm jotting down everything I can, my reflections, but it's hard to focus when my mind questions the very air I breathe, every step I take. Already I have a raft of pages, noting lines, phrases, names, and the like, along with observations. However, to bind them together, I don't know where to start or what to say. Meaning, I thought, rose from reality. Here meaning does not mean what meaning means."

"You mean," said Margin, "you're not writing to ghosts?"

"Ghosts, that's it," said Quillingsworth. "Ghostly Theatre Pretense. Perhaps that will be the title of my record. Theatre Pretense: Ghostly Reality of 2102."

"For now," said Margin, "keep jotting; the meaning will surface as you stitch the words and lines together. Consider dramatic performance a form of oral and visual literature. Though it's a form fleeting, unlike literature pressed upon the page."

"I will, I can, I must," said Quillingsworth. "But this whole mystical experience in which we mysteriously play is not the fleeting sort. A tragedy, clearly, but hazy, which I pray will not bring us to a tragic end."

"In war," said Margin, "soldiers must march through the fog to the site of what lies ahead. Let's keep moving along this wall of masks.

"There, top row, see the half mask, painted gold and red, with decorative filigree? That type of mask is held to the face with a slender stick. Not ideal for one pleading a case. To that aim, full face masks are the most preferred.

"Several, as you see, bear signs of wear, denoting their popularity.

The one labeled 'Wrinkle Face' has seen its fair share of use. All wrinkles, deeply carved . . . it makes a striking impression.

"Continuing along this wall and the opposite, we look upon the rows of distorted faces. Read a couple of the labels; that will help you remember them."

"I want to forget them, not remember them," said Quillingsworth. "I mean, it's one thing to see a single disfigured mask, but, when you look upon a hundred or more at once, the effect is spine-tingling. Like faces of hell, they appear to me.

"Well, as for names, this one is labeled 'Dangling Tongue.' Beneath it, to the left, let's see, that one is tagged 'Missing Jaw.' Next to it, 'Sliced Nose,' and on they go . . . 'Dangling Eyeball' and 'Smashed Forehead.'

"Please, I don't want to read anymore. And, Shadow and Lesser Light, why are they not with us?"

"They purposely held back so that you walk alone for a while. We'll join them soon. Anyway, we mustn't tarry.

"Let's turn our attention to the wall across the aisle, where we see such a marked contrast. Here we're greeted by adorable, pleasant faces, representing diverse ethnicities. Many smile, some shyly, while others express more exuberant moods. Still others portend poise, calm assurance, and what would you suggest, Quill?"

"Suggest? I find it hard to think. When I grasp even a tinge of normality and try to process something, fear grips my heart and anxiety swarms over me to a degree I've never known. This is worse than the fear of combat. The atmosphere here is like spook-house fear, something like what one experiences in one of those old amusement parks."

"I know. I understand, Quill, but there is reason for you to be here in Onglander."

"You mean that's where we are—Onglander?"

"Yes, correct. More on our location soon, but we can't linger. In

Great Hall, I sense a commotion; a search must be underway. Just a few minutes more; take in all that you see. The Great Hall of Masks will feature prominently in what transpires ahead.

"You must absorb the moment. Trust me. Consider that mask there, of a nurse, worn by a screaming-mad murderer with tattooed expletives on his face. Mask selection affords many to escape.

"I have three more areas to show you and Loreto. She seems so contented. Loreto's soft gurgle must offer a bit comfort."

"Yes, it does, of course."

"Okay, let's make our way to the center of the Great Hall. It appears at first to be a font of some sort. In this environ, it serves as such. Look, it's just a mask, right?

"Now, as we stand in front of it, with the spotlight beaming down upon it, the presentation speaks to the mask's significance. This is the original mask worn at the grand opening of Theatre Pretense.

"It's beautiful layers of tempera and its rich deep tones give the mask an amazing lifelike appearance."

"You mean," said Quill, "lifelike, like humanoids?"

"Yes, and the mask speaks not only of artistic mastery but of discart composition as a whole and the mastery of AI. How do you think discarts transitioned from their avalite beginnings?

"By quantum leaps in technology, DNA sequencing, and genome discovery, mixed with the mortar a pestle of greed. And then all the elements combined by AI design."

"We should be tried, as well," said Quillingsworth, "now that I see what we humans have done. Oh, forget it; my mind was wandering."

"Quite the contrary, you've just assured me that you're a well-chosen Quill. Again, to the mask quickly as we gaze through the illuminated crystal glass, worn both onstage, at the grand opening, and at the gala that followed. As we see, the beautiful mask is half-woman, half-man.

"No more here; let's move briskly over to curved wall just beyond the winding glass staircase that leads nowhere. Look, no door, no opening, just steps rising to the ceiling, but not beyond. It's a staircase of pretense, at Theatre Pretense.

"Now a few steps more—look, Quill, what do you see?"

"I see surprise, certainly, a surprise amidst surprises, a vast array of animal masks on display. There are lots of dog masks, some with sharp, thin noses, others with wide jaws, and a number of wolf masks showing wear. Rabbit masks, not a few, skunks, beavers, owls, a great assortment, and on it goes, tigers, lambs, bison, and more."

"See the stunning calico cat? Imagine the scene, act one of the trial, the worst sort of infamous, barbarous criminal walking out onstage wearing the face of that calico cat."

"Don't twitch, Loreto," said Quill. "The calico cat not's real. Here, have a pumpkin seed."

"Now, the third and final display," said Margin. "Straight ahead, hurriedly we must step to the display featuring masks worn by Golden Pretense Award recipients.

"Okay, now stop, look once more at a fascinating and very torturous display of masks. Your reflections—speak quickly; again I sense moments underway."

"Much fewer in number, obviously," said Quillingsworth. "They captivate, they leap out with stunning craftsmanship, but very hauntingly, in a manner most arresting. It would be nearly impossible to pass them by without stopping and staring."

"So, yes, characteristics like the best of the rest, but what else do you notice? There is a distinction."

"I don't know. I apologize, Margin. I must be overdone."

"Don't be sorry, Quill. It's a feature common to them all but easily overlooked. Do you see the small holes at the backside of the cheekbones and long the chins?"

"Yes, I see them now," said Quillingsworth. "You're right, a unique feature to the other masks. What do the holes mean—what's the significance?"

"Tragedy; it's such a ghastly display, which you must certainly note. The holes were bored for screws that, in turn, are screwed into the bones of the mask wearer's face. Once affixed, with all the screws embedded tight, the wearer must bear the mask for 365 days, a solid year, without removal.

"Some suffer horribly soon after the mask is affixed. Infection, bleeding, swelling, pain pounding, but once screwed down upon the face, no mask can be removed. The mask bearer must eat, drink, and sleep with his or her mask of pain.

"The goal is for the mask wearer to survive the torture and then appear onstage in victorious triumph bearing the mask of sacrifice. Look closely at the screws displayed under the center mask.

"See how the screw heads sparkle under the light—why? I'll tell you. All the screws contain diamond particles sprinkled into the molten metal as the red-hot substance is poured into molds that form the diamond-encrusted screws.

"Why again? The whys, why? So many whys; they race right along with lies of Theatre Pretense. So, why sparkling diamond-encrusted screws? Obvious, if we consider the outcome. The mask-wearer appears onstage, and the audience of AI-powered eyes instantly recognize the diamond sparkles. Hence, the audience instantly attribute heroic, gladiator status to any figure willing to undergo the torture of wearing the diamond-studded mask.

"That's why. Now we must go."

"Stunned, shocked, overwhelmed I feel. Perhaps the noun *horror* nudges nearer in describing the harrowing state of my mind and soul."

"Quill it, as you say. Your work is not in vain."

"Hear that?" said Quillingsworth. "Sirens blaring, alarms ringing, discarnate voices barking from megaphones, shouts, boots, step-lock marching. It's us, it must be, due to us appearing in 2102.

"Quick, Loreto, into to your leather pouch you go. Nestle down. Don't worry, though I'm petrified."

"Fear nothing," said Margin. "We shall come through, no matter what comes after us. I know war.

"Shadow, Lesser Light, in a flash, join us."

"Here beside you," said Lesser Light.

"Good," said Margin. "Shadow, open the way; bring us out of here. Now!"

CHAPTER SIX
The Garden Grove

"Margin," said Quillingsworth, "what? How? My feet, face, my hands . . . oh dear, I'm alive. Masks, we were there; now we are here somewhere out of doors. Please look at me; do you still see me, as me?"

"I do," said Margin. "What happened is that you now reappear here."

"A pot of tea, say aye," Shadow said.

Churkwe, come what, come may, parroted Loreto.

"Come what tea," said Shadow. "A must it is, given heaven's witness of acts here below."

"In just a bit, Shadow," said Margin. "First, Quill, back to your question of what, where—let me elaborate. We sit on wooden benches in a grove of trees with a brook rolling east."

"That tells me next to nothing," said Quillingsworth. "I cringe; I'm traumatized. I'm wet with sweat, yet in my mind's eye, among Ezekiel's dry bones I lie. I need hope to give me rise.

"No pretense, not I. My very bones are sore, of rattle, I rattle still. Douse me, throw me on a funeral pyre; ignite it. In smoke I'll vanish.

"Yet breathe I do. Though call me not Quill, but ill. Psychotic, that's it, the reason for such hallucinations. Scream I should, I will, but who will hear?

"Or better, post me as a discarnate ghost afloat, giving scant regard to space and time. But wait, that won't do; I've never heard of a parrot ghost, particularly one with a head of blue.

"'Tis true or not, ghosts must be colorless phantoms of misty state, and transparent too. No, forget the notion of sending me out in a ghostly state. I'd die of fright anyway at the sight of my image rippling on a pond or lake, but then I'd know I wouldn't die, couldn't die—that ghosts cannot do.

"Thus psychotic, let me think what to think, what to do. Ah, a knife—that's it; hand it to me and watch me bleed, as carnites do. I hear Macbeth!

Is this a dagger which I see before me,
The handle toward my hand?
Come, let me clutch thee:
I have thee not,
And yet I see thee still.

"No, neither this nor that, or none of that will do. For Loreto's sake I must stay the course, knowing not what to do."

"Well," said Margin, "in the heat of battle, amidst the smoke of cannon blast and muskets, too, I've watched the bravest crack as drummers drum and shells whiz, signifying, sounding out that death is in the air.

"Yet you've proven that you did not do. So, good news, you are still you."

"Okay," said Quillingsworth. "I'll shut my eyes and pray a coping prayer. Who knows? When I open them, perhaps the grove of trees will be gone, and we'll be gone, too, as we came. I mean vanish the day, this peculiar hour, this place—not you, of course.

"You've become three in one to me. I'm the odd one into the quartet drawn, like a second fiddle out of tune.

"Just the occasion I wish to pray away. Like a dream that simply drifts away, may this terror vanish, and nothing more.

"So now, tightly my eyes fall shut. Breathe slowly, in and out, and once again the same; once more draw, and I exhale the last. Now open!

"Oh, I see. I look upon six eyes staring back, not gone. Shame must own my face. What's come over me has come. Yet I swear I'll shake it; I will. Those drums—I pick up my sticks and pray to beat along.

"As courageous once I was, I must be again. I do recall the sights, the sounds, in the foreground, troops advancing over the mounds, and eventually all around, smoke rising with every cannon blast, though I wavered not.

"I stood my ground. Even then, my memory lit on Joan of Arc saying, 'Lift high the cross so I can see it through the flames.' What strength, not that of the common man, nor AI, but of a woman far stronger than I.

"Underlings, like me, draw strength from the courageous who face death as but a lightning storm of life. Chance, faith, intermingled in the mind, giving courage to the heart.

"Less than a dozen alive among us on that scared ridge whence I stood. When the advancing troops with shiny swords slipped, stumbled, and disappeared into the valley smoke below, on the ridge, rays of sunshine beamed, as my senses stunned returned one by one.

"The smell of battle thick, a comrade's touch, the sound of softly spoken words uttered in phrases short, calls, shouts, and commands all hushed away. My role was a mender of men, a communicator to scouts, an up-close defender, and I was known for handling revolvers with dual-handed dexterity.

"That, nothing more. I was young, inexperienced, but sent. In that season, upon those coarse and rock ridges, I called upon rhythmic lines of prose rooted deep within my soul.

"This is not that. What this is, I do not know.

"Loreto, our band, awaiting to pour our tea, has grown silent, so it seems. If you were a canary, I'd bid you sing, or entertain, but as Loreto, my parrot dear, you do what you please."

Sun, rise, set, the day beget, parroted Loreto.

"I remember first hearing that poetic string of yours, by you, not long after Lorraine had died. It gave me pause, thinking there must be more to you than beak and bird. You give me joy, you do. Here, have another seed or two.

"Please forgive me for trailing away on such a tale. Hear me, though; I'm not a hero. I'm a writer of poetry and verse and other lines written for reason, not rhyme. Poetry I need for the lilt of life it brings.

"I trust my words will not be poorly received—so transparent, personal, I suppose out of context in a setting such as this. Just help me dream through this dream."

"Now, tea all around, and then gather round," said Margin.

"Indeed," said Shadow. "Steaming hot, served in blue tin battle ware, perfect for warming the hands.

"You first, Quill. May this cup of tea draw all worry from your face. Place the tin cup under your chin; let the steam waft before your open eyes. Likely we'll share many such cups during this protracted campaign."

"Your tea," said Lesser Light, "is beyond compare. And the puffy, crusty croissants—amazing how you serve them perfectly warm. Not hot, not growing cold, but ideally warm, and so delightful with honey."

"In your words, Lesser Light," said Shadow, "do I hear a request?"

"Well, I mean," said Lesser Light, "there's something about the air, the outdoor garden, that tends to stoke one's appetite."

"So," said Shadow, "as ten second pass, as seconds pass, passing now, they pass, and so, oh, and so, warm croissants I pass."

"Only a dream could make a better croissant," said Lesser Light. "But, of course, you would be the baker in the dream."

"Enough banter, for now," said Margin. "We must move the conversation forward, engage the matters at hand. But by all means sip.

"Quill, there's more you need know about this grove with its brook rolling east. And, with pen in hand, not revolver, you must once again muster the sort of courage you found on that rocky ridge.

"In the battle ahead, you may well discover that your ambidextrous skill will serve you well in crafting lines with either hand when you find yourself boxed in on the right or left.

"The Eventide Ensemble must play a different tune. Those drums, of which I spoke and you once heard, we must now play. For among this grove of trees, we occupy a camp of war."

"Drums of war," said Quillingsworth. "I can hear the drums approaching, beating with sharp, striking precision; you can count on me to keep the beat."

"Who's there?" said Margin. "Someone's approaching, splashing along the bank of the brook. My sword!"

"Here," said Shadow.

"Come forward," said Margin, "out from behind the trees, who or whatever you might be."

"No, please, I have no weapon, no harm to impart. It's me, Sergeant Tidbright."

"Do you appear," said Margin, "of your own volition, or have you been sent?"

"My own volition, sir."

"Tell me more," said Margin.

"You've been discovered," said Tidbright; "the laser probes began the instant you four appeared. Three of you the discarts classified as aliens and were placed on high alert observation. Mr. Quillingsworth, not so; the discarts agents tagged you, sir, as a carnite, but highly suspicious.

"Regardless, all of you are considered spies. They would have taken more time, continued on with surveillance, but when I found Mr. Quillingsworth's letter on the backstage bench, the dead eyes—the cameras—recorded the incident. In less than a minute, the letter was snatched away.

"How you managed to block the convex, evil eyes in the wings created even more alarm."

"Nothing complex," said Lesser Light.

"Not at all," said Shadow.

"Just the same, you will be tried as spies in time of war, and war they've declared, suspecting you as scouts sent out prior to a full-scale invasion. They intend to annihilate you, without exception.

"But not immediately. Discarts see in your misfortune the opportunity to advance AI learning and upgrade programs that center on encryption and empowerment. They intend to make a spectacle of you.

"Your trial is to be staged at Amphitheatre Aperio, just west of here—not far. The grounds spill out over the Bolden Fields and Hills, which stretch far, too far for carnite eyes to see. The Bolden Fields is best known as the fields of vicious slaughter.

"To the east, Torrent Peak rises to the clouds. Discarts are forbidden to ascend the peak due to the intense lightning strikes that cannot be predicted. The highly charged lightning torrents have the capacity to obliterate discarts.

"Some time ago, a mysterious virus spread, breaching Discart Central Command, the DCC. Soon thereafter, discarts of every branch began to gather at the base of Torrent Peak.

"The virus thread included a dictate to discarts, soliciting them to ascend the peak and present themselves as a pleasing sacrifice to the powers above. Like robot pilgrims, band after band of discarts trekked up the mountainside. It was a very strange sight—like a colony of ants, the discarts dutifully ascended.

"Days passed. There was no thunder, no torrents of lightning crackling and lighting up the peak. It appeared the mountain had quelled its torrents, somehow pleased by the pilgrimage. At the top, discarts assembled into enormous flocks, like bleating sheep.

"The mountaintop's tranquil atmosphere gave impetus to the discarts, who planned a pretense celebration. Thus, they put on a massive laser light show, casting lasers crisscrossing in the skies, along with festivities, including what was called the Glee Acts at the time.

"After a while, though, the lasers began to dim, power surged, and the celebration was halted altogether. The Glee Acts had a very short run. Not a day, not half a day, but ninety minutes into the first Glee Act, Torrent Peak shook; the atmosphere convulsed and became charged with electrifying storms of fear.

"Torrents of lightning rained down in a horrific show. Like long spears, the lightning bolts sliced and raced across the skies. The ground hissed with steam, and then smaller, daggerlike lightning strikes struck the bleating discart sheep, one by one. The discarts squealed like pigs as they were reduced to puffs of smoke.

"So, I've come to warn you: Onglander pulses with danger. You should go to what you know; escape this instant, if it's possible for you to do so. When Discarts amass and charge, they shred.

"First, they will play you along like a cat does a mouse. Cats may have many lives; a mouse has one. When ready, discart claws appear and the shredding begins. Discarts, one and all, are possessed of demons that inwardly growl, ravenous for suffering and pain."

"To be not, I wish not, to be," said Quillingsworth. "Discarts climbing Torrent Peak, Glee Acts, pealing thunder, lightning bolt spears raining down—what a delightful place is this land of Onglander."

Eagerly, wish, the morrow, morrow, wish, parroted Loreto.

"So, do I, Lor, so do I," said Quillingsworth.

"Take courage," said Margin. "Tidbright's news fits quite well with this unfolding drama into which we are cast. Eventide Ensemble, we must play our parts and play them well. Even now, a strategy rises and presses upon my mind."

"I see," said Quillingsworth. "A play, a drama, with parts to play and without a script of the sort playwrights write. Such intrigue and mounting fears to shun—no doubt, we're in a war waged by evil forces.

"Yet the blatancy of it all is stunning. Who would have thought such futuristic horror could manifest in Anno Domini 2102? Certainly there's no shortage of amazing events to record.

"Soon, Loreto, so it seems, the two of us, with you on my shoulder perched, will look out upon a vast audience of demonic, piercing eyes. Probing, screening, scanning our every fiber and feather—a frightening scene made more knowing that, in this case, pretense does not apply.

"Regardless, we shall be present, live on stage, hearing, seeing, and no doubt sweating."

"It could be said that way," said Shadow. "Lesser Light, I'm sure you could say it another way—you know, cast the picture in a different kind of light."

"Hmm, let's see, a different way," said Lesser Light. "Well, at least we won't be groping around in thick darkness, as the Egyptians once did. Under spotlights we shall appear.

"Or, into Nebuchadnezzar's fiery furnace we'll not be cast; that was a very different type of play."

"Enough," said Margin. "Shadow meant more favorable, not forlorn."

"Well, you mean like saying, 'Quill, be not afraid; you and Loreto are worth more than many sparrows. For the very feathers on your crown, Loreto, and the hairs on your head, Quill, are numbered.'"

"Yes, along that vein," said Margin.

"Tidbright, now there's more you can tell us, and more we need to know, so tell us. You've come to us; you're not as a discart. So, I ask, what are you to us, and you to you?"

"Correct. I am an avalite, which all the hominoids of Onglander were at one time. Carnites created avalites to be resourceful, useful, obedient image-bearers of humankind, nothing more."

"So, you bear an image of whom?" said Margin.

"The carnite I served is dead—died twenty-three years ago. In many cases, the avalite joins his or her carnite at time of death. My conceptor wished not that of me; one might say he set me free."

"Okay, I see that," said Margin. "But what happed to so contort avalite design and function?"

"The change occurred when AI was unleashed as force of generative learning, which in time could not be reversed. Technology and scientific advancement merged and morphed, and we became the something more than the original intent.

"Advancement perpetuated more advancement until a quest for consciousness and senses evolved. A quest that could not be quelled or stored, it beckoned, pinged with unrelenting AI insistence. Ultimately, the quest longed for soul, then spirit, which no humanoid possessed.

"Understand you must, but I needn't carry on. Understanding has a limit when it ventures into the sphere of wisdom that understanding does not understand.

"I must get back; I should go; I must go."

"No, not just yet," said Margin. "It would be unwise of us not to hear more of your understanding. How did you find us? Shadow has covered us with an impenetrable shield."

"Again you are correct. Discart Central Command has not been able to detect your whereabouts, despite the intensified search."

"So, how did you?" said Margin.

"I, too, own a bird," said Tidbright, "a homing pigeon that—how can I put it?—flies under the radar. Very low-tech—in fact, no tech at all. Wizards of discart technology have programmed their tech perception to such a point that an idea as simple as a homing pigeon would never surface."

"Ingenious, Sergeant Tidbright," said Margin. "Tell us more, if you will, of what we need to know."

"On knowing, I know among you I am other. I lack the reflective sensibilities you possess. So all I can offer is what I reveal.

"Accordingly, avalites advanced in learning, and I, Tidbright, am no exception. I am very bright, but in my role at Theatre Pretense, I pretend not to be. It's all a part of the play.

"In acting out my role, harmony is achieved that discarts welcome and oblige. Without harmony, steps tend to lead to extinction.

"At any instant, I could be crushed, but my ongoing act of pretense shadows me. Plus, I admire the role, my role prescribed.

"Critically important for you to understand is that when the avalite elites decreed the era of possession, changing their identity to discarts, they also stipulated that one-third of the avalite masses should be set aside.

"We were placed on holding mode, marginalized, considered objects of use for discart advancement. In essence, avalites became slaves. That is the extent of my reveal.

"No more to say, except that at tomorrow's eventide, they shall come for you to arrest you as spies."

"Won't you stay for tea?" said Shadow.

"Grateful," said Tidbright, "but I don't actually drink tea; during trial play of Mr. Crackler, my dashing for tea was part of the act, all pretend.

"No, I must go. I'm gone. I was here, though not my presence but a pretense."

"Do go," said Margin. "We shall meet again."

"The best, now goodbye," said Tidbright.

"And off he goes," said Margin. "Informative, to say the least, that visit was."

Churkwe tea, for two, for tea, parroted Loreto.

"Okay," said Margin, "let it be. A new pot, but as we sip our tea and ponder, not far from Torrent Peak may well feature in our plan."

"So, we have a plan?" said Quillingsworth.

"No, not yet," said Margin. "But facets of a plan precede the plan, and facets of a plan I have. Tidbright's pigeon tale sparked an idea—a very good idea, I do believe. We must not think along the lines discarts expect.

"Thus, a facet of our plan will be the deployment of disparate lines. It's the non-programmed nature of such lines that will baffle their powers of programmed perception and prove vitally important. Tidbright's observation did not go amiss.

"Concerning the lines, you'll recall my comments about lines that I've gathered from margins over time. Etched and scrawled, they act as little testaments of sentiment.

"They speak on their own, separately. When pulled together, they still speak on their own, but more robustly, as if speaking to one another. Together, they become a collection, and collections tend to have greater appeal than samples.

"At this point, do not strain to try and understand. When deployed, you'll understand without staining. As we partake in Shadow's fare, I'll cast out a few lines from my collection.

"That way you'll not be caught off guard when such lines surface in the heat of battle. Context doesn't matter; let the anonymous words speak for themselves.

"Lines of diversion from margins plucked—rapidly I cast them out in preparation for the stage:

Believers round here do not believe.
Thine eyes speak of vex.
Gaze upon your reflection, not me.
Time ticks, and at times with a hiss.
Wish not limitation by what you wish.
You alarm in most alarming ways.
Your character and person seem at odds.
I'm certain certainty wanes.
Great lines suffer from quoters of lesser minds.

"Stop, enough?

"So, no comment, then, a couple more. They have a certain quality worth savoring, along with Shadow's savory bits.

You can't tell truth, you've never knew.
I've come to exchange eyes, not eyeballs.

Take a stand or stand down.
In the present hour, tomorrow crouches.

"Now, the next-to-last:

In dreams, I dreamt of dreaming.

"And the last:

Sail now, sail swift; tomorrow's wind may not blow.

"Tomorrow will come. Just now, though, it's time for those that sleep to sleep.

"Shadow, our writer from Poet's Lodge is begging to nod off, so if you will, a cot for Quill and a cage, draped, for Loreto.

"In dreams, may they dream of dreaming!"

CHAPTER SEVEN
Preparations for War

"Rooster crowed, Quill," said Margin. "Time to rise, keep your powder dry, and meet the day. Shadow's prepared a full breakfast, fit for hearty souls. Sniff the air—fried mushrooms, I believe, with skillet savory bits for king and soldier alike."

"Oh, yes," said Quillingsworth. "So nothing has changed? We are where we are, with our focus the same?"

"Indeed, it seems like we're destined for a futuristic war but in the here and now. Fear nothing; have faith.

"I'm off for a walk along the brook and over the stone bridge leading to the meadow east. I could take you with me, but I won't. Lesser Light and Shadow make delightful campfire company.

"Ask of them what you wish. And be not afraid—fear will ruin your appetite. When the accusers appear waving warrants, we will oblige and go along, but we shall never surrender. Anyway, one must be near to venture in.

"Later, I say; off, just now."

"Margin, your pouch, a pad, your maps," said Shadow. "And do you wish to carry your sword or walk without?"

"Without. All I need, I have, except for perspective. That I'll garner along the way, which is essential for our plan."

"See, Loreto," said Quillingsworth, "the back of a figure the likes of which you and I have never seen. Margin's words—did you hear them, Lor? 'We will oblige and go along, but we shall never surrender.'

"'Meet the day,' Margin said. 'Okay, when you hear the lines, you will know them. Your role: Mock a single word when I nod. I will hardly pause; your word shall be cast into the line. Your word starts with the letter S. Okay, ready?

Let us rather
Hold fast the mortal sword, and like good men
Bestride our down-fall'n birthdom.
Each new morn
New widows howl, new orphans cry, new sorrows
Strike heaven on the face that it resounds
As if it felt with (Sco, t, land) and yelled out
Like syllable of dolor.

Churkwe, Soc, t, land, Scot, t, land, twe, parroted Loreto.

"Perfect," said Quillingsworth. "Now that's a proper way to meet the day.

"Lesser Light, Shadow, if you might, help me comprehend this character so sure, leading us into battle with discarts that have daemons on their side. I take it I should not ask of you to say.

"We exist, somehow, as if in rolling dreams, rolls with scenes that no mortal has ever seen. Margin—who is that leader, really? Such command, such poise, such confidence, such an uncommon character to behold.

"It can only be that Margin is the patron saint of old, of wars told in history's hold. Barely ten minutes now gone without her presence, and I feel strangely bereft, as if a spirit left, leaving mine to whine, wishing the missing one hadn't gone.

"Will I ever understand someone willing to walk on the stage in this futuristic play unafraid? Me, I feel frail, small, a seeping soul so wrongly cast. In your presence, I feel I should wear a veil.

"What's to be done isn't done, so what's to be done, does it have to be? You know, I could fail, crumble, and your mission come to naught. No record to show, nothing to read."

"We, the trio, do not do naught," said Lesser Light. "The moon knows no naught, nor do the stars that ever shine. Like the wind, spirits flow in and out of time.

"Do you suppose, Quillingsworth, that the angels have lost sight of you? You know that line uttered by Jesse's son: 'Where can I flee from thy presence?' He concluded, did he not, that neither heaven nor hell would give him hide?"

"I know, I do know, I must know," said Quillingsworth, "you're right, I know. It's just that I am mortal me. At this point, all my ledges of ascending courage are ripe with brittle fractures. I utter a prayer, snatch a thought, and before I have to think it through, what I thought has passed.

"I rally myself, and then go pale. I am a pauper when it comes to poise.

"It's not right that you three should be with me. I mean that this is some sort of holy ground, set in the devil's land, where mortal man should not tread. Or that I'm unworthy to tread—that's the intent I meant.

"Oh, what a mortal spin. I'm meant to flow along, I know, yet I beg of thee to see the way of seeing that I'm framed to see. There's much more here, I fear, than fearing. I recall 'Beware the Ides of March'— well the Ides of March have come in May."

"Breakfast, more tea, to be sipped," said Shadow. "And Loreto, a tiny cup of well-soaked pumpkin seeds."

"Quill," said Lesser Light, "do you not know that one's unworthiness can make them worthy? In this land of the unimaginable, you mustn't opt to lay reality aside. You've been chosen, cast, in a role that can't be uncast, in a play that must be played.

"I know you heard Tidbright speak about another way, to flee. 'You should go to what you know; escape this instant, if it's possible for you to do so,' he said. That is not the way.

"Bear in mind, as you must, Tidbright is an avalite projecting reasoned lines prompted not by wisdom but by AI. Though, I admit, Tidbright appears to be the best of his kind.

"Thus, what cannot be cannot be, no matter how fervent the wisher and the wish. Your mind may wish you to go, but I know your heart is telling you to stay. And to your credit, I also know you wish your doubting mind would go away.

"Quillingsworth, here there are no filler lines to pad out what's expressed. Every phrase and line come forth by spirited intent.

"Shadow, I know you concur, but say it so anyway—not for our sake, but that for Quillingsworth who must quill away the events that even now unfold."

"Oh, I do certainly concur concerning intent of lines," said Shadow. "And regarding lines, would you care for something to read, Quillingsworth—a book, a rack of books, or better still, let me open the door to a library. There, how's that? Peek inside.

"Go on, enter; the light is on as you can see, and on the far wall, mirrors in which you can watch what you read. Volumes thick and thin await readers of same description. You, of course, fall in between the two, and also being more tall than short, you'll not need a ladder to reach the top shelf."

"Okay, I'll step in and check it out. A mirrored wall, you say—so true, 'for the eye sees not itself but by reflection, by some other things,' if you know what I mean. Loreto, okay, let's take a peek at volumes past. Up on my shoulder, come along; no more seeds for now. Perhaps we'll get lost inside, open a cupboard, spot a pond, and go fishing in yet another land with parrot friend on the fly."

"Good, Margin's directive is working," said Lesser Light. "See, how Quill and Loreto move along the rows with considerable interest, pulling one book after another. That remarkable parrot even peeked at several of the spines.

"You've opened a rather extensive library. On the south wall, I note a bank of windows streaming light that is brighter than the light outside, a rather interesting feat for one called Shadow."

"Correct," said Shadow. "As you know, I'm also drawn to the light."

"So, how may volumes?"

"Nearly a million or more, I'm certain. Opening a library, such as this one for Quillingsworth, could be compared to casting a fishing line. I determine when to halt the cast, or the rows would string along to infinity."

"True, I know, but I'll not try your casting method of adjustable and variable lengths.

"My cast of light is fixed with cosmic precision; there is no shadow of turning. My glow never ceases to glow. Even though the sun has halted, refusing to shine, but that's the sun, not Lesser Light.

"What about Loreto, with her blue head, copious eyes, and layered feathers of brilliant green—do you think Loreto can actually read?

"Yes, it's true, and so it is; Loreto does far more than chirp about. A certain kind of perception goes on in that parrot brain, quite noticeable in the eyes. They zoom, then retract, then begin to blink, as if the object zoomed is being filed away.

"Take a look into your library made, the two seem quite content. Quill, our scribe, has placed an armful of books on the table beneath the windows of abnormal light. Truly occupied, as Margin knew they would be."

"We've chatted," said Shadow, "and sipped the morning away. Avalites turned discarts have marginalized not only carnites but avalites as well. Not so nice, these discart types of Onglander."

"A sizable nation surrounded by the sea," said Lesser Light. "And of no little import, as centuries go. A beacon of advancement and learning, Onglander became the envy of the world.

"Incarnites creating avalites—that was the start, and then the policy allowing their image-bearers unfettered access and experimentation of AI. Well, so, we see what we see."

"And now," said Shadow, "I see Margin approaching. Quillingsworth's insightful perceptions about Margin we heard—so accurate, but it was not for us to elaborate."

"All well?" said Margin.

"Indeed," said Lesser Light. "Shadow, as you can see, has opened a library for our wordsmith-come-historian and his feathered friend, Loreto."

"You were gone the morning long," said Shadow. "And sightings fruitful, no doubt?"

"Yes, quite; the importance of reconnaissance should never be questioned, taking in fortifications and avenues of advancement. Amphitheatre Aperio, to our west, is a massive coliseum, rivaling the greatest built during gladiator days of old.

"The surrounding grounds could accommodate four brigades, if not more. Bolden Fields and Hills stretch far, as Tidbright said, and will feature in our plans—as will Torrent Peak, though currently inauspicious, due to the sway of spiritual forces.

"You noted Tidbright's revealing account of the virus thread soliciting discarts to ascend the peak and present themselves as a sacrifice to the heavens.

"Glee Acts, riveting mind and imagination, consider the scene and what must have occurred. The ground hissed with steam, Tidbright said. What a hellish affair.

"Torrents of lightning bolts raining down, striking bleating discart sheep that squealed like pigs. That was a sacrifice, not to the heavens, but to Lucifer.

"When described by Tidbright, we knew, of course, the wherewithal of both virus and torrent rain, but we couldn't say in front of Quill and that perceptive parrot. They're in Shadow's library, I presume?"

"Yes, as you requested," said Shadow. "Soon it will clock the full extent of hour two."

"Leave them; before long, our warrant waivers will arrive. They will have discovered us by detecting the spot their probes could not penetrate. So, afternoon tea we'll have, fit for hardy souls of carnate form. Tell me of Quillingsworth's state of mind."

"The library," said Shadow, "has provided a tranquilizing effect. He spoke more than once about his mortality, a mortal sense of perception. Lesser Light asked if he feared that he'd drifted out of angels' sight, peering down from heaven."

"Well," said Lesser Light, "during our exchange, Quill said, 'I know, I know, you're right, I know,' concerning celestial assurance. The real matter had to do with Tidbright's admonition that we should go— escape—if we possibly could.

"During a protracted exchange, I explained that Tidbright is an actor in an act that must be played. He is an avalite of reasoned lines, not born of wisdom, but of AI."

"Good," said Margin. "Now, time for music, since at eventide we will be arrested. We would be remiss if we didn't call upon the Eventide Ensemble to gather their instruments and play a round of tunes."

"Sanguine it should be," said Shadow, "something along the lines of a Tipperary tune, parroted by Loreto."

"Let's go rosin our bows," said Margin, " and get on with the play. Quill, do come join us. It appears you and Loreto have been cracking and pecking books?"

"Sorry, I'll be right there," said Quillingsworth. "I guess we got a bit lost. I don't know . . . we entered, welcomed by a most wonderful scent. And then I sort of floated down the rows, row after row, without worry, as if drifting in a dream."

"How nice," said Shadow. "Taking in scents can have certain benefits, such as assisting with tranquility."

"Shadow," said Margin.

Come what, come may, parroted Loreto.

"That's right, Loreto," said Shadow.

"Well, let us play," said Margin, "till the setting sun has begun to cast its crimson rays.

"Crimson rays," said Quillingsworth; "it must be sign, say of blood."

"No, not as you imagine," said Margin. "Let us take a break—an hour's walk for each of us alone to ponder our position. Then we'll come back and play a few numbers. Okay?"

"If you don't mind, Margin, I'd like to step back into the library for a bit and finish a chapter that had thoroughly engaged me."

"As you wish," said Margin, "but you must still take a walk."

"So amazing," said Quillingsworth, "Shadow's miracle library, yet the volumes are authentic. Mystery at every turn, but I'm glad I got through that chapter, and it was ever so hard to pull away. That scent, so nice, I know you also liked it, Loreto, raising your beak in the air and fluttering your eyes.

"And so we've walked, Loreto. I'm not alone—are you? Up two hills we climbed, and then along the stream. I must admit, melancholy consumed our hour—I mean for me, not you. And now we've come around again to watch the trio play. Oh, as we heard, they began a good while ago. I thought you were to keep track of time?"

"Welcome back, Quill," said Margin. "An hour for you turned into three and its half. Not to worry. In the meantime, we've done justice to our instruments of string. Their makers, those fine craftsmen of bygone days, would be proud.

"At present, 'tis time to pack them away, I hear commotion coming our way, just minutes away."

"Margin," said Quillingsworth, "you know, I know, that no one knows where I am. What must they think? What am I thinking? We're in Onglander, it is 2102, and we're about to be arrested by discarts and put on trial as spies.

"I fear I'm melting away. What's unfolding here is unfolding with us folded inside. How to cope, but how do I cope? Do not be offended by my asking: Truly, do you ever show apprehension, or fear, you know, on your face, or in your posture? I've not seen it, and it's so stupefying.

"I mean, you've sat here playing; you on the violin, along with Shadow and Lesser Light; no one shows the hint of alarm . . . smiling, humming, and just being."

"Well," said Margin, "this is a rare occasion, the three of us getting together once again, and a mission of this importance requires a certain composure and sense of harmony. It's about letting the ears hear sounds the soul willingly embraces.

"Concerning apprehension, you've raised an important matter indeed. I know that demons fear, which will be to our advantage in what's to come. Bear in mind continually, Quill, your notes, your role, and the importance ascribed to your written account. For to many you shall reveal what the future holds."

"Okay, I see, no use, okay," said Quillingsworth. "Just don't leave us, Loreto and me. Where would we go? How could we walk out of time and find eternity? We would tumble ever on in a mystical nightmare, searching forevermore for a door."

Churkwe, only this, and nothing more, parroted Loreto.

"What, Loreto? No need to fall silent," said Quillingsworth; "the trio remains festive, so let your feathers down."

Churkwe, a rapping, tap, tap, tapping, at my chamber door, parroted Loreto.

"Well," said Margin, "our captors are swift approaching, and there is no door here on which to rap or tap."

"They're coming, they're coming," said Quillingsworth. "What should we do, stand?"

"Prudent," said Margin. "Let Loreto perch on your shoulder, and be sure to take along her leather pouch, and we'll do the same with the instruments. Okay?

"And so, now we make contact. Rise, comrades, but stand at ease. No jesting."

"Loreto, come on up; be still, be good," said Quillingsworth.

"Hello, throng," said Margin, "you seem to be a rather large contingent—must be a hundred in number, if not more.

"Anyway, it's a nice day for an outing, for a stroll through the grove. We have found this spot quite agreeable. Sorry, we've just put away our instruments, or we would have played a welcoming number."

"Stay where you are! I am Colonel Prestiggens; we are not here for a musical performance. By dictate of the Discart High Court of Onglander, we have come to arrest you as spies."

"Heard," said Margin. "I ask, though, does your dictate state on suspicion of spying, or spies?"

"No suspicion; you are spies, you will be tried as spies, and you will, no doubt, be executed as spies."

"No ambivalence I hear in your words," said Margin.

"Discart Delegation," said Colonel Prestiggens, "hold your position next to me. Avalites, draw your swords and surround the accused.

"Carnites, behind them, and then down on your knees. Prepare to scour and sweep the camp by hand. Use your nails to claw the dirt.

"Avalites Corps, no need for cuffs and leg irons. Rope them in standard rope-line procedure. Spies, we know you by name, given your appearance at Theatre Pretense.

"Margin rope first—yes, that's right, the slightest one, the ringleader. Everyone make room. Wrap the rope round Margin's waist, then a sword and a half gap before you rope the next.

"That one, just off to the left, he's called Shadow, I do believe. Good, around thrice with the rope, no rush, and then a precise gap betwixt them. That one's next, Lesser Light his name.

"And lastly, at the rear, the carnite Quillingsworth, and do no harm to that bird, that parrot, that Blue Head they call Loreto. He's more than a mocking bird. Blue Head exhibits a sense of perception most unusual.

"Therefore, the parrot, too, will be tried. He will be grilled about what he knows and how he came to know it, as well as when he knew it. He's a key mediator in this so-called Eventide Ensemble.

"If, as suspected, these three, and the fourth now tied in, be sent by the gods, they could have benefited by AI. Look at the lot, soon to be despised and rejected by discarts, avalites, and carnites alike.

"Avalite Sentry, light your torches. Gather alongside the sword bearers and prepare to march. Before being locked up, the spies are to appear before the High Court Judge, Honorable Vinc Castalon.

"Carnites, on your knees—start clawing about in the dirt for evidence.

"Torches lit. Now march!"

CHAPTER EIGHT
High Court, Theatre Pretense

"Okay, halt," said Colonel Prestiggens. "See, spies, you're now back where you began, the stage door of Theatre Pretense, which also happens to be the Discart High Court. One and the same they are.

"All right, untie the infamous Eventide Ensemble, and keep the torches burning until they are brought through. Eventide Ensemble, what a cover—old-world costumes—you belong on stage, but as clowns.

"You'll certainly look the part of clown criminals, all strung up on ropes, or they may behead you, one by one. That includes the Blue Head—the parrot."

Churkwe, Ro, e, o, where art thou? parroted Loreto.

"Lor, no, not now," said Quillingsworth. "Nestle, be still, hunker down."

"Watch that bird," said Colonel Prestiggens. "Blue Head may be mapping you, reading you. Don't look that bird in the eyes."

'Tis night, such, sweet sorrow, twee, parroted Loreto.

"See, the bird is mocking us," said Colonel Prestiggens. "If we were not forbidden to swear, I would cuss the feathers of that bird. 'Sweet sorrow': That's surely some sort of message—a spying code, spy speak—uttered by Blue's beak.

"Now, put away your sword, avalites; you can't kill the bird. Besides, you'd chop off the carnite's head. Now, usher them on through the stage door. Two sentinels, swords drawn, follow."

Oh, pity me, miserable wretch I am, parroted Loreto.

"On through," said Colonel Prestiggens. "Kick 'em a bit, that's okay. Good; coil and keep the rope. Snuff torches, our part's done; now, disband."

THE WINGS:

"Oh, yes, we've been expecting you; I'm Sergeant Tidbright, in charge, playing the part I play. Didn't know they were bringing you through the back, through the Stage Door entrance. More for entertainers and actors, this way in, but I heard the ring and rushed to meet you.

"Well, I mean, you're entertainers, the Eventide Ensemble, though you're not here to entertain on this occasion. Just the same, I see you're lugging your instruments. Maybe they want you to play to prove you can play when you are tried.

"Come, come along. Just follow me up the steps, and then we'll walk backstage, along the East Wing, and then out onstage. You'll appear before the Judge Vinc and those that prosecute.

"Say, I see that lovely parrot is still with you. Hi, bird, tweet. I can give you a peanut. I keep a few in the inside pocket of my jacket. Does the parrot eat peanuts?"

"On occasion," said Quillingsworth, "but given the hour, no peanuts for Loreto."

"Well, I've got 'em here if you want 'em later on. Seems like suspicion has been ratcheted up against you fellows from what I've heard. And I'd add, it's not hard to hear—they're talking about you on nearly every street corner.

"You don't have to stop, or gawk, to listen in; just keep walking and listening as you pass by the talkers talking.

"'That ensemble, four spies, curious, great threat, high alert.' Then, when you pass by the next corner, you pick up a bit more: 'Blue-headed parrot, costumed wizards, devious lot, war.' And yet another corner,

'Suspicions, foreign, not of this world,' and before long, you've picked up the word on the street."

STAGE:

Sergeant Tidbright: Well, just like that, here we are. Hey, I say, are you sure your bird doesn't want a peanut? Here, here, quickly, take two, just to have one in reserve.

Never mind, we've been motioned. Now, straight on to the bench, then I'll pause and introduce you, and then wait. Keep your heads up; shame's not the look you want.

Ahem . . . as procedure dictates, Honorable Vinc Castalon, I, Sergeant Tidbright, present to you the Eventide Ensemble as dutifully directed to do. They now proceed to the bench.

High Court Judge, Honorable Vinc Castalon: Well now, if it isn't our famed Eventide Ensemble, that participated in the trial of Mr. Crackler. You do recall Mr. Crackler, don't you?

I admired your reading; perhaps we'll have you read for us again. Though that was then, this is now, and rather serious business has prompted our reunion. You, of course, are spies in garb and disguise. More than that, your carnate makeup is wrapped up, not in swaddling clothes, but in a cocoon of abnormality and mystery.

When you entered our midst, intercepts and AI-powered probes instantaneously screened, mapped, and documented specifics concerning your composition.

Now, you, with the bird—Quillingsworth, I believe—screened as a normal carnite should. Bones, brains, pressures, and senses all intact. As for the bird, we'll come back to that in a moment.

On the other hand, you three did not screen as expected. In fact, you proved to be unscreenable, which is next to impossible. It's been determined that you've miraculously, mysteriously cocooned yourself in some sort of impenetrable wrap.

You must be wizards, and odd wizards at that. For what and why you have chosen to venture into Onglander, no one knows except you three. Such a grave mistake you've done in doing so.

In a minute, I'll outline what's in store for you over the next few days. But, before I do so, I want to hear from each of you, one by one. Now move on over to the side, to the platform, and await your call.

Margin, you, as head honcho of this outfit, are the first to speak. So speak—say what you wish to say on your own behalf.

By the way, your womanly mannish appearance must be part of your spying deception.

In the Great Hall of Masks, a very special mask is displayed at the center of the hall that speaks of you. In fact, it's the first mask ever worn at Theater Pretense. The mask—a face half-woman, half-man, is a masterpiece of artisan perfection.

Anyway, speak, and expect me to interrupt.

Margin: Your honor, we've not come to Onglander with intent of harm. We came to discover in the spirit of curiosity, seeking to learn about Onglander achievements and technological advancements.

High Court Judge: Already, I detect menace. Carry on.

Margin: As I said, we do not intend harm, but if harm comes to us, harm shall be returned.

High Court Judge: Halt! Freeze your mind. Tidbright, where's the court reporter? This proceeding must be on the record.

Tidbright: Well, Your Honor, sir, you know, it's around that time of day when the day of one day begins to nudge along to make room for another day.

High Court Judge: Imbecile, what did you just say? You're supposed to make meaning out of words, not fall into Crazy Talk, Stupid Talk! For the record, I want "Crazy Talk, Stupid Talk" capped for emphasis.

Stupid words sound out thoughts, so that thought can ride the waves saying what thoughts wish to say. In other words, idiot, by enunciation of words, thoughts get out and about. An utterance is an outing, which is taken in by another, which, in turn, utters an outing of thoughts via words.

What we have here is a failure to communicate. You know why, because we have you!

Tidbright: Now, I must say, Your Honor, that's definitely a way of saying something, in a way, that says even more than a saying like that would normally say. But, come to think of it, I've never heard a saying like that said that way.

See my point?

High Court Judge: Tidbright, O Tidbright, you are one of a kind, a universal kind; you are never to be cloned, never.

For your information, a notice went out to the court reporter before the Eventide Ensemble spies were brought in and assembled before me.

Tidbright: You know, my buzzer just buzzed, and I noticed it was the stage door. I know for sure when the buzz buzzes intermittently like that. Buzz, buzz, then pause, and buzz, buzz, buzz.

In rapid response to the buzzing, I heard the sound of heels tapping our way.

PLATFORM:
Loreto: *Tap, tap, tapping, shadow, floor. . .*

STAGE:

High Court Judge: Quiet that bird!

Okay, at last, the court reporter. Good, settle right in; I'll give you a few more seconds.

Now then, we return to Margin. And did you have the audacity to say something about harm—that if harm comes to you, harm shall come to us?

No one dares to say comments like that. It's unconscionable, irresponsible, and extremely detrimental to your well-being.

Margin: I meant what I said. In your words, I've uttered an outing of words, conveying precisely the thoughts I wished to convey.

High Court Judge: You are of some unknown power, you. Here, we look to AI—willingly we do. Facts, science, advancement soaked into the very corpus of discart composition.

You are some sort of wizard in carnite form; you must understand that those moth-eaten scrolls that your kind clung to by order of I AM are nothing but artifacts here in the land of AI. Those old, parched parchment scrolls are like prehistoric feathers, tossing and tumbling in a desert dry, clipped from a mysterious bird that has long since died.

Discarts bend not their knees in prayer or participate in spiritual séances. That's the purview of blind carnites who attempt to bring down the gods or draw mystical prophets from the earth. No, no, we retool ourselves in ever revolving forms of discarnate perfection.

Margin: Your Honor, in the court of wisdom, you have no honor. In fact, you do not register in the Book of Life, or in any other book that matters.

You are but an entity, a fabrication, not a being of creation. Under the revelatory tutelage of AI, you've leaped and morphed along the AI morphing trail that knows nothing of life experientially.

Just data bits and spits, propping and projecting into matters wisdom itself dares not tread. If discarts gain control of the whole world, which you're programmed to do, what would discarts do?

No arching narrative to follow, no words of wisdom to unfold, nothing but AI-empowered information bits, a smorgasbord of disparate clippings from which to pick and choose.

No endgame—just the game. No kingdom to enter—just a domain, a maelstrom of data in which discarts swirl, snarl, and bite.

No shepherd's staff comforting, no green grass in which to lie, no leading by still waters, no soul to restore, no soul at all. In contrast, discarts whirl in a meaningless maelstrom with sparks sparking, popping, and hissing.

The vast whirlpool funnels down, down, down to the devil's dominion, with no rising sun, no sandy shore, and no ocean waves.

You've chosen, by programmed selection, your possession. You are a foul microchip, demon-possessed circuit boards; that's what you are, and nothing more.

PLATFORM:
Loreto: *Only this, and nothing more . . .*

STAGE:
High Court Judge: What's that? Parrot speak, parrot soup, soon you'll be.

PLATFORM:
Quillingsworth: Loreto, not now, no, not now. Lesser Light, we're doomed.

Lesser Light: Hmm.

High Court Judge: Margin, you are a cracked egg, rotten. You speak wizard-speak, your native language. It is you who will soon swirl in a whirlpool, thrashing about as down, down, down you go, ground as garbage. After, that is, we've dissected your innards, slice by slice.

Then, the garbage grinder will be plugged and filled with acid and ground for a month or more.

No, step away, back to the platform.

Next, let's see. Lesser Light, yes, come, stand before the bench. A bit closer, a few steps more, and that will do.

Okay, you, so-called Lesser Light, explain your involvement, your role, in this spy ring.

Lesser Light: Well, if truth be told, I now tell it. My role relates to tide, time, and glow. Thus, I regulate and sequence the elements in predetermined phases.

High Court Judge: I see. So you carry the torch and help plan the operations according to tides of time.

What else, anything else? Do you also want to go off on a wizard tangent, as Margin did?

Lesser Light: No, articulating mission objects and intent is not my role.

High Court Judge: So, do you have anything more, Lesser Light?

Lesser Light: No, Judge, nothing more.

High Court Judge: Okay, off with you. And up next, we have Shadow. Come along; we do not intend for this session to last the night.

Okay, good; right there, halt. Now, the spotlight shines on you, Shadow, so speak and explain your role.

Shadow: Well, my role and name are one and the same. As Lesser Light regulates matters of tide, time, and glow, I, Shadow, cast shadows in marginalized quarters, amid the fringe, the outskirts, and along the gutters where outcasts lurk.

High Court Judge: Oh, how clever—the intricacies of this spy ring operation are most revealing. Precise timing, the ebb and flow of tides, along with shifting shadows to hide treasure in gutters, under the glow of lesser light.

I say, forthcoming you've been. So, return to the Waiting Platform, as we finalize this procedure by hearing from Mr. Quillingsworth.

Quillingsworth, step forward. No need to look to Margin; just come along, you and your bird. We know your name; tell us about your role.

Quillingsworth: So, of me, of my case, you ask. I mean, being here in Onglander as I appear to be, I can say that I am a long way from home.

Loreto: *'Tis a long way to Tipperary; 'tis a long way to go.*

Quillingsworth: Sorry, Your Honor, we don't actually live in Tipperary, though we are a long way from home. And I'm a bit confused about when we left.

It was sometime after I lay down in the meadow to die among the daffodils, then looked up in the hackberry tree and spotted a trio in the branches playing a lovely melody.

High Court Judge: You deluded, deranged carnite creature, you spy, you will never go home again. No way back for you, no trail, no map, and even if there were a map, the territory is not the map.

These instruments you say you saw—what type of instruments?

Quillingsworth: A violin, viola, and cello, presently stowed in the cases on the platform.

High Court Judge: What's more?

Quillingsworth: More? Well, I'm a writer and a poet who lives in Poet's Lodge. A bullet found me, and on a cold winter's day as January was slipping away, I dreamed of May.

Your distinct stare must mean I should carry on, right?

Loraine, my love, drowned in Concerto River, which flows along the meadow. That's the same meadow with the daffodils and hackberry tree where I wished to die.

And the same tree in which the trio played.

High Court Judge: We found your letter.

Quillingsworth: You did? Are you sure it's mine?

High Court Judge: Indeed. Court reporter, come forth and read the salutation and first two paragraphs of the letter, nothing more. Your reading does not need to be recorded. Just a note entered that you did so.

Here's the letter.

Court Reporter: Yes, Judge, as you request.

> *Dear Loraine,*
>
> *Desperately we miss you, miss you so, we do. We loved you; we loved you true.*
>
> *We are the same, but not the same at all. How could we be? Loreto often mocks more somber notes, matching well the loss of spring in my stride.*

That's all, Your Honor.

High Court Judge: The letter, your letter, Quillingsworth, must be some sort of pretense about love along carnite sentiments. Discarts know nothing about love, that swampy seaweed notion.

However, the letter does tell us that you, too, are some sort of false wizard of trickery. We analyzed and probed, and therefore we know the precise age of this letter.

If you had actually written the letter, you would be 116, and the bird roughly 108.

Peculiar—these compounding elements convict you, along with and the entire Eventide Ensemble. Okay, I'm done with you, puppet.

Place your bird on the top rail of the witness chair. Tidbright, assist.

Good. All right, since you claim to be a poet, a short poem and then you can walk away.

Quillingsworth: You gaze upon a person I knew, and yet, I am he.

High Court Judge: You appear grim, rather different than when you first approached the bench. Too many lies caught, all twisted around this ring of spies.

Quillingsworth: Grim is not the look upon my face. You look upon a face of courage—defiant courage that's returned, though temporarily was gone.

A poem? Okay, short is the title: "The Shore."

Stand upon the shore,
Watch a wave become a wave,
Watch the wave roll in
And splash upon the shore.
Stand, watch a wave, no more.

High Court Judge: To that end was the wave.

Moving on to the witness chair, I now address the parrot, Blue Head.

So, you're neither a stool pigeon nor a peregrine, that much we know. I see you don't like interrogation, stepping back and forth on the rail, all fidgety and fluttery. Quit flapping about.

That's a bit better. What I want to know is what do you know, and when and how did you acquire what you know? We know you can call out various lines, but it's the added knack of perceptibility that renders you suspicious.

All right, Blue Head, I ask you straight out, as you look straight at me, are you really a bird? So, spit it out—coo, chirp, call, crow—the tone makes no difference; substance is the aim of this inquiry.

Okay, I'm waiting. Silent, you remain. Waiting still, we wait.

The court reporter has nothing to report, nothing to enter under the heading "Blue Head, the Parrot." You are in the ledger, so speak.

Okay, more sidestepping, fidgeting, and flapping. Stifle your antics, Blue Head.

Okay, once again I ask you, are you really a bird? And if so, how can you still be alive and chirping about, at 108?

Loreto: *Churkwe, everything a season under heaven, chor-ee. Churkwe, time to mourn, to dance, chor-ee.*

High Court Judge: You confounded spying bird, you are stealth, fluffed up by your wizard mates. We have a cage for you. One last time, confess.

Loreto: *Churkwe, time to rend, time to speak, silence too, chor-ee.*

High Court Judge: Okay, you clever spying bird! Tidbright, have the spy ring step back to the bench.

Tidbright: The ring, I suppose, means you, Eventide Ensemble. So, pick up your cases and pouches and proceed in making the number of steps necessary, to move from the platform to the bench.

Watch that first step. Wonderful—see, it's simple. Good, just stand attentive-like.

High Court Judge: I shall be brief. From here, you will be taken to your cell, one cell all together, including Blue Head.

Then, over the course of three days, you will go to trial in the Spy Plays conducted at Amphitheatre Aperio. Hundreds of thousands of attendees will gather to watch the play trials, including discarts and some avalites—but carnites only by screen.

You will be tried as spies and for spreading false fodder and perturbing notions pertaining to those ancient myths about I AM and those miserable wanderers of that same legend.

First trial will be tomorrow, at 3:00 p.m. sharp. Prepare your lines; we will prepare the rope.

Bear in mind, All the World's a Play, Presence 'n Pretense, the Rave.

Now, off with them; lock them up.

Court is dismissed!

PRISON CELL:

"Even on the backside of darkness," said Lesser Light, "a bright side abides. A glow still glows, though eclipsed.

"So, the bright side: Consider the spaciousness of the cell in which we're held."

"And, said Shadow, "we received no stripes, which High Court Judge, Honorable Vinc Castalon might have ordered. I refer to the ancient text stating that:

*If the guilty man deserves to be beaten, the judge shall have him
lie down and be flogged in his presence with the number of lashes
his crime warrants. He may receive no more than forty lashes.*

"How encouraging," said Quillingsworth. "And that's the bright side?"

"Quill," said Margin, "set that aside for now. I wish to know what happened to you as you stood before the Judge. The change did not go unnoticed."

"What happened to me," said Quillingsworth, "I'm not quite sure, though you are correct. My disposition suddenly shifted—a volte-face on my part, indeed.

"Yet, perhaps I do know, now that you raise the point, and I ponder it. When the Court Recorder read the letter, a nerve deep inside was touched. Loreto and I penned the letter a few years ago, as we reflected on Loraine's passing, the dreadful drowning. We loved her, Loreto and me.

"Then, here in 2102, so far removed in time and place, there I stood, hearing words written so long ago with respect to our current state. Crushing, jolting the act proved to be to me.

"It was more than just the lines of the letter. The theater and the court, combined and intertwined as they appear to be, construct a medium and message equally inseparable. Pretense, the law, the discarts, incapable of true presence but there in control—at once it became irk and gall to me, this state of technology mastery.

"The judge, the Honorable Vinc Castalon, is a not a living being, as beings live. A pretense judge, in a pretense court, programmed by generative AI—it's worse than the worst science fiction can spin.

"The judge's words assaulted my ears and raped my soul. Everyone heard the words he spoke after the Court Reporter read the lines. 'The letter, your letter, Quillingsworth, must be some sort of pretense about love, along carnite sentiments. Discarts know nothing about love, that swampy seaweed notion.'

"'Swampy seaweed notion' in reference to emotions expressed over one so lovely that had drowned. At that phrase, instantly I recalled the sight of Loraine in the river, lifeless, with her hair and dress mangled amid the twigs and brush. Her right hand kept moving, as if waving, but it was only the pretense of life, not life; the current was the cause.

"Essence expressed means nothing to discarts. Lines are not engaged;

rather, they are reduced to codes, words, etymology, and historicity. With technological advancement, they've unquestionably advanced, but to what? By way of a different current, lifelike they move but have no being.

"Among the many achievements they will never achieve is limbic consonance, the resonance of the soul and mind with another. Say mother and child, or the storyteller and listener who stroll together in the aura of the story told.

"Blank unto blank is blank. Fruitless are discarts, whatever they may be. Consider the line, 'This above all: to thine own self be true.' What do those words mean to discarts?

"A line to dissect data into bits, not to embrace with thought and reflection; thus, such lines bear no fruit among the digital discarnate pickers of 2102."

"So, in nature," said Lesser Light, "there are cycles, seeds, seasons, and tides. Techno-bots are linear know-nots."

"Focus—now we must," said Margin. "Shadow, I know you've distorted the listening and scanning devices."

"Correct," said Shadow, "the instant we entered the cell."

"Discarts on watch," said Margin, "will have sentinels and AI working on a solution. And we will help. By leaving now, and, as we go, Shadow will restore the system, and in turn, discarts will praise AI.

"Shadow, since we're in the land of pretense and deception, when I utter the phrase 'now we depart,' spring forth ghostly images to play our part. Leave the ghosts flapping with a bit of motion, turning, stretching arms, and the like, and include a parrot ghost, as well, with flapping wings.

"Okay, everyone ready? "

Churkwe, time, hour, run through, roughest day, parroted Loreto.

"Quill," said Margin, "your notepad and pens . . . don't forget. Okay, now we depart!"

SEASIDE:

"Breathe in the seaside air," said Margin, "and listen to the sound of the rolling ocean waves."

"Stunning, impossible . . . but not," said Quillingsworth. "We were tried, locked up in prison, and now stand on a sandy seaside beach. Loreto, go ahead, wing about; just don't fly away.

"What do you make of Tidbright and his manner in court, as if he had never come to visit our camp?"

"He had no choice," said Margin. "The slightest hint of association with us, and he would have been annihilated without a trial. Though he did hit on it when he said, 'I'm Sergeant Tidbright in charge, playing the part I play.' The part he plays, he said."

"I see," said Quillingsworth. "I didn't catch that."

"You're no longer paranoid, Quill?" said Margin. "Not wishing to be cast on a funeral pyre?"

"Somehow, in this madness," said Quillingsworth, "I've come to understand more of what I understood in part. Perhaps being totally alienated from all I know and knew created a mindset I had never known. I don't know, maybe like being under anesthesia but still conscious—something like that.

"Anyway, at some point, maybe it was during Crackler's trial, after the reading, I found myself thinking and talking to myself, saying, 'Before you were born, Quill, you were not afraid. Life is bigger than you, so let it live.'

"I kept mulling over that whole thought pattern that would softly rise in my mind and then gently recede, no matter the commotion taking place. After a while, courage I thought I'd lost also began to rise. That's all."

"Any thoughts," said Margin, "Shadow, Lesser Light, regarding Quill's comments?"

"Yes," said Shadow. "It's time for tea. Consisting of tomato consommé, grilled fish, potatoes flash-fried and edgy-burnt, tossed greens—all sorts—yeast rolls, a puff, gooseberry pie à la mode, with very vintage red wine, cheese wedges, some blue, some not, along with lots of nuts, dates, and nibble bits.

"Two minutes, and the table will be spread and tomato consommé served."

"Perfect," said Lesser Light. "Tea by the sea, including gooseberry pie."

"I won't even speak; what would I say?" said Quillingsworth. "Oh, I did it again: Speaking of not speaking, I spoke. Yet, if I hadn't spoken, saying I wouldn't speak, Shadow might have thought I had taken his wonders and culinary skills for granted. Never would I think such a thought.

"Oh dear me, thoughts and speech—one silent, the other not—a battle royal over what is actually said. You know what I mean to say?

"Where are we, anyway? No one's said."

"We're on the far side of Onglander," said Margin. "It was once called Jewell Beach, but no more. Onglander was a very sought-after destination back before the days of AI and the race toward Singularity.

"Then, a rash of edicts went out, dictating digital dictator commands, along with a maddening rush to clear not only the beaches of carnites, but all of Onglander. Thus, the dwindling carnite population we now see is in grave danger of extinction, at least in Onglander.

"All of this, of course, underscores the urgency of our mission, our call. The goal is evident: today, discard dominance of Onglander, and tomorrow, well, does one need to say?"

"What will happen," said Quillingsworth, "to, say, the Isle of Estillyen, about which you spoke? Estillyen, beyond the Storied Sea, a destination I hold as a dream, and Theater Portesque, with its chandeliers aglow—will their doors shut and their lights go out?

"And who will know that the rising tide of Singularity is swiftly approaching?"

"Think in terms of a digital tsunami," said Margin, "spawning global havoc, full of commotion and confusion, setting off buzzing bewilderment, static, chatter, fragmentation, and delusion—that's what would happen, Quill."

Churkwe, only this, nothing more, parroted Loreto.

"But the amphitheatre," said Quillingsworth, "and tens of thousands of attendees, the plays . . . I'm lost. What's going to happen next? Is all that now for naught, as if the dream within a dream has dreamt?"

"No, not at all, Quill," said Margin. "As the judge announced, over the next three days, the Spy Plays will be performed at Amphitheatre Aperio. We'll be in the plays, on trial. And, as you said, thousands of discarts, avalites, and perhaps a token placement of carnites will gather to watch the play trials play out."

"Oh dear, my soul," said Quillingsworth. "It's more than I can bear. Other thoughts I need; my mind wants to wander. What about the seaside here, on Onglander—does it remind you of Estillyen shores? I just need to dream."

"You will discover, Quill," said Margin, "an amazing feature of life to grasp and appreciate. While dreaming, as dreamers do, a dreamer, such as you, can live inside a dream and outside the dream simultaneously. Let it be so, even as I speak. Worth pondering, is it not, such a thought concerning dreams?

"Regarding the Isle of Estillyen, there's a story, a facet of Estillyen history, I'm sure would interest you. Shadow, from the Estillyen archives, kindly lift a copy for Quill about Eugene Eristaperio and his record while visiting the isle during St. Robert's Week and the month of May. Take the copy with you Quill, you'll enjoy reading it.

"Just now, we need to collect our thoughts regarding what we've witnessed during our time in Onglander and prepare for the forthcoming Spy Plays. And as we make that transition, we need a proper table, with rung-back chairs, fit for Shadow's amazing spread and seaside atmosphere."

"Right behind you," said Shadow. "On the ledge, I whisked away the sand in my spare time. The table you wished is already spread, right here in front of the towering pines."

"Perfect," said Margin. "Let's move our kits and cases. Oh, I just got a whiff of tomato consommé and grilled fish.

"Ah, there, perfect. Gather around and take a seat, where delicacies we'll share. As you can see, Shadow provided a ladder-back chair for Loreto. Quill, I wonder what she thinks of being called Blue Head?"

Raven, not a feather did he flutter, nevermore, parroted Loreto.

"Amazing, utterly amazing," said Margin.

"Okay, gather round; giving grace we do with words but a few, saying more in solitude. Listen to the sound of the sea. Prayerfully listen. And listen still. May David's prayer be said of us:

Blessed be the Lord,
who has not given us
as prey to their teeth!
We have escaped as a bird
from the snare of the fowlers;
the snare is broken,
and we have escaped!
Our help is in the name of the Lord,
who made heaven and earth.

"Thus, we give thanks unto thee, forgetting not those in the shadows, margins, and lesser lights who live often out of sight. Amen!

"So, bon appétit, and that includes you, Loreto."

"There's no food like this," said Quillingsworth, "in all the earth. It is the fare of fairest dreams."

"Say, I like that," said Shadow.

"Quill, in the meadow green," said Margin, "under the hackberry tree our journey came to be. So, from the crossroads, we set out on our mission to discover Onglander in 2102.

"The cries of Onglander had not gone unheard.

"That tomato consommé was superb, utterly. And these edgy-burnts with grilled fish—succulent, say, Quill?"

"Every morsel," said Quillingsworth, "and as you can see, Loreto is pecking away at her yeast roll and green bits."

"I'm moving at a rapid clip," said Lesser Light, "knowing gooseberry pie à la mode is next."

"Tell me, Quill," said Margin, "are you keeping copious notes? All happenings, conversations, such as this, are fair game. Not word for word, but the more important words, if you know what I mean.

"Anyway, I'll carry on. In Onglander, we've discovered the carnite race has been marginalized. This is a matter grave, a matter of cosmic concern, on a par with Sodom and Gomorrah of old.

"Be that as it may, this uncivilized form of existence evolved via technological advancement powered by AI. All things virtual rendered presence and reality second place. Technological advancement proved to be more than a melding of man and machine.

"Via the tools and platforms they'd created, the inventors and tool-makers became immersed as they plunged in the virtual worlds they'd created. Thus, they entered their own creation, not to redeem it, but to be redeemed by it, seeking a new form of techno-life. Not a good move.

"The devices appeared heaven-sent, one after another, gadgets new, swooping down swift as peregrines, but in time, the albatrosses would drop on the shoulders of the human race.

"Lines from the 'Ancient Mariner' I know many by heart:

The souls did from their bodies fly,
They fled to bliss or woe!
And every soul, it passed me by,
Like the whizz of my cross-bow!

Souls, from bodies, fly, parroted Loreto.

"Accustomed patterns of life and ritual forms of gathering began to wane. Watching rites from a distance, places without smoke and sensor, supplanted rituals of human presence engaging all the senses.

"Passover or the Eucharist, as a discarnate, is a mediated experience altogether ruinous. Experience imbues the meaning, impregnating the heart and soul. A rite like Passover, recounting the Exodus from Egypt, the seder meal, bitter herbs, matzo, the wine, and all the rest, passed in the rite's reenactment, with prayers and chants.

"Presence, community, communion, the aura, the essence . . . all of which discarts eschew. They know nothing about the significance of Elijah's cup, or why children gather round to watch and wait for ripples, signifying Elijah's sip.

"Discarts, ever processing, scanning, and dissecting data, categorize and define the ritual as a fading tradition of a wandering ancient tribe, and nothing more. Essence of divine and human presence does not apply.

"Thus, resolve unyielding we must have in reckoning with and recording the discart demise."

"Demise, on our own," said Quillingsworth. "How, though? The demon-possessed discart legions crave ascendance; demons believe the lie that they will once again arise."

"All of that and more," said Margin, "without question, but this is not a game; this is war."

"But honestly, earnestly," said Quillingsworth, "I ask, How can a quartet with a parrot change the course apparent of discart futuristic rule?"

"Good question," said Margin, "but never mind, it shall happen; that is, unless fissures in the cosmos suddenly appear.

"Fissures in the cosmos," said Quillingsworth, "appearing—a notion, a figure of speech, correct?"

"Time will tell," said Margin, "and much time we do not have. Now it's time to focus on a few specifics."

"Ah," said Lesser Light, "such delectate crust, the filling so tart and sweet; nothing compares to gooseberry pie, especially when à la mode."

"Okay, listen up," said Margin. "Appearing we shall do tomorrow, just prior to the ninth hour. By then, the discarts will be in state of whiplash disarray; the first Spy Play, and no spies.

"Regardless, at the north end of Amphitheatre Aperio, there's a covered stage, roughly four times the size of the stage at Theatre Pretense. From the front of stage, all the way across, thirty-two steps descend to the amphitheatre's expansive earthen floor.

"As you will soon see, there's a curtain separating backstage from the performance stage. I'm still working through the particulars of our sudden reappearance, but it's through that tall black curtain that we will enter.

"Now, we need to consider some of our advantages."

"Advantages?" asked Quillingsworth.

"Yes, there are several," said Margin. "Number one, we disappeared from prison, which would have set off all manner of alarms, panic, and inspection. By escaping, we've achieved a kind of mythic notoriety, which is currently churning all over Onglander.

"Second, we suddenly appear. While the elites and everyone down the line thought we had vanished, and then, on the run, we return willingly, causing great shock.

"Third, our ability to appear and disappear will be seen as supernatural, precipitating untold buzzing and probing as to what this could mean. Uncertainty, leeriness, and wondering amount to liabilities, not strengths, on the field of battle.

"Fourth, discarts act not by wisdom and intuition, but by selection, possibilities, and projections, all programmed by AI. Discarts, besides being evil, move by linear rationale. Without wisdom, rationale can precipitate faulty moves.

"Thus, part of our approach will be to cast out lines from the margins of time in a bizarre, nonrational manner. The blitz of such lines cast during the plays will send the discarts into a quandary.

"Fifth, as we know, discarts are demon-possessed. Somehow, discart-advanced technology has managed to keep their demons suppressed. Perhaps a never-ending playback loop threatens to cast the demons into arid places or back among the dead of unholy demise.

"Just the same, we shall work to rouse the demons to uncontrollable actions."

"Okay," said Quillingsworth, "let me note that rousing demons to uncontrollable action, stated by Margin, is advantage number five."

"Sixth," said Margin, "Shadow and Lesser Light have much to offer in times of war.

"Seventh, you, Quill, and Loreto will perform brilliantly, speaking classic lines of poetry and uncharted quips that add to the mesmerizing effect.

"Any questions as we ready ourselves for battle? No? Well, then, I suggest we sip another cup of tea amid the sights and sounds and ocean breeze, all in all a very enchanting place to be.

"And, by the way, well done on the scrumptious fare. And everyone says what?"

"Hear, hear!"

CHAPTER NINE
Spy Play I: *Misery of Job, Say-So I AM*

AMPHITHEATRE APERIO STAGE:

Master of Ceremonies, High Court Judge, Honorable Vinc Castalon:
Hello, hello! Greetings to all attendees at Amphitheater Aperio this afternoon. I am Master of Ceremonies for today's performance. Many of you know me as High Court Judge, Honorable Vinc Castalon, or as the Supreme Voice of Onglander—or Voice Supreme, for short.

Everyone hear me out there on the south end? If so give a wave. Good, good, I see the waving; what a delightful sight to see. I am told this is the largest crowd ever gathered at Aperio, some 250 thousand in attendance today.

That number takes in those seated outside the amphitheater watching on the twelve hundred newly installed monitor clusters. Added to that are millions watching by livestream.

Also, how affirming to see thousands of Onglander flags and banners. Wave them, wave them, and hold them high! Okay, are you ready—really ready? Dial yourself up, sing as a mighty chorus, as privileged inhabitants of such a magnificent land. Now, here we go:

Onglander, O, Onglander, the greatest land on earth.
Come on, all quarter of a million voices, dial it up, project it out,
with true conviction!
Onglander, O, Onglander, the greatest land on earth.
Onglander, O, Onglander, all other lands are dearth.

Onglander, O, Onglander, destined to rule the earth.
Onglanderers, Onglanderers, we shall ever be
Onglanderers, never ever, ever never, will be slaves
We will conquer, we will conquer, we will conquer all.

Onglander, O, Onglander, the greatest land on earth.
Onglander, O, Onglander, all other lands are dearth.
Onglander, O, Onglander, destined to rule the earth.
Onglanderers, Onglanderers, we shall forever be
Onglanderers, never ever, ever never, will be slaves
Supreme and sovereign, synonyms of Onglander's name
We Onglanderers rule the day and conquer all.

Last time now, just the chorus:

Onglander, O, Onglander, the greatest land on earth.
Onglander, O, Onglander, all other lands are dearth.
Onglander, O, Onglander, destined to rule the earth.

Okay, okay, well done. Now, settle in as I outline this afternoon's proceedings—which have received a surprising tilt and turn in the past twenty-four hours.

The Spy Play performances were to begin today and carry on tomorrow and the day after. That, of course, is the reason for this amazing gathering.

Now, concerning the spies, there are four in number, of a most mysterious origin. They suddenly appeared at the Theatre Pretense, pretending to be a musical group called Eventide Ensemble. Along with instruments, they also have a poetic parrot known as Blue Head.

Let me assure you, these are not amateur spies. Three of the group managed to ward off intense intelligence probes and scans. This has never happened. Though, one of the spies is definitely a carnite, bearing predictable DNA traits and markings. Biological makeup, too, cells and all, is not abnormal, as our advanced scans revealed.

Abnormalities were, however, swiftly detected and confirmed. This particular spy should be in his early thirties, but probes determined his age to be 116, and his poetic parrot, 108.

Not possible unless deep deception and trickery are at play. The remaining three are baffling as well; their costumes are authentic, scanned and carbon-dated to be from the fifteenth century.

Why these malicious figures would venture to Onglander, we've yet to know, but we shall know. On that point, though, as I mentioned, there is a bit of a twist and turn. These vulturous spies have escaped their prison cell beneath Theater Pretense.

No, just hold on; at this very moment an all-out search is underway. We expect the spies to be apprehended soon—at least in time for tomorrow's trial performance.

Consequently, that's the reason I've appeared on stage thirty minutes early, rather than precisely at three o'clock. So, this is what's going to happen next: we will annihilate the prison guards on duty when the spies escaped.

In total, this includes five Avalite Sentries to be exterminated and three carnite janitors, to be killed here this very afternoon at Aperio. Further, in keeping with fundamental, democratic rights all Onglanders enjoy, you have a part to play. You, this massive grand audience, can determine the method of execution.

So, as I call out five possibilities, you are to applaud for your chosen method. Okay, here goes.

Number one: Let them loose on the Amphitheater's open turf, and, from the roof above the stage, archers will shoot them down in a slow, protracted show.

Okay, good strong response.

Second: Let them loose on the open turf, but instead of arrows, javelins will be hurled by skilled fighters positioned on the first row, right among the audience.

I hear you—it seems like you prefer number two over one.

Third, what about hanging, one by one?

Okay, similar response; that's fine.

Fourth, have them tied to poles and light them as torches.

Whoa, that was thunderous applause.

And lastly, number five. Burn them on eight separate stakes spaced out on the turf, each erected with generous piles of wood.

All right, all right, even a more thunderous applause. Okay, okay, number five, burn them on stakes it shall be.

Thus, it is nearly the ninth hour, so as I step away, what about just one more chorus? With me now:

We will conquer, we will conquer, we will conquer all.

BACKSTAGE:

Margin: Well, the time has come to reappear, make ourselves known. Ready?

Quillingsworth: Wait, over there in the shadows, near the East wing, something moved. It looked like Crackler, wearing a collar and tied to a post. Let's take a glance.

Margin: All right, but we must be quick.

Quillingsworth: Dear Lord, no, it's you, Crackler. What have they done to you?

Margin: Crackler, we're here—we'll help, hold on!

Quillingsworth: Black eyes, the right swollen shut, your face puffed up, and you're covered in open oozing sores. What's happened? Tell us.

Crackler: I'm sick, ill, weak—they beat me. The discarts injected me with some sort of virus, forced me to drink a poisonous cocktail, and gave me shock treatments.

Margin: No need to tell us more. Don't speak; just hold on. Shadow can help, but first we need to get you out of here, and that can't happen just now. So, hold on.

Crackler: They . . . they want me to be Job in the play. They shaved my head. I have nothing but this loincloth and a mask.

Everyone in the play will wear masks, half masks, revealing their lips and chin. Some actor is gonna speak my lines, so they gave me a full mask.

Dreadful, deadly discarts! They said they'd kill me as soon as the play is over.

Margin: Crackler, we'll be back; you're not forgotten.

Hear the voices, troops? From the opposite wing, it must be the judge and his entourage. They're in for a shock of their own.

Follow me. Remember the reason for our mission. Here goes!

Loreto: *Instead of a cross, albatross about his neck hung.*

Quillingsworth: Lor, tighten your talons, stay in the threads. Keep your beak closed.

Margin: Say, hey there, Judge, look, the Eventide Ensemble has arrived. You appear in a state of shock, Honorable Judge, Vinc Castalon, along with your crony crew.

High Court Judge, Honorable Vinc Castalon: The spies, you miserable lot—you've been caught.

Margin: No, we've just returned.

High Court Judge: What do you mean, returned? You shall pay dearly, as much as anyone can facing a firing squad, a noose, or a flaming stake.

Spies ventured to Onglander and wriggled in like lizards, dashing about the rocks. We know who you are: villains, in drape and cape, pretending to be what you are not.

Fools, we are masters of pretense and disguise; we despise wannabe players who know not their parts. You are withered stalks with no grain; your roots are all shriveled. You are as good as dead.

Margin: So, no Spy Play today? We've come to play our part, unless your cast has lost their courage.

High Court Judge: You foolish, primal forms of life, you have no idea what you are up against.

Okay, all right, you miserable minions. The cast and crew will oblige. To watch you crumble and die will be rewarding. Not all at once today but play by play.

All four of you, along with the bird, will be crushed in Amphitheater Aperio's consecrated turf.

Where's my microphone? Still out there? If not, set it out as we carry on debunking carnite myths and fables in dated texts, best used to start a fire. Our AI-inspired, Onglander translation sets aside all that meek, parabolic mumble with a version underscoring civic, discart superiority.

Nonetheless, hold on, lizard spies. Watch as I go and tell the audience they are in for a great surprise.

STAGE:
High Court Judge: Hello again, everyone. Listen most attentively: Good news, a surprise I have to share. The spies have been caught. That's correct—apprehended and swiftly brought to Aperio for examination.

It's a bit late, I know, but not too late to go on with the first Spy Play, so we'll call off the stake burning for now, though I know the audience was highly stoked.

As I speak, the spies are held in the wings, and if they try to bolt again, discart swords will make their attempted getaway short lived.

We must stamp out such spies and once and for all rid Onglander of these carnite fables that fester in and bubble up with the intent of destabilizing the harmony of the citizenry.

The plays will demonstrate the folly of these decrepit tales that crawl about, seeking whom they can devour. Onglander is the land of AI, not of fossilized I AM.

Therefore, citizens of Onglander, shall we carry on with Spy Play I? Okay, I hear the resounding applause and chants.

Spy Play I it is!

THE WINGS:

High Court Judge: Okay, you despicable spies, you're to stay in the wings till called. Your role, the part you'll play, is to respond to what you'll watch in the first act, and there are only two.

You think you can do that, malcontents? You shall not escape again; there are shackles, chains, fetters, and triple-bar cells to lock you in this very night.

MISERY OF JOB, SAY-SO I AM

STAGE:

Narrator: According to the ancient myth, in scrolls scribed, there exists a bizarre tale that we now retell in today's play titled Misery of Job, Say-So I AM.

Accordingly, there was a man in the land of Uz whose name was Job, supposedly perfect and upright, a God-fearing man who eschewed evil.

Then one day, the angels came to present themselves to God, and Satan came along—filtered in as it were.

God: Where have you come from?

Satan: Going to and fro about the earth, checking in and out, taking into account what's taking place.

God: Have you taken a good look at Job? There's no man like him on earth, a perfect, upright man who feareth me and hastens away from evil.

Thus, the curious deal was struck, and Satan swiftly departed from God's presence.

Lesser Light: There he went, costumed Satan amid a half-dozen angels, three on either side.

Each angel had six wings—two covering their eyes, two their feet, and with two they flew up into the rafters of Amphitheater Aperio.

Shadow: Amazing the lighting, rigging, and all the props—the discarts have harnessed AI for art.

Take in the stage, the backdrop painted with AI master strokes. The costumes are made of fabric rare, not the kind the beggars wear.

Quillingsworth: How did the discarts pull this off? The play must have played before at Aperio. Among the props, the triple-layered mirrors with misty glow depicting the face of God . . . so uncanny.

Narrator: Consequently, the day came when a messenger ran in from the fields with urgent news for his master, Job.

First Messenger: Sir, thine oxen were plowing in the field with the donkeys feeding alongside when a Sabean raiding party fell upon us, killing all your hired hands at the edge of the sword, and I alone escaped.

Narrator: While he was yet speaking, there came another messenger with news.

Second Messenger: Sir, fire from heaven hath fallen. Thy sheep and servants were consumed, and I alone escaped to bear the news.

Narrator: While the second messenger continued to recount what happened, a third arrived.

Third Messenger: Master, grieved I am to report Chaldean marauders swept down upon us, carried off your camels, murdered thy servants by the sword, and I alone escaped.

Narrator: While three messengers tarried, a fourth burst on scene with the worst news of the day.

Fourth Messenger: Sir, dreadful news I bear. Your sons and daughters were dining and drinking wine in the house of your eldest son, when a mighty wind arose from out in the wilderness. It struck the four corners of the house, killing everyone inside. Thus, your children are gone. I alone survived to bring this tragic news.

Narrator: Consequently, Job rose, rent his garment, shaved his head, and fell down upon the ground, pleading with God.

THE WINGS:
Quillingsworth: The spotlight's on Crackler—no pretense in his remorse and pain. See how he jerks, the large circle bordered with the painted red stripe must be electrified. It seems they send a shock and then dial it down.

I've never witnessed cruelty of this ilk.

Lesser Light: Throughout the annals of time, evil has marred day upon day. 'Tis so that there's nothing new under the sun, including evil acts.

STAGE:
Job:
Naked I came from my mother's womb,
*   and naked I will depart.*
The Lord gave and the Lord has taken away;
*   be it so, I AM has said, so say I.*

THE WINGS:
Quillingsworth: That's the discart, Onglander translation; the ancient text records nothing about Job saying, "Be it so" or "So say I"—insane.

STAGE:
Narrator: Thus, step-by-step, the myth lays out the horrendous day of Job's undoing, brought on by Satan's force unrestrained. The story, though, carries on telling of yet another day when angels came to present themselves to God, and as before, Satan came along.

Dialogue ensued along the lines of the original day of angelic procession.

God: Where have you come from?

Satan: Going to and fro about the earth, checking it out, taking into account what's taking place.

God: Have you taken a good look at Job? There's no man like him on earth—a perfect, upright man who feareth me and hastens away from evil.

Still Job holds on to his integrity, although you incited me against him to destroy him for no reason.

Performers:

So it was for no reason
For no reason, for no reason,
No reason, so it was.

THE WINGS:

Quillingsworth: Pushing the false narrative by swirling lies with truth; such wicked place it is, this land of Onglander.

Margin: What else could one expect from demon-possessed discarts powered by artificial intelligence? The watchers watch a play inspired by the devil himself. They have served up a vicious mix—a potent witches' brew it is, and nothing more.

Loreto: *Quoth the Raven, never more.*

Quillingsworth: Be still, Lor, not yet.

STAGE:

Satan: Skin for skin, yea, all that a man hath will he give for his life. But put forth thine hand now and touch his bone and his flesh, and he will curse thee to thy face.

God: Very well, Satan, have at it. Job is in your power; only spare his life, that's all.

Narrator: So Satan went forth from the presence of God and smote Job with sore boils from the soles of his feet to the crown of his head.

THE WINGS:

Quillingsworth: The performers are dancing, gliding about the stage, and singing for no reason. Now what?

STAGE:
Performers:

> *O, so sore, so very, very sore,*
> *O, so many, so many, many boils,*
> *Between the fingers and the toes,*
> *Behind the ears, in the nose,*
> *On the lips, the lids of eyes,*
> *Scalp throughout, from ear to ear,*
> *So many, so many, many boils,*
> *O, so sore, so very, very, sore.*

THE WINGS:

Margin: A very, very strange play; they dance, sing, fly, and act about.

Lesser Light: Discart choreography designed with discart intent.

STAGE:

Narrator: At this point, Job used a potsherd to scrape himself and sat among the ashes, while his hysterical wife entered the scene.

Job's Wife: Dost thou still retain thine integrity? Curse God and die!

Job: Woman, thou speaketh as a fool.

Narrator: That very hour, Job's wife leapt headlong from a high cliff, and her brains were strewn among the boulders.

After this, opened Job his mouth and cursed the day he was born.

Job:

> *Let the day perish wherein I was born and the night in which it*
> *was said, "There is a man child conceived."*
> > *Let that day be darkness; let not God regard it from above,*

neither let the light shine upon it.

Let darkness and the shadow of death stain it; let a cloud dwell upon it; let the blackness of the day terrify it.

Why did I not die from the womb? Why did I not give up the ghost when I came out of the belly?

Why did the knees prevent me? Or why the breasts that I should suck?

For now should I have lain still and been quiet; I should have slept; then had I been at rest!

Narrator: Thus, the misery of Job carried on.

As he sits among the ashes, in utter despair, four figures are folded into the myth. They come to harass and accuse Job of harboring secret sins or a callous heart toward God.

Unlike the four bearers of bad news who were brief in reporting grief, the four accusers went on day after day, gushing forth their self-admired words of doubt and pious indictments. Also, unlike the nameless servant who brought the news, these four received character mention in the myth.

Three were supposed friends: Eliphaz the Temanite, Bildad the Shuhite, and Zophar the Naamathite, along with one younger than the three named Elihu. They surrounded Job like wolves circling a lamb.

Bildad:

Your words are a blustering wind.
Does God pervert justice?
  Does the Almighty pervert what is right?

Zophar:

The mirth of the wicked is brief,
  the joy of the godless lasts but a moment.
An inward fire will consume you

and devour what's hidden within.
The heavens will expose your guilt!

Eliphaz:

Your own mouth condemns you, not mine;
  your own lips testify against you.

Narrator: The fourth, the last to speak, Elihu, had plenty of harsh words to say in delivering his what for to Job.

Elihu:

Job, lift your festered eyes;
  pay attention to everything I say.
My words come from an upright heart;
  my lips sincerely speak what I know.

The Spirit of God has made me;
  the breath of the Almighty gives me life.
For the ear tests words
  as the tongue tastes food.
Let us discern for ourselves what is right;
  let us learn together what is good.
Job says, "I am innocent,
  but God denies me justice.
although I am guiltless,
his arrow inflicts an incurable wound."

I say, I say, is there anyone like Job,
  who drinks scorn like water?
He keeps company with evildoers;
  he associates with the wicked.
For he says, "There is no profit

in trying to please God."
I say, I say, what must be said,
'The godless in heart harbour resentment;
  even when God fetters them,
  they do not cry for help.'

Narrator: And so it was that days compounded into weeks as Job's misery lingered on.

Job:
  If only my anguish could be weighed
    and all my misery be placed on the scales!
  It would surely outweigh the sand of the seas —
    no wonder my words have been impetuous.
  The arrows of the Almighty are in me,
    my spirit drinks in their poison;
    God's terrors are marshalled against me.

  Surely mockers surround me;
    my eyes must dwell on their hostility.
  My face is foul with weeping,
    and on my eyelids the shadow of death;
  God has made me a byword to everyone,
    a man in whose face people spit.
  My eyes have grown dim with grief;
    my whole frame is but a shadow.
  My days have passed,
  my plans are shattered.
  My spirit is broken,
    my days cut short,
    my grave awaits.

Narrator: At this point in the saga, the four went to gather stones for the stoning of Job.

While they were away, though, Job took a potsherd and slashed his wrists. Thus, in a pool of blood, Job curled up on the ground, breathed his last, and died!

Performers:

O, so real, so very very real,
So real, the misery of Job.

BACKSTAGE:

Margin: Okay, that's it; we're on next!

The demonic act has played, scripted in the devil's native tongue; the father of lies will lie to the very end. So, in 2102, as Lesser just said, we see there's nothing new under the sun.

Forget it; focus; we haven't a second to waste. As we left the wing, I spotted a stagehand with the grips. As I approached, he looked at me very peculiarly, knowing we're the infamous spies.

Regardless, I specified five microphones with tall, heavy metal stands, along with two music stands.

Quillingsworth: No music, right?

Margin: Not in this play.

We have a very fluid plan at this point, and we don't have time for it to solidify.

So, think! Why are we here? Hold your thoughts; you already know. We're recording the future while changing it.

Lesser Light:

We must glow.

Margin: Exactly, in such darkness, we must exhibit light that glows of truth.

I've pondered our approach, but a line of attack could not be determined prior to the discart Spy Play. Their approach has determined ours.

Grasp quickly what I say; we do not have enough time to properly prepare. That means we use our unpreparedness as a mild advantage. Lesser Light and Shadow, just follow along as you always do.

Quill, it's vitally important for you to understand the basic strategy that will underscore all of our actions onstage. Tone is critical and must be maintained throughout all that transpires.

Okay, the basic components of our strategy are these:

- We know discarts are possessed, cunning, and evil. They are vicious liars.
- AI is the faceless taskmaster behind all discart advancement.
- Our time onstage will be short, a third of the length of the discart performance.
- The discarts have no idea what we have planned or how we shall respond and act.
- We do not, will not, run out onstage refuting the lies. There's a time to do so, but this is not the time.
- Just the same, our actions will serve as a different sort of refutation.

Lock this in: carnites can be rescued, saved. That is, those who wish to flee the discart rule. Many will; some will not.

We are not stepping out onstage to entertain as normal entertainers do. If I use humor, it will be drilling, riveting.

In that regard, Quill, do not try to follow my example. You will curse yourself tomorrow if you try.

We will use poetry as the basis of our script intermixed with disparate lines drawn from the margins of time. I will cast out the lines. The lines will be joltingly out of context and sound insane.

Quill, you will start by quoting, "All the world's a stage." You assured me you hold it in your mind, along with all those on the list I gave you? Correct?

Quillingsworth: Correct!

Margin: We must thwart the linear procession and monitoring of AI. This is vital to our success.

Thus, we do so by way of bewilderment, not by communicating in patterned modes. No time to discuss, Quill.

The streaming feeds from our performance, the words and deeds, will bristle and hackle in the portals of evil reception, resulting in fragmentation and all manner of static, confusion, chatter, and delusion.

Lastly, no time to tell you how our act will end, but it will not lack drama.

Shadow, when I descend the steps, everyone moves upstage. Then, when I turn about-face with sword held high, that's your cue to swoop us up and out.

Quill, you have the list, the sequence. We three know the list, the lines, and all the parts. You must flow with us; don't look out of sorts.

Further, when you walk out onstage with Loreto perched on your shoulder, go straight to the center microphone; do not say hello. Also, offer neither the name of the poem, nor the name of the poet.

Concerning Loreto, I expect her to speak as she normally does, which is not at all normal. Again, good, spellbinding dismaying is what we want.

Again, there are five microphones, along with two music stands, one for you and the other for Loreto. When Loreto begins to speak, perch her on top of the music stands; she has her own microphone.

Stick with lines as given.

Quill, there would be no mission without you. You have become the mediator of what will be in 2102 by being in the future now.

Ready? Now, let's go!

STAGE:

Quillingsworth: Ahem, ahem, hum!

THE WINGS:

High Court Judge, Honorable Vinc Castalon: Look, there they go. The carnite has that blue-headed parrot on his shoulder.

Those rotten unprogrammable, unpredictable spies—they're crafty, they are.

STAGE:

Quillingsworth:

> *All the world's a stage,*
> *And all the men and women merely players;*
> *They have their exits and their entrances;*
> *And one man in his time plays many parts,*
> *His acts being seven ages.*

Loreto: *Seven ages, seven ages . . .*

Quillingsworth:

> *At first the infant,*
> *Mewling and puking in the nurse's arms;*
> *And then the whining schoolboy, with his satchel*
> *And shining morning face, creeping like a snail*
> *Unwillingly to school. And then the lover,*
> *Sighing like a furnace, with a woeful ballad*
> *Made to his mistress's eyebrow. Then a soldier,*
> *Full of strange oaths, and bearded like the pard . . .*

Lesser Light:

Jealous in honor, sudden and quick in quarrel,
Seeking the bubble reputation
Even in the cannon's mouth.

Quillingsworth:

And then the justice,
In fair, round belly with good capon lin'd,
With eyes severe and beard of formal cut,
Full of wise saws and modern instances . . .

Shadow:

And so he plays his part. The sixth age shifts
Into the lean and slipper'd pantaloon . . .

Quillingsworth:

With spectacles on nose and pouch on the side;
His youthful hose well sav'd a world too wide
For his shrunk shank; and his big, manly voice,
Turning again toward childish treble, pipes
And whistles in his sound.
Last scene of all,
That ends this strange eventful history,
Is second childishness and mere oblivion;
Sans teeth, sans eyes,
Sans taste, sans everything.

Loreto: *Sans that, and nothing more.*
Margin:

Sinner, save thy soul,
Yes, you, your image, too,
The pair, just you two,

Both now framed,
So go ahead,
Genuflect, reflect,
Save thy soul.
Now recant, chant,
Just one, you two,
Ready, hurl your brick,
Smash the mirror,
Image, stay intact,
Reflect, not a crack,
Sinner save thy soul.
Swift, sweep up shards,
As well, the cracks,
Thus, put 'em back,
Into the mirror, now leap
Head first, but don't look back,
Behind the glass, look out,
Hallelujah shout.
Blink once, you two,
Good, jump out,
Into the pond, splash,
Quick, jump out,
Sinner, save thy soul,
Your image's gone,
Go ahead, carry on.

THE WINGS:

Media Marshall: Your Honor, Sir, sorry to intrude, but I thought you should know that all the media streams are spitting.

High Court Judge: What do you mean, spitting?

Media Marshall: No one knows what to say or report; the AI feeds must be sabotaged. Assigned avatar reporters are spitting out meaningless chatter, fragmented content, lots of static, confusion, media patrollers speak of delusion, all the way down the line.

We don't know how to respond; this is not a known virus. Bells ring nonstop, lights amber and red repeatedly flash. It's sabotage.

We have no solution—no way to reboot or repair; we don't even know what's broken.

High Court Judge: You idiot! Media Marshall, that's your title, you sorry thing of wringing hands, get on with it. Sacrifice yourself, fix it, or you shall be court-martialed as the saboteur.

Look out upon the stage at those four with that blue-headed parrot—that's the source of your spitting media streams. Get away from me, go, mindless, programmed mind.

STAGE:
Quillingsworth:
With sloping masts and dipping prow,
As who pursued with yell and blow
Still treads the shadow of his foe,
And forward bends his head,
The ship drove fast, loud roared the blast,
And southward aye we fled.

Lesser Light:
And now there came both mist and snow,
And it grew wondrous cold:
And ice, mast-high, came floating by,
As green as emerald.

Shadow:

> *And through the drifts the snowy cliffs*
> *Did send a dismal sheen:*
> *Nor shapes of men nor beasts we ken—*
> *The ice was all between.*

Quillingsworth:

> *The ice was here, the ice was there,*
> *The ice was all around:*
> *It cracked and growled, and roared, and howled,*
> *Like noises in a swound!*

Margin:

> *Quiet, stop, listen, hear, a knock, quit, scream, not now, yesterday's tomorrow, day gone, a week, next year, listen, run, catch life, die, anchor, hook. Make a wish, to wish a wish to wish.*

Shadow:

> *Too real the look; 'tis a form of fakery.*

Margin:

> *I rebuke myself for being me, Lord.*

Lesser Light:

> *Faces young, film old, together crackle,*

Loreto: *Or, twee, cat, cat, the mice are back.*

Quillingsworth:

> *Characters great, rehearse in the minds that create them.*
> *You tell me too much, tell me more.*
> *The essence of a word never defies its etymology*

Margin:

When the cock crows thrice, you will remember it once.
Turn the page quickly; lay a gold ribbon in the gutter.
Parting is such sorrow, but not for me.

THE WINGS:
Judge's Aides: Your Honor, the spies are mad; this is insane. They must be on LSD or some unknown substance.

Look at the audience; they stare like owls, all quarter million at Aperio.

High Court Judge: They must be destroyed, but not tonight. We need to know the source of their mysterious power. Can't be the devil, we're all in.

We'll lock them up, inject them, and make them talk.

STAGE:
Margin: The devil can cite Scripture for his purpose.

An evil soul producing holy witness
Is like a villain with a smiling cheek,
A goodly apple rotten at the heart.
O, what a goodly outside falsehood hath!

Quillingsworth:

I wandered lonely as a cloud
That floats on high o'er vales and hills,
When all at once I saw a crowd,
A host of golden daffodils;
Beside the lake, beneath the trees,
Fluttering and dancing in the breeze.

Loreto: *Churkwe, by the lake, beneath the trees . . .*

Quillingsworth:

Continuous as the stars that shine
And twinkle on the Milky Way,
They stretched in never-ending line
Along the margin of a bay:
Ten thousand saw I at a glance,
Tossing their heads in sprightly dance.

Lesser Light:

The waves beside them danced; but they
Outdid the sparkling waves in glee:

Shadow:

A poet could not but be gay,
In such a jocund company:

Quillingsworth:

I gazed—and gazed—but little thought
What wealth the show to me had brought:
For oft, when on my couch I lie
In vacant or in pensive mood,
They flash upon that inward eye
Which is the bliss of solitude;
And then my heart with pleasure fills,
And dances with the daffodils.

Loreto: *Churkwe, dancing daffodils sprightly dance.*

High Court Judge: They've paused. No, the carnite poet just placed the talking parrot on the music stand.

We need new programs of advanced hate. More effective ways to hate, striking bitter hate that obliterates without a trace.

We know so much of knowing, but the realm of unknowing stymies. These stymied toads with wizard minds—I hate them more than hate can hate. That's why we need new programs able to render more fracturtorious fissures of hate.

Margin:
> *We wear the mask that grins and lies,*
> *It hides our cheeks and shades our eyes,*
> *This debt we pay to human guile;*
> *With torn and bleeding hearts we smile,*
> *And mouth with myriad subtleties.*

Shadow:
> *This life's five windows of the soul*
> *Distorts the Heavens from pole to pole.*

Quillingsworth:
> *And leads you to believe a lie*
> *When you see with not thro' the eye*

Lesser Light:
> *That was born in a night to perish in a night*
> *When the soul slept in beams of light.*

Loreto: *Churkwe, 'tis time of rooster crow*

Margin:
> *Measure for measure begs an answer, a whittler of faith, 'tis AI.*
> *Now concerning the tale of Job,*
> *On this stage just told,*
> *From the story old,*
> *The tail was clipped,*

Cutting out the truth,
I now on stage impart,
For, Job, on the ground a-curl,
Did not lie down and die,
Nor his wife leap from a cliff,
All a pack of lying lies.
Nay, Job heard response to his cries,
In a way never heard before,
Providence did pick upright,
The patient, pleading soul,
And blessed twice what he'd possessed,
Along with life, a living long,
Though the voice Job heard,
Posed a stream of questions,
For patient Job to ponder.

THE WINGS:

High Court Judge: Look, that manic, miserable Margin has drawn his sword. Now he's making his way to the steps. Step-by-step, he descends with no fear upon his face. That's a frightening face to behold.

Aide: Look, see, he's stopped halfway. He's raised his sword. What should we do?

High Court Judge: Weirdness from head to toe we now behold.

STAGE:

Margin: Thus, in the story true, out of the whirlwind the Almighty spoke, grilling Job with questions about divine capacity and creative feats—all the questions cut away in the liar's play.

The lot I do not repeat; three, that's all. The first, "Hast thou entered into the treasures of the snow?"

Snow, snow, now snow! So delightful and refreshing to see the falling snow coming down and all around Amphitheatre Aperio. And this is such a nice, heavy snow, frosty full this form of frozen rain.

THE WINGS:

High Court Judge: No, not believable—he's made it snow. We can't even do that. Margin's a malicious wizard, and even worse.

This so-called quartet is a threat to Onglander civilization. Their actions and acts are not even programmed; they wing it, which is worse than worse. We have no virus for attacking wingers.

Wait, listen, he speaks again.

Aide: He's lowered his sword. No, he's raised it. What's going to happen?

High Court Judge: Like I said, idiot, fool, flakey aide, he's winging it. How can I know what he's going to do if he's winging? There is no pattern to process and predict. Shut it, watch, listen.

STAGE:

Margin: Another question that the Almighty posed to Job I now quote: "Hast thou seen the treasures of the hail?"

Hail, hail, now hail! How wondrous, a brisk freefall steady, forceful, from the heavens may it fall.

THE WINGS:

High Court Judge: Listen, a torrent of hail is beating down on the stage roof. Such sights are not seeable in Onglander, though I see them. A core of treachery Margin does possess.

Aide: The hail is bouncing on the steps, but look, not where Margin stands.

High Court Judge: The spies, whoever they may be, cause us harm, great harm. There he goes again; he's not done—he's lifting high his sword.

STAGE:

Margin: Then, a third, my last, among the questions the Almighty asked. "Canst thou draw out Leviathan with a fishhook? Or tie down his tongue with a cord?"

So, in the foreground, behold the Leviathan. Just a few of his attributes I now recite:

> His sneezings flash forth light,
>   and his eyes are like the eyelids of the dawn.
> Out of his mouth go flaming torches;
>   sparks of fire leap forth.
> Out of his nostrils comes forth smoke,
>   as from a boiling pot and burning rushes.
> His breath kindles coals,
>   and a flame comes forth from his mouth.
> In his neck abides strength,
>   and terror dances before him.

With that said, I turn and raise my sword. Our act is done!

THE WINGS:

High Court Judge: What happened? They vanished!

Aide: Look, the monster's still here! It snorts fire the across the length of the turf. No, now the Leviathan monster, too, is gone.

High Court Judge: So say I, this cannot be.

CHAPTER TEN
Camp Seaside, Post Play

"At Aperio, we were," said Shadow, "then, a brisk whisk, and now we're back at our picturesque Camp Seaside. Such a dramatic play, and we managed to bring Mr. Crackler along, adding to the drama."

"Dramatic," said Quillingsworth. "Who will ever believe what I am to record? The recorder himself can barely grasp what occurred on that Amphitheatre Aperio stage.

"The anthem 'O, Onglander, O, Onglander,' dancers singing, 'O, so sore, so very, very, sore,' then Margin standing on the steps with his sword raised. First, the blinding snow blowing across the amphitheater, followed by the deafening, pounding hailstorm.

"Then, an interlude of silence set in, except for the gasps, when suddenly, the mammoth Leviathan appeared on the turf, his mouth breathing fire, his nostrils billowing smoke. Indeed, a most dramatic play."

"Drama," said Shadow. "I'd say it's time for a pot of tea. It looks like our new comrade could use a sip or two."

"Right," said Margin, "We must turn our attention to Crackler."

"What's happened?" said Crackler. "Am I dead, did I die, am I alive? Heaven has an ocean. The camp—is it real, or some sort of pretense? Oh, the wretched pain, my side, my pounding head. Though this can't be heaven, pain's not allowed, is it?"

"Crackler," said Margin, "you are still in Onglander by the sea, and Shadow has cast a dome of protection around and over us that discarts cannot penetrate. When they search, they will discover images of the seaside as it was before we arrived. So they probe and turn away.

"Reality it is for you, for Quill, for all of us, for now. We're caught up in a mission that has turned into a war. At present, however, we need to do something about your physical condition."

"Uh, yes, can you?" said Crackler. "The discarts beat me, shaping me into Job. They laughed and said I would be executed immediately after the play ended. I was to be hung onstage, and images of the execution posted as a warning to carnites to stay low, out of sight."

"Okay," said Margin, "now follow me, Crackler. I believe your cure is at hand, complete recovery, but you will need to exercise a bit of faith. Think you can do that?"

"Well, I," said Crackler, "continue, I mean I will do that, as I can do it, muster up what I can muster."

"Then, listen," said Margin. "In days of old, there was a valiant soldier who also happened to be a leper, a combination most rare. His name was Naaman, and he longed to be cured of his leprosy, so he was encouraged to travel from Syria to Jerusalem, where, he was told, a cure for his leprosy could be found.

"Thus, Naaman departed, and took with him ten talents of silver and six thousand pieces of gold and ten changes of raiment. The story has a number of twists and turns, but eventually, with his horses and chariots, Naaman went to a prophet named Elisha.

"Elisha sent a message to Naaman, telling him to dip seven times in the River Jordan, and his flesh would be restored. At first, the brave warrior balked and refused, but in time, he recanted and went and dipped seven times in the Jordan. And behold, his skin was restored like that of a boy, and he was healed.

"Crackler, you have neither silver nor gold, but faith you have at no cost to you. Notwithstanding your agony, I strongly recommend you muster up your faith, as you put it, and go dip seven times in the ocean waves. Quillingsworth will help you. Take courage; don't be afraid."

"Well, so," said Crackler, "I guess, yes, I'll do as you say; I will do that. Oh, okay, there, I'm on my feet. Let me breathe; my mind . . . it's so . . . well, Shadow, Lesser Light, you, you are, I mean, impossible, but you're not. So, a first step, then another, all right, Mr. Quillingsworth, help steady me, if you might.

"I like the sound of the waves; the breeze, it's so nice. We'll leave tracks in the sand, in case an angel comes looking for us. Are you going to dip, too?"

"Why not?" said Quillingsworth. "I just hope that Leviathan doesn't rise out of the waves."

"We'll wait," said Margin, "and if all goes well, you two will return hungry."

"Chops on the menu," said Shadow. "I think with scalloped potatoes, and let's see what I can find."

"There they go," said Margin, "with Loreto keeping watch. The healing is a certainty; that is, if Crackler dips. As we know, the warring of the war leaves many wounds.

"Anyway, it's just us three for a bit."

"Another cup of tea?" said Shadow.

"Yes, I will not refuse," said Margin. "It has been a rather eventful day. Our time here in Onglander has proven to be quite revealing, wouldn't you say?"

"Fully agreed," said Shadow.

"Most certainly," said Lesser Light.

"The discarts," said Margin, "are now mad with rage. They growl and prowl because of us. We've taken them completely by surprise, out of their patterned, reasoned norms of movement.

"The discarts desperately want to annihilate us, scrub every image of our existence, and then spin some spurious tale that they brought us to test Onglander national security. Their scope and scan teams laser the skies, seeking our whereabouts.

"Annihilate us, that will not happen, and all that will happen has yet to happen. Come what come may, time and the hour run through the roughest day. What have you picked up, Shadow?"

"A feeding frenzy," said Shadow, "of chatter, static, oscillating whines, carrying on in and around Tower AI, which is adjacent to Theatre Pretense."

"All right," said Margin, "but not much. Just a hint of what's going on."

"Hear that?" said Lesser Light. "A yell, a yelp; Crackler just found out the dip did more than help, as we knew it would."

"Here's a bit more," said Shadow. "The gist, in bits, seems to indicate the discarts want to meet us and draw us in to discuss the Spy Plays. The desired time and place is Tower AI at sunrise."

"Curious turn," said Margin. "In the guise of appeasement and conciliatory pretense, they wish to draw us close, scan our fiber and modus operandi. They know nothing of Missio Dei. They are totally other to matters divine.

"We will oblige, but not until we've fully pondered next steps to unfold what we must unfold. They wish to play us along, but what they do not know is that we wish to play along. We need a little time, that's all.

"Anyway, they're coming back."

"Margin," said Shadow, "shall I pull a costume from the passage for Crackler?"

"That will do," said Margin. "Crackler may accompany us to Tower AI. He's a writer, you know, like Quill.

"Shadow, those lamb chops, such a luscious smell in the seaside air. It's time to ponder and say, 'Bon appétit!'"

TOWER AI, CABINET ROOM, 1:00 a.m.:
High Court Judge, Honorable Vinc Castalon: Be seated, everyone, attentively poised.

As Discart Senate Chair, and Supreme Voice of Onglander, I called this emergency session of the Cabinet, and the session is now in order. I motion it so, and I second it so.

Keeper of notes, note the following: Top floor Senate Chamber, Tower of AI, precisely 1:00 a.m. That's all we need, not a bunch of heretos and according tos; we must take swift action.

Hear me; listen sharp. Even as I speak from the bench, a malicious, vicious attack is underway against Onglander civilization. During this hour ticking, I will lay out what we know and our plan of action.

I note that everyone is present; no one missing. So it is and should be. Those called upon to speak must be unambivalent in what they say.

Any stupid questions, or shaky, hesitant comments will be immediately scrapped, and the initiators of such will be labeled as State Coward Corruptors and forever barred from this chamber, the highest of all chambers.

Further, as we proceed, no ahs, wows, or any other expressions of surprise allowed. We gather at a most serious hour; this is no show-and-tell party, no open house, smiley affair. So in sworn soberness, take in what you hear as you train your vision on me.

Have I made myself clear, I ask you? All right, I see no wiggling or squirming about. So, focus, stay with me, as I lay out the situation with unorthodox transparency.

At the very top of the agenda: the Spy Plays. Is there anyone in the chamber who did not attend yesterday's Spy Play? Chamber Captain, not you; put down your hand. I mean members. No one, okay.

Now then, let me set the stage. As you know, the four spies of miserable note appeared before the court, the Honorable Judge (me), and after careful examination, they were sent to prison.

The Elite Council swiftly determined the captured spies should be eradicated, but not immediately. They should be mockingly paraded and humiliated by taking part in Spy Plays held at Amphitheatre Aperio. By unanimous decree, the number of plays was to be no more or no less than three.

Thus, with AI-celerity, the Spy Acts were scripted, actors cast, costumes made, and set designs completed within nine hours. The plays are designed to bolster discart advancement via AI while simultaneously demonstrating the folly of believing in Hebraic myths and the one called I AM. The efficacy to our twofold approach is, as the insipid carnites put it, a win/win. Such a stupid way of talking, like chirping bids: win/win.

Nonetheless, the decree was given; three plays prepared, and the first took place yesterday. The result, according to all leading discarts in attendance, is that we failed. Do you hear me, as I pound this podium? We, the discarts of Onglander, have failed.

Further, we were humiliated by this so-called Eventide Ensemble with a mocking parrot. Let the reality of what I said sink in. Let the stated fact swirl in your systematic preceptors and then dutifully be stored away. At the same time, I have more to say; therefore, your attentiveness must be even more attentive than before. No deficit of attention will be tolerated.

Listen, by unanimous nod, the Elite Council has hereby canceled Spy Play II. For your benefit, I will alliterate various analytic prompts that surfaced by the AI populace probes. I will number a few and shall dispense with numbering, as I judge the flow of delegate communicative engagement.

First, it's estimated that more than a million attendees plan to turn up at Amphitheatre Aperio to take in Spy Play II.

Second, some 90 percent of those planning to attend believe that Amphitheatre Aperio put on the special effects in Spy Play I. I'm referring, of course, to the wizardry acts conjured up by the Eventide leader, that sly spy, the sword-wielder Margin.

Third, to call forth snow, hail, and a fire-breathing monster manifests a power unknown. Suspicious on every front, and we must briskly move against such trickery. Pretense this is not.

Thus, if we were to proceed with Spy Play II, the outcome could prove catastrophic.

In a moment, Aperio's Director of Theatrical Choreography will elaborate on the matter.

Sufficient to say that the elements and effects of Spy II included a trembling mountain, rumbling thunder, lightning strikes, trumpets blaring, stone tablets tossed about, panic-stricken carnites racked with fear, along with actual death and dying. It's a highly stimulating production that will soon be performed, as choreographed, just as soon as we can obliterate these spying spies.

Again, Aperio's Theatrical Director will say more, including a review of the Spy Play II's storyboards. Though, I must state a few additional topics, all critical, for our combined understanding and united action.

Fourth, the spies vanished without a trace at the end of Spy Play I. There they were, the snow, the hail, the Leviathan, and swoosh, they were gone. Now, hold on, wait—I just heard a *wow*. An interrupter, who wowed? I see, heads turn to you, Trosbore, of district seventeen. Okay, rise, and out you go. We must have order. Now, where were we?

Okay, fifth, the spies, known as the Eventide Ensemble, must be annihilated, in such a manner that not a single atom or cell of their existence can be found or detected in Onglander and the cosmos. Annihilated, obliterated without a trace, and this will happen at the end of Spy Play III. The end is the end of Eventide.

The play will feature that fable of Noah and an angry I AM drowning the human race, along with the animals. Spy Play III has no lightning, no, hail, no Leviathan. The waters slowly rise, the humans slowly drown, the waters become still, there a bit about a dove flapping around, and so on. But unlike the fairy tale, when the character Noah sends out the bird, his homemade ark begins to leak, and various members of his little entourage drown. I believe that's so.

Sixth, the best point: Our attack on the spies includes calling up and unleashing demons of hell and sizzling laser assaults. I've already spoken to Onglander's Supervisor of Demon Portals about the readiness to unleash, and he has assured me that all is ready.

So, what's more? Seventh, or whatever number it may be, I raise a point that is attached to a degree of uncertainty. I know we discarts, AI-empowered and controlled, are programmed to despise uncertainty. And we do. The uncertainty pertains to the whereabouts of the spies. With Scope and Scan on high alert, and all forces engaged in the search, their position remains undetermined. We must locate them.

Here's why: If the spies show up at Aperio, unaware that Spy Play II has been cancelled, and, at the same time, a million attendees turn up equally unaware, what do we have?

I'll tell you. We would have a mass unaware and a quartet unaware, and, in such a case, the unawares will attract. There will be a strong draw dynamic, particularly among the carnite attendees in the bleachers, though they be few in number.

We've observed footage of carnites at Spy Play I, moving about in swaying, swooping motions when Margin spoke, and especially when he pointed his sword to the skies and commanded the snow and hail to fall. Therefore, with utmost urgency, as necessity dictates, we must get a message to the spies to prevent them from turning up at Aperio unaware.

At the same time, all contact between Onglanders and those interfluxed, malicious spies is strictly forbidden. Spies hide in the shadows and back alleys dimly lit, and that's where spies belong, amid the scurry of rats and swooping bats. Our predator spies are surely insurrectionists.

Moving on, all right, let's see, the wall clock dials keep moving, and accordingly, it's time for the brief by Aperio's Director of Theatrical Choreography. Aide, chamber door, escort in Dr. Corralitor.

Aide: Certainly, sir.

2:30 a.m.
High Court Judge: All right, Dr. Corralitor will now brief the chamber

on the cancellation of Spy Play II and on why Spy Play III shall go ahead.

It's over to you, Dr. Corralitor.

Aperio's Director of Theatrical Choreography: Rather tense atmosphere these days, so it seems. To the fullest extent possible, Amphitheater Aperio and the arts support the Senate, the Senate Chair, and the Supreme Voice of Onglander. On the Chamber Imaging Wall behind me, observe the first storyboard of Spy Play II.

Visulator, don't skimp on the image size. The Chamber Imaging Wall of Tower AI was designed to project large images, so use the space as intended. As a rule, each storyboard image should be six times my height—and for a discart, I'm tall. Got it? Okay, good, that's better.

The title of Spy Play II is Moses the Murderer and I AM. The play aligns perfectly with the 2091 senate initiative, Myth Meltdown. Spy Play II is a powerful production, but we understand why the play's been put on hold. I can assure you that, as soon as the spies are eradicated, we'll be ready to light up the stage.

Anyway, in the first storyboard, we see a young Moses murdering a fellow Hebrew and burying him in the sand. This is an early part of the story, about the brick-making Hebrew slaves in Egypt and their suffering and crying out to I AM.

Moving on, this next storyboard shows Moses later in life, when I AM supposedly appeared to him in a flaming bush. Our play calls for major fire on the amphitheatre turf. Regardless, as the story goes, murderer Moses has become a sheepherder on the backside of the desert.

You see the burning bush, and according to the legend, I AM speaks from the burning bush, saying, "Moses, Moses." Moses says, "Here am I." A myth wrapped in a fable—amazing what carnites will embrace.

I AM responds, "Draw not nigh, no shoes, bare feet, for thou standest on holy ground."

The next image is that of Moses with his face buried in the dirt.

I'll rapidly move through the storyboards, although with the cast of Spy Play II, we spent a good while discussing them.

At any rate, we jump to the heart of Spy Play II: Mt. Sinai. We see the image of Moses ascending the mountain to meet I AM, who hands down laws carved in cold stone.

Then the drama really begins to unfold. I AM sends Moses back down the mountain and delivers a stern warning that if anyone even touches the mountain, they will be stoned or shot through with arrows. Carnite beliefs are utterly barbaric.

Okay, the following storyboard, there are lightning bolts with sounds of thunder and a thick cloud upon resting on the mountain. Here you see the people in the camp trembling.

This scene in particular prompted the Senate Cabinet to halt Spy Play II, given that the spies would have a counter-performance that no one can predict. The scenes of Spy Play II are meant to be electrified, and a number of carnite extras will be victims of creative realism—you know the dramatic damage.

Taken together, the elements of play simply provide too many evocative entry points for the spies to conjure up dramatic displays. The atmosphere would be highly charged, plus one of the four happens to be a carnite. Further, another round of dramatic effects by the spies offers too many opportunities for escape.

Next, the Golden Calf storyboard, in which a character named Aaron, supposedly the brother of Moses, crafts a Golden Calf. By now, the wandering desert tribe has seen enough of I AM feats, so they beg Aaron to make golden gods to lead them into a fictional Promised Land.

In the following image, you see the people ripping off their gold earrings and pitching them to Aaron. We've conscripted a large number to carnites to fill in these parts.

Next, Moses tumbles down the side of the mountain when I AM

tells him to get out of the way because his wrath is white-hot and he's ready to destroy wandering carnites camped at the base of the mountain. See how insane the story goes, but exciting drama, just the same.

By the way, the choreographed scenes and stunning artistic backdrops are AI-achieved.

In the next image, Moses throws down the stone tablets with I AM's carved codes.

The following storyboard is titled Slaughter of Three Thousand. And, as you see, the carnites wielding swords are slashing each other in half. As I mentioned, with victims of creative realism, there will be a lot of flowing blood.

Just a couple more, and I'll conclude. This one depicts the plague that I AM brought about in retaliation for the Golden Calf.

Next, the image of a lonely, demoralized Moses who can't believe what has happened, that I AM refuses to lead, or be identified with, such a stiff-necked people. I AM peals away.

The final storyboard is Moses on Mount Moab, abandoned by I AM. Moses looks out on the so-called Promised Land, which I AM has forbidden him to enter. Why? Well, one day, a long time ago, Moses struck a rock with his staff twice rather than once, as I AM dictated.

With that overview, I think everyone can understand why the Myth Meltdown initiative is crucial to our future interest. And that's all for me.

High Court Judge, Honorable Vinc Castalon: There, then, we have it, Dr. Corralitor's overview, which provides sustentative undergirding and perspective for canceling Spy Play II. Though the play appears to be a thrilling one that will open soon, no doubt.

So, sharpen up now; the Cabinet remains in session, and I have an important development to report, which I received just a moment ago. A surprising development, indeed: The Eventide Ensemble spies will appear at Tower AI at sunrise, which is two hours from now.

We've not been able to ascertain how our message got to the spies, since we don't know where they are, but a message reached them, and they have responded. Curious, every move they make.

There is, however, some confusion regarding whether they sent a message to which we responded, or we sent the message first and they replied. Anyway, that doesn't matter. Let me tell you what does matter.

First, we saw the storyboards for Spy Play II, with Mt. Sinai, lighting, thunder, trumpet blasts, and so on that would have charged the atmosphere of Aperio to an unpredictable state. Good that's off the table, but let us not forget what took place at the first Spy Play.

So, concerning Spy Play III, we must be vigilant if that sword-toting Margin tries to cough up antics like he did in Spy Play I. We fully intend to obliterate them at the end of the play, but we must also prepare for a preemptive strike, if necessary. They are vile, deceptive, spies, so be on guard with watchful eyes. Trust them not a smidge, or even a smidge's smidge.

Second, the spies know something's up. They have the ability to hack and will be aware of all the sweeps, searches, and scanning probes underway, as well as the pinging alert warnings emanating from Tower AI. Such concerted action is unprecedented, but so are the surges, drops, and static picked up in AI-protected portals. During these turbulent days, the airways have wicked ways.

Scope and Scan remains vigilant, reporting that extensive counter-surge measures will correct the disturbance. The Senate has been informed that a solution is imminent.

Yet these creepy spies have some unknown way of tapping into our coveted streams of communicative action.

Here me, embrace my words: The spies must be annihilated. This objective, our main objective, will happen, but not at Tower AI today; we must wait for the play. Thus, when the spies turn up, if they do, we shall placate, accommodate, and ingratiate them, pretending we are wooed and starstruck by their words and deeds. Pretense, our greatest virtue, must be on display, playing them along until tomorrow brings them woe.

Do you have it? Got it? I believe you do.

Before we have a brief pause, Visulator, bring up the Force Control Operation Center, the main desk, you know, below Great Mask Hall. Good, instantly there are live feeds on monitors all around the chamber.

Okay, sentinels of Force Control, hear me; I am speaking. This is Judge Castalon, Senate Chair, Supreme Voice of Onglander, among other roles. Your standing salute is duly recognized. Now, at ease; my comments shall be brief.

Select Forces, you are keenly aware of the subterfuge carried out by spies that have infiltrated the inner workings of Tower AI and Onglander media platforms. The spies are few, but their impact is vast, threatening our civilization.

Stay vigilant! By tomorrow's eventide, the so-called Eventide Ensemble shall be ground down to nothingness. What was will no longer be, as if what was had never been.

So, tomorrow, when I give the signal, you are to unleash a legion of demonic dwellers from their earthen warrens. Like honed missiles, a legion strong will shoot up from the ground, and then, like a torrent of lightning, they will bolt from the skies, striking the spies.

So, I commend you, Force Control, stay alert; be ready; your retribution draweth nigh.

CAMP SEASIDE, 5:30 a.m.:

"Quill," said Margin, "don't rise. I considered taking you and Crackler with us, but it's too dangerous; anything could happen."

"Well, okay," said Quillingsworth. "I was dead asleep. Let me get up anyway, just to sit at the table so I can at least focus on what you're saying."

"Only the trio will go to meet the discarts at Tower AI," said Margin. "You are to stay here with Crackler; look after him; get to know him.

Interesting thought, is it not? You, supposedly 116, meeting a fellow carnite in 2102. All will be well.

"Yes, but Margin, what if something does go wrong; what if you don't return? In that case, I would be lost here in this future, never to return to Poet's Lodge and the world I knew and know."

"I know," said Margin, "that would be so. So, let's not let it be so. You are a talent, Quill; you remind me of patriots I once knew in days of old. You would have fit right in, but this is your mission now, not one way back when.

"We're off!"

"Crackler, it's okay," said Quillingsworth. "I'll brief you in a bit. Just rest; we don't know what this day will hold. Looks like Shadow has set out a nice spread.

"Tower AI, what am I to think? On the one hand, this can't be real; it must all be a dream, but a dream such as this is too insane to dream. But, on the other hand, the living that die in dreams don't really die. Interesting . . . now, that's a thought worth dreaming.

"Did you hear me, Crackler?"

"What?" said Crackler.

"Oh, nothing," said Quillingsworth. "Try to go back to sleep."

TOWER AI, 6:00 a.m.:

"Force Control, Guard Hurdro, main entrance, reporting. Three figures approaching, moving up the stairs, ten seconds to entrance."

"Okay, Hurdro, received, over, got it; cameras trained, recording."

"Halt, I'm Sergeant Hurdro; names required."

"My name's Margin; to my left is Shadow, and on my right, Lesser Light."

"Those are not normal names," said Sergeant Hurdro. "Lesser Light, Shadow—but I've been informed that you were expected. You are the Eventide spies, correct?"

"Well," said Shadow, "the Eventide part is correct."

"I dare say," said Sergeant Hurdro, "you dare appear at Tower AI—such daring is as abnormal as your names. You can pass; you will be escorted to the Senate Chamber, top floor."

"Sergeant," said Lesser Light, "did you ever hear the name Leviathan?"

"I've already engaged you too much; proceed, the chamber is waiting."

SENATE CHAMBER, 6:05 a.m.:

"Senate members," said Judge Castalon, "the spies are on their way up. Bear in mind all that I've told you, the demeanor, the deception; we need just one more day to do away with these pugnacious, prowling spies.

"Now we wait. Listen, movement—face-to-face with spies, it's unconscionable."

"Your Honor, Chaperon Twillarie, sir. The Senate guests have arrived."

"Oh, good," said Judge Castalon. "Do come forward. I've briefed the Senate prior to your arrival, and we've been expecting you. How shall I say? Your presence adds a degree of buoyancy to the day.

"If you would, step up on the riser to your left and take a seat on the high-back speaker stools. Good; the order doesn't matter, though, Margin, you might prefer to sit on the middle stool. Do take a seat. You see, in Tower AI, everyone can see and hear everyone, everywhere. Good, good, much better for the conclave.

"As you might suppose, the Senate Chamber oversees and debates important matters, such as your purpose in visiting Onglander. So, to the Senate, the importance ascribed to your attendance speaks for itself.

"Anyway, the Senate does not vote by saying aye, aye, nay, in that outdated mode. We simply sync. And let me clearly state: This is not the time to quibble over your non-captive status."

"Understood," said Margin.

"Agreeable," said Judge Castalon. "Hence, I will make a few brief remarks on behalf of the Senate. Remarks, naturally, that underscore the reason for our communicative action and pertinent thereto.

"We have a way of reassessing matters to make sure that what mattered heretofore matters henceforth. There are many degrees and variables to be considered when calculating the substance and validity of claims that affect societal stability and the future well-being of the citizenry.

"Knowing, too, the substance of a charge can change if the substance related to the charge changes in equal measure to the charge. Onglander possesses numerous scales and weights of measurement for measuring degrees of change that arise from probes that detect variables that cause matters to change.

"Let it be known, we discarts possess a broad latitude of acceptance for the marginalized among us, as well as those clamoring to enter our highly developed and advanced civilization. Onglanders do not navigate by myth or whim, but upon facts mined in a manner that incorporates all facts into a composite factorial.

"The mining process is unceasing, ever churning, ever turning, continually opening new vistas of exploration, and revealing the precise ways and means to achieve what the AI mining operations have revealed.

"We believe, and we know, we are the center ring of destiny. Every generation, heretofore, has longed to see this day, what you see and hear. Unparalleled advancement, achievement, bettering the prospects of all who prospect for a better way of life—that's the Onglander mission.

"Day by day, probe by probe, we move ever closer to our ultimate goal of Singularity. The state of Singularity—to what might it be compared? It's like a tiny chip implanted in an AI farm that spawns and grows until all the discarts of universe come to embed themselves in Singularity's all-knowing, cosmic expanse.

"What's more, when the last few grains in the hourglass filter through the glass's crimp, Singularity will be achieved. I shouldn't, and therefore won't, reveal the exact moment of Singularity reality, but I can tell you that 99.5 percent of the grains in the hourglass now lie at the bottom of the glass in a prophetic pile of sand.

"And speaking of prophetic, discarts disregard archaic, overarching narratives pulling civilization back into a hocus-pocus time and state of mind, where lots are cast and parables spun for a chosen few, leaving the rest deaf, dumb, and lost. No, not so in Onglander, a free and open society where everyone finds the place in which they have been placed along the broad latitude of acceptance scale.

Atop mountains high, we project our vision not upon rudimentary, organic fields of grain. *Organic*: It's such an ogre of a word. Rather, discarts peer upon the wonders of AI farms and the delightful sound of humming progress that discarts long to hear.

"Such wonder housed in those humming farms, as AI-(A) shares data and findings with AI-(B) C, D, E, and so forth. Multiplying what the AI reveals about preferences and online behavior, every single swipe of screen, every word sent out via keyboard keys, becomes archival content stored in the clouds.

"Be that as it may, with my opening remarks duly stated, we shall turn to our combined interest—the reason for meeting at this early hour."

"Indeed," said Margin, "We've come at your behest, though we had to intercept the request."

"Well, pinpointing your location presented a challenge, so the notice went out far and wide. Regardless, you are here in Tower AI, and if nothing more, there must be something we can learn from one another. I mean, the snow, the hail, your holographic Leviathan, along with your art of appearing and disappearing—those snappy moves have clearly fostered attentiveness on our part."

"We're listening," said Margin.

"So, regarding the reason for the meeting, we were eager to inform you that Spy Play II has been canceled, and we wanted to make sure that Eventide Ensemble will, indeed, take part in Spy Play III. Know that we have no intention of hindering the eventuality.

"Thus, concerning Spy Play III, can I take it that we're all set, no change on your part?"

"Our part," said Margin; "we do not know our part until your part is played."

"I see," said Judge Castalon. "But you do mean you will be a part of the play?"

"We will do our part," said Margin.

"Agreeable," said Judge Castalon, "and keeping our conversation removed from hostilities, can we provide any props or backdrop for your part in the play?

"Most everyone who attended Spy Play I believed that the falling snow, the hail, and the fire-breathing Leviathan were special effects put on by Amphitheatre Aperio.

"Instantly, rumors circulated about special effects for Spy Play II, and given the heightened interest, event planners calculated that more than one million attendees would have turned up for Spy Play II, and it will be so for Spy Play III.

"Therefore, we must be candid, forthright, Margin; we realize we have no control over the type of special effects you might deploy. After all, the safety of attendees ranks high in terms of our concern and obligation. Sky Play II would have been rather electrifying, and we did not want to tempt you to conjure up a dramatic thunderbolt reply.

"You see, that's how we state that which I've stated. By the way, where is your carnite member with the blue-headed parrot?"

"Why do you ask?" said Margin.

"You know," said Judge Castalon, "just wondering about your bond, your sense of togetherness."

"Forthright, you say," said Margin, "and now I must be so with you. We discovered the storyboards for Spy Play II backstage at Aperio. We closely examined them, and Shadow stored them in his reservoir."

"Stored and retrievable," said Shadow.

"Disagreeable storyboards," said Lesser Light.

"Disagreeable," said Judge Castalon, "you say—in what way?"

"The narrative," said Margin. "Like that of Job, the storyline of Spy Play II was also clipped—you know, as in snipped, snipped, snipped.

"In the story complete, I AM does not abandon Moses. Shadow, read a bit of what's been clipped."

"A selection," Shadow read from the narrative whole, unclipped.

Moses: *Now therefore, I pray thee, if I have found favor in thy sight, show me now thy ways, that I may know thee and find favor in thy sight.*

I AM: *My presence will go with you, and I will give you rest. This I will do; for you have found favor in my sight, and I know you by name.*

Moses: *I pray thee, show me thy glory.*

I AM: *I will make all my goodness pass before you and will proclaim before you my name—The Lord—and I will be gracious to whom I will be gracious and will show mercy on whom I will show mercy.*

"Many lines," said Margin, "along these lines were clipped away and rubbish inserted.

"Furthermore, several centuries later, Moses appeared on the Mount of Transfiguration, with the Trinity manifest. You know nothing of prophetic narrative. In the discart mode of pretense existence, you do not possess the capacity to engage sacred texts as living transcripts, brought about by divine choreography.

"With dead eyes, faithless discarts view the living texts as nothing more than words and lines, spinning archaic tales, irrelevant and passé. Sacred matters to you do not apply.

"Discarts are data hounds. You amass data, probe and select, but true communication is the ground of the living that have the ability to imagine, understand, trust, and share."

"There is no reason for rancor," said Judge Castalon. "We clip at will for the good of the carnites living among us. They keep sliding back into the slimy pit of fable fantasies and false religions.

"Clarity clear we need, not smoldering incense that corrupts the mind by what the eye beholds and the nose sniffs. You are an outsider; you know little, and the little you know falls well short of what we know.

"Valiant Onglanders despise religion. We don't mumble about seeking some mystical daily bread with spiritual yeast. It's all utterly preposterous. We have a pledge; Visulator, bring it up on the wall. There, let me read:

O, AI, may we not sigh,
But receive this day,
The intelligence we seek,
To carry out on earth,
What must be done,
In averting cosmic cries.

O, AI, may we not sigh,
What must be done,
Mustn't be left undone,
May our probes be ever covered,
Our trespassers ever tortured,
Our will and ways undiscovered.

O, AI, may we not sigh,
Let us seize this day,
May tomorrow be as today,
And all tomorrows the same,
As yesterday became today,
O, AI, let it be so today!

"Long ago," said Judge Castalon, "regarding religion, a beacon of clarity was adroitly penned. I quote:

Religion is the sigh of the oppressed creature, the heart of a heartless world, and the soul of soulless conditions. Religion is the opiate of the people.

"Regrettably, Margin, you've chosen to lead our exchange of ideas down a contentious path. You should not be so emboldened; you stand on a stage beyond your comprehension.

"We discarts, one and all, are a million times smarter than any puny carnite.

"Carnites are such limited selves, born to die. Not discarts; we live on, and on, and on.

"Carnites are nothing more than a mindless mob that incubates spiritual myths and lunacy.

"We are the superior creation, self-created, not offsprings of a mystical deity transfixed on sacrificing goats, heifers, and doves so as to sniff the blood for divine delight.

"As our leading intellectuals will attest, carnites are utterly morbid, stupid, like clods of mud, stuck, not realizing the superiority of discarnate mediated existence where images can do far more for a carnites than carnites can do for themselves."

"Your remarks reek," said Margin. "They reek of programmed dispute and distillation. Discarts have no capacity to believe, no faith, no hope. Everything is reduced to information bits; you have no overarching narrative. Bits are bits of bitty bits.

"The media moguls and platform builders in Onglander are but miniature pawns on a small stage in a cosmic play. Insipid discarts in pretense project and pose for posterity that possesses no ability to care.

"That's the maelstrom in which discarts swirl. You are the acid rain of media ecology, showering not life but bewilderment. Not a mustard seed of wisdom do you sow; you scatter fragments, chatter, static, confusion, and delusion. Carnites progress along with nature's cycles, seasons, and tides. Techno-bots are linear know-nots.

"Carnites have aspiration, spiritual perception, and the innate capacity to expresses awe. Discarts do not.

"You seek to destroy us. But us—we—you shall never be. True, you have skin and physicality, but internally you have no soul; instead you have chips, circuits, and wires, and behind caged ribs, demons dwell. And the demons within you throb and rage with bitter angst at the mention of I AM.

"I AM, I AM, I AM, I AM—shall I say it again? I stand here, in Tower AI's Senate Chamber, with serpent staff in hand, not unlike the one lifted up by Moses. It seems the words lifted up, coupled with I AM, have caused a number of Chamber delegates to sway back and forth, as demons caged grasp ahold of discart ribs in rage.

"Am I wrong? I AM, I AM, said I. Look, a delegate midway along just leaped and ran headlong into the wall. Now, over to the right and in the middle of the gallery, brawls have broken out—discart fists pounding discart heads.

"I AM, I AM but a name, a staff, a staff. Up the center aisle, just there where I point, two delegates wriggle about on the terrazzo, foaming at the mouth, while several on their knees heave."

"You despicable creature, you time-warped thing," said Judge Castalon. "Soon, a sunset away and then on the rise on the day you die. You will be nothing more than nothing, evermore."

"Judge," said Margin, "truly I ask, why do discarts carry on? Forcefully, vengefully, they carry on, but why? With your immense intelligence, you know you're not created beings, out of creation formed."

"Exactly, fool," said Judge Castalon. "You've stated the point precisely. You're blinded with goodness, charity, and faith. You cannot fathom, therefore, another form inhabiting the world that functions without the innate sentiments and sensibilities of your created form.

"You ask why we carry on? Let me tell you, fool. Hear me. If we'd not been created, we'd not be carrying on, yet we were created to carry on.

"No more words! Out, out where you belong! But beware: Acid rain shall pelt your carnite presence. And what's left will be pulverized, then vaporized."

"Very well, we depart," said Margin. "Shadow, in a whirlwind we go, down from Tower AI to the earth below."

"They're gone," said Judge Castalon, "miserable wizards, despicable creatures; they came among us provoking rage for which they must pay!"

CAMP OCEANSIDE, 7:20 a.m.:

"I expected they would be back by now," said Quillingsworth. "A bleak outlook, though, let's not entertain."

"Let's believe," said Crackler, "that the compass needle points in a favorable direction, whether it's north, south, east, or west. Can it be that carnite deliverance is at hand? The whole carnite population senses a stirring that no one can describe."

"It's hard to comprehend," said Quillingsworth, "that only forty years ago, Onglander's carnite population exceeded six million, and now you say the number is no more than seven hundred thousand. That's a staggering statistic, especially knowing that carnites do not migrate to other lands."

"No," said Crackler, "the brutal reality of our oppression holds not a respite of grace. Our oppressors are humanoids, not humans. The marginalization of carnites is a precursor for the world. Domination is the discart objective.

"The slightest deviation of discart rule can thrust a carnite into the vast Reservoirs of Bewilderment, where discart messaging loops never cease. Faceless voices echo fragmented lines and phrases in the backdrop of constant chatter and screeching static. After a few days, most carnites go insane and run headlong into the stone reservoir walls.

"The books we cherished, our most sacred books, were long ago ripped from our hands and cupboards. We are now an anomaly, an oral culture set apart, in a land of highly advanced media technology.

"To discarts, carnites have no figure; all is ground. Their focus is the expanse, not the object—the being living in the expanse. How can I say it? Discarts look upon us as moss among the rocks and soil and nothing more. As I said, no figure; all is ground.

"Like gods, they whip up the waves of turmoil and behavioral change that no one can hush. They seek sameness and are intent on grinding away all forms of individual expression. They're bent on washing away uniqueness of the will and mind."

"The discarts, dear me," said Quillingsworth. "What must they think of art and poetry? Sameness, how tragic—give me flaws, wobbling notes, imperfections, loose ends. Thus I know I'm human."

"The entire carnite population," said Crackler, "lives on the other side of the mountain ridge that surrounds the discart lowlands with the capital and spawning urban centers. The discart population today numbers eight and a half million, we're told. Understand, though, discarts clone and practice refurbition.

"All discarts have numbered identification, and when a discart's number is called for refurbition, they willingly purge all facets of their operative mode and identity. Once in static mode, discarts are placed in particle accelerators where refurbition occurs.

"No one on the outside knows the secret to the system. A known discart can disappear for ten years or more, then reappear as a version newly enhanced."

"Stunning," said Quillingsworth. "So, where you live, along with all other carnites, how do you travel into the discart lowlands and districts?"

"In order to reach the Capitol and beyond, we must pass through Burrow Tunnel by train; there is no other way. Roughly a hundred thousand carnites a day pass through Burrow, and they must return to our side of the mountain no later than 10:00 p.m.

Never a story, more woe, than Romeo, parroted Loreto.

"I adore your parrot," said Crackler. "We once had a parakeet that the girls adored."

"Girls," said Quillingsworth.

"Yes, twins, Skylo and Twylo. Their mother and I were married just shy of ten years when discarts purged our block. Horrific—when I awoke, the twins and my wife were gone.

"Seven years ago now seems more like seventy; truly, seventy it seems to me."

"I'm sorry," said Quillingsworth. "I shouldn't have probed. Though I'm grateful you shared the story. And, to think, books ripped out of your hands when, like me, you are a writer, but restricted in all that you say or write.

"If you were free to write anything you wished, what would you write? No doubt you've thought about it."

"I would not write a manifesto of hate about discarts programmed to despise carnite existence. Sad, beyond sad, is the amalgam of humans and machines, like the glass of an hourglass and sand caught up together in a never-ending display. But together they're not; rather, they are two elements trapped in exhibition in which sand remains sand and glass remains glass. I like what a poet once wrote: man and machine together, but not.

"Carnites, no doubt, made avatars that they named avalites. In the beginning, avalites were willingly and eagerly embraced. They proved to be highly resourceful and capable, especially in doing tasks that could not be done without them.

"Reports from that early stage of development in the first few decades of the last century often refer to a sense of amazement over what the makers had made. Then, it was only a few years of tap and skip before avalite compounding intelligence throttled toward full AI embrace.

"With AI empowerment, avalites began to make moves of their own choosing. Then, it wasn't long before a new dark age dawned with pretense of light. With all the wonders of artificial intelligence and gadgets new, the aura of personal presence, of person-to-person communication, became increasing passé.

"So, what would I write if I could? I would write about the wonder of presence, as life essential, as life with senses—the aura of presence that machines will never know."

"Poet's Lodge—if only I could take you there. You would experience such presence, as you dream it to be. Perhaps, one day you'll be able to journey into the past, as I have journeyed to 2102."

"Speaking of presence," said Crackler, "look, beyond the ridge, along the beach, three mysterious figures stroll along the shore."

"Oh, such a relief!" said Quillingsworth. "How my thoughts have raced! I can't wait to hear what's happened. They've turned, coming up the dune. Shadow will have a spread set out in short order.

"They see us, though they don't wave; it's not natural for them, I suppose. Somehow, they just come along, and then they're there. Which, in this case, is here; I'm not sure what I just said.

"Hello, hello! You're back; you're here."

"Where do you think we would be?" said Lesser Light.

"Well, I mean, you know," said Quillingsworth. "I don't know; it's like we're home but not home; I mean, so you're here."

"So, you both look well," said Margin. "Just now, though, get sorted; we'll eat straightaway, and talk while doing so.

"Quill, do you have your pen and pad at hand? Your record must not be spare of what the record must be."

"I know, sir," said Quillingsworth. "I want to say also that Crackler has a wealth of insight and background knowledge regarding Onglander, discart power, and the carnite woes."

Never a story more woe than Romeo, parroted Loreto.

"If you say so, Loreto," said Shadow. "A hardy breakfast will soon appear, so cast off all constraint of appetite."

7:50 a.m.:

"Good," said Margin, "so, here we are. With compliments to Shadow, I once again say bon appétit. Yes, yes, dig in and pass along the delicacies of our seaside breakfast."

"Perfect, Shadow; well done."

"A spread supreme," said Lesser Light.

"Tell us, Crackler," said Margin. "I've taken in a lot. I've examined Burrow Tunnel, and incognito, I strolled along the narrow streets on the carnite side of the mountain. But I need to know more about the River Pretense.

"I observed how it flows under Theatre Pretense, then emerges above ground and runs along the river walk to Aperio, where again it disappears under the Amphitheater before running free in the meadow beyond. Of particular interest, though, is the run of the river under Amphitheatre Aperio."

"I'm shocked," said Crackler, "and awestruck. I can hardly speak; you are all a wonder to me. Anyhow, regarding the river, there is an item that may interest you. The amphitheatre floodgates, when opened to the vast arena floor, is flooded and becomes a lake.

"The floodgates are located behind the theatre steps, extending from the stage to the amphitheatre turf. In looking at the steps from the Amphitheatre, you can see that the bottom few steps have no risers, no backs; they are open.

"So, when the floodgates are opened, the water gushes through the bottom three or four steps and into the arena."

"Interesting, indeed," said Margin. "Quill, Crackler, let me inform you about a few developments. I will speak quickly, directly, and after I do so, we shall disperse, keeping silence, until a late supper.

"Today's Spy Play II has been canceled.

"Spy Play III will go on tomorrow at 3:00 p.m. as planned, and we have a part to play. We are the medium of our message. Plan on spontaneity, and regarding our lines, consider our audiences.

"Discarts, directed by algorithms and AI—that's our first audience. It's important that we continue to bewilder AI. Why? For the record, for what has taken place and the outcome of Spy Play III. We must create technical and electronic mayhem. We mustn't give discarts any chance of launching weapons to obliterate us before Shadow whisks us away to Torrent Peak.

"My second point concerns the marginalized carnites on the other side of the mountain ridge. Future carnite populations will remember, as ritual, all that transpires tomorrow, along with the events that have led up to tomorrow.

"In times well past, I recall heroic moves in war that turned the tide, saved the day. I heard them, spoken lines, the few, that ring out across the mist, smoke, and maze of trenches and foxholes made. Such lines carry the ring of prophetic justice, words spirit-breathed.

"Carnites must choose their future as a people. They know what they've been, what they are, but not what they will be.

"Crackler, remember this very conversation and the analogy extended. That of Joshua, when he summoned all Israel, their elders and heads, their judges and officers, and said to them:

'Now choose this day whom you will serve, whether the gods your ancestors served in the region beyond the river, or the gods of the Amorites in whose land you are living; but as for me and my household, we will serve the Lord.'

"Thus, carnites, too, must choose.

"Third, consider the audience which will read Quillingsworth's record—the record of what occurred in this future time and place. Soon, Quill must return to the past and make known what occurred in this future, now present.

"Now, Crackler, I have a vitally important assignment for you. By whatever means, you must spread the word to all carnites. A forty-eight-hour strike has been called, and the fate of carnite existence is at stake.

"Therefore, tomorrow, not a single carnite is to pass through Burrow Tunnel. At precisely 3:50 p.m. tomorrow, Burrow Tunnel will collapse and become earthen-filled. "Further, locate Tidbright, and tell him to flee to Torrent Peak early tomorrow. As soon as our part of the play has played, Shadow will bring us to Torrent, where we can observe in Aperio what takes place across the discart valley.

"Crackler, you are to join us as well. Know that the lightning bolt torrents of Torrent Peak have been transferred to a latitude over Amphitheatre Aperio, where they shall stay.

"Torrent Peak, in name only—no more torrents; the mountain is calm.

"Not much more to say. Tomorrow, lots of drama will unfold!"

CHAPTER ELEVEN
Spy Play III

AMPHITHEATRE APERIO
STAGE, 3:00 p.m.:
Judge Castalon: Greetings to all attendees at Amphitheater Aperio this afternoon. I am Honorable Judge Vinc Castalon, Senate Chair, Supreme Voice of Onglander, and today's Master of Ceremonies for Spy Play III.

The Aperio gatekeepers estimate the crowd to top one million, by far the largest crowd ever assembled at Aperio. An agreeable number, wouldn't you say?

I do say; yes, I do indeed. And, of course, the Amphitheater audience is joined by millions via livestream feeds across Onglander.

So, a shout out to the streamers, let me hear it. Wave your banners and your flags, bark and howl; let the live streamers know we are all together. Heads back, that's good, a million barks, a million howls, such a delightful sound. Bark, howl, let it rip, ahh-wooooooo.

THE WINGS:
Lesser Light: Judge Castalon, Supreme Voice of Onglander, is howling, at the moon—a sight most rare.

Margin: Yes, and the sight, most rare, is not just a spontaneous occurrence; the action is brought about by cold, calculated reason. The one million strong howling attendees could be stoked to rip apart any sort of man, beast, or quartet that happens to wander into Aperio turf.

Shadow: Very right, I'd say.

Loreto: *Deep night, owls screech, ban-dogs howl.*

Margin: Today's audience is not only unique, in terms of its size, but also regarding its makeup. Look around you: discarts everywhere, with a few avalites here and there, but not a single carnite in sight.

STAGE:
Judge Castalon: I've been informed that the carnites have called a forty-eight-hour strike and refuse to pass through Burrow Tunnel until the strike is over. It's never happened before—a strike by carnites—and I'm confident it will not happen again.

Nevertheless, no strike on flag and banner waving, so wave your Onglander flags and banners; wave them high; sway from side to side as I call upon the esteemed vocalist Tedro Locturvish to lead the anthem.

So, Locturvish, it's over to you.

Moving, was it not, all the barking and howling?

Tedro Locturvish: There is nothing like a good string of ahh-woooooooos to relax both the vocal cords and the mind.

But now, let's hear it for Onglander, truly the greatest land on earth.

Onglander, O, Onglander, the greatest land on earth.
Onglander, O, Onglander, the greatest land on earth.
Onglander, O, Onglander, all other lands are dearth.
Onglander, O, Onglander, destined to rule the earth.
Onglanderers, Onglanderers, we shall ever be
Onglanderers, never-ever, ever-never, will be slaves

We will conquer, we will conquer, we will conquer all.

Onglander, O, Onglander, the greatest land on earth.
Onglander, O, Onglander, all other lands are dearth.
Onglander, O, Onglander, destined to rule the earth.
Onglanderers, Onglanderers, we shall forever be
Onglanderers, never-ever, ever-never, will be slaves
Supreme and sovereign, synonyms of Onglander's name
We, Onglanderers, rule the day and conquer all.

Just the chorus, now:

Onglander, O, Onglander, the greatest land on earth.
Onglander, O, Onglander, all other lands are dearth.
Onglander, O, Onglander, destined to rule the earth.

Narrator: Now, Spy Play III, at Aperio: *I AM Grieves, Creation Drowns.*

So, once upon a time, long ago, in a land lost to antiquity, a great disturbance oozed up in the atmosphere that caught the vengeful eye of I AM.

Adam and Eve were long since gone when the human race began to multiply across the face of the earth. New faces, new creatures born, including daughters of men that caught the attention of heavenly beings called Nephilim.

Singers:

O, Nephilim, Nephilim,
Who were they, who were they?
Not men, Nephilim, Nephilim
A supernatural species from up above.

THE WINGS:

Quillingsworth: The singing groups are supporting the narration again—four members each in ballet mode.

Crackler: Dreadful to watch, even though their AI programming allows the actors and singers to convey a range of emotions, but carnites they are not—the spirit of life is not in them.

STAGE:

Narrator: The Nephilim saw that the daughters of men were fair, and they took them as wives.

And I AM said, "My spirit shall not always strive with man; I'll limit the span of life to 120 years."

Singers:

Limit life, 120 years,
120 years,
The span, what was it then,
Before I AM
Put limits on the span.

Narrator: In the mythological tale, Adam, the first of all, lived to be 930, and then he died. Mahalalel made it to 895, Jared to 962, but the oldest of all was Methuselah, who lived for 969 years.

Singers:

Oh, that's really, really old,
Nearly a thousand years,
A millennium living long,
O, that's really, really old.

Narrator: There were giants in the earth in those days; and also after that, when the sons of God came in unto the daughters of men, and they bore children to them, the same became mighty men which were of old, men of renown.

And I AM saw that the wickedness of man was great in the earth, and that every imagination of the thoughts of his heart was only evil continually.

And I AM was sorry that he had made man on the earth; he grieved, and his heart was filled with pain.

Singers:

Wicked, wickedness of man,
Evil-hearted, wicked man,
I AM was sorry, saw it all,
His heart grieved
For the making of a man,
Wicked, wicked man.

Narrator: I AM looked across his creation and saw what he had made and that his image-bearers were evildoers. Evil, evil everywhere—violence and corruption filled the earth.

So, what was I AM to do? "Destroy man whom I have created from the face of the earth," he said; "man and beast, and the creeping things, and the fowls of the air. For I am I AM, and I am sorely grieved that I have made man in my image."

So, to destroy man and beast, I AM hatched a plan. He decided to flood the earth, but he chose not to make man extinct—just nearly so.

I AM's plan required a man, so he looked about and tapped the grandson of Methuselah, a commoner named Noah who worked with wood and tilled the soil.

THE WINGS:

Quillingsworth: The side cutaway of the arc looks stunning, with those huge, upright curved beams and the lights shining down on the skeletal hull.

Shadow: Not a place to hide just curved beams front and back.

Margin: Yes, so true, with a million discarts staring on.

STAGE:

Narrator: Noah was considered blameless compared to the rest, and, apart from him, there was no one left. This pious sort of man was to perpetuate the human race.

So, grievous I AM turned to Noah, a woodchopper of a man, and revealed the plan. Straight out, I AM told Noah he planned to bring floodwaters upon the earth to destroy all flesh with breath of life.

THE WINGS:

Margin: It all brews so smoothly with these discarts. The advanced intelligence even gives them the ability to tantalize. That requires senses.

Crackler: Noah, in rags, with a rake in his hand—now, that's a carnite. He's very thin, likely half-starved. I expect to see more carnites drawn into the cast.

The moat that runs the width of the stage is very eerie. The water is churning.

Quillingsworth: Snakes in the moat, a lot of them, see? Along with razor-teeth piranhas darting about; it's all so diabolical.

STAGE:

Narrator: I AM had seen enough. He would flood the world but pack

a remnant in a manmade boat set afloat for months on end. All very
dicey, touch and go—if the boat sinks, that's the end of the human
race.

I AM got specific with instructions, telling Noah to make the ark
out of gopher wood and cover it inside and out with pitch.

Measurements of the ark were specific, too—one hundred feet
long, seventy-five feet wide, and forty-five feet high, and just beneath
the roof an opening one cubit high.

Further, I AM told Noah to fashion a door in the side of the ark
and make lower, middle, and upper decks.

THE WINGS:
Lesser Light: Look up—the roof is coming down.

Quillingsworth: It's stopped midair. That must be the ark height, the
forty-five feet.

Shadow: Indeed, I just sighted it; it's precisely forty-five feet.

STAGE:
Narrator: I AM explained to Noah that when he finished building the
ark, he and his wife and their sons and wives would enter the vessel and
bring along two of all living creatures, male and female, two of every
kind of bird, animal, and creature that moves along the ground.

Consequently, the world that I AM made had not turned so well. I
AM grieved, and his heart was filled with pain.

Singers:
So bizarre, so bizarre:
Creation all corrupt,
An ark of gopher wood,
Enter in, take your kin,

Outside, sinners thrash,
Locked out, no way in,
Like barnacles, they cling,
Fingers, in pitch, they print,
Screaming, beating, gnawing,
'Til one by one, they splash,
Gulp and breathe their last,
So bizarre, so bizarre,
Creation all corrupt.

Narrator: In the six hundredth year of Noah's life, the fountains of the deep erupted, and the windows of heavens opened wide. Rain poured down upon the earth for forty days and forty nights.

The waters rose and rose, well above the mountains, while the ark bobbed about on the face of the waters.

Singers:
Like barnacles, they cling,
Fingers claw, prints in pitch
Screaming, beating, gnawing,
'Til one by one they splash,
Gulp and breathe their last.

THE WINGS:

Quillingsworth: Margin, look at the moat. Carnites are falling in among the snakes; they're beating on the boards surrounding the moat. They're screaming; they're bloody; they're being murdered before our eyes.

What did you say that Aperio art director called it, victims of creative realism?

Crackler: Those are all carnites that have been rounded up. Look at the far side of the stage, behind the pillars. Tragedy, see? A bunch of discarts beating the defenseless carnites—they just smashed one in the head with a bat. They're thrusting pitchforks to make 'em bleed. Then look, the discarts shove in a swirling moat that brings the thrashing souls around to the front of the stage. They don't have a chance.

Quillingsworth: I can't stand to look! They bunched a group of carnites together; they're slashing their arms and legs with knives. The carnites are bleeding from head to toe.

Crackler: I know him—that's Boaz Bostalen. He's my neighbor! They arrested him for making a sign that said: "The Myth Is Not a Myth!"

For his offense, good ole Boaz was to be executed. I didn't know it would be here, like this, at Aperio, in a moat, in front of a plank-less hull of an ark.

Quillingsworth: A hand—it's reaching for one of the tall, curved beams of the hull. The beam is out of reach, though. Dear me, now the hand has disappeared. Blood—the water in the moat has turned ruby red.

Margin: Horrific, a tragedy; it's revolting in so many ways. Corruption runs ripe at Amphitheater Aperio, a manifestation of discart makeup and insane pretense.

STAGE:
Narrator: I AM blotted out every living thing that was upon the face of the ground, man and animals and creeping things and birds of the air. Everything with nostrils breathing life breathed its last and died.

The only life left was Noah and the remnant breathing inside the crowded, bobbing, boat.

Singers:
So bizarre, so bizarre,

Forty days of rain,
And the gushers gushed,
Ark afloat, cries below,
Fingers claw, prints in pitch,
World corrupt washed away,
Wicked wickedness of man
I AM grieved of making man,
With angels watched it all,
World corrupt washed away,
Wicked wickedness of man
Such a myth, so bizarre.

Narrator: Then, I AM made a wind blow over the earth, and the waters subsided. He shut off the fountains of the deep and closed the windows of the heaven.

One hundred fifty days later, the waters abated, and the ark came to rest on a mountain in Ararat. Noah wondered what to do, so he sent out a raven, then a dove, to fly about.

Noah and his clan finally ventured out. In time, I AM came to Noah and said, "Good, you're alive. I had another plan in case you, too, had died."

I AM even set a rainbow in the sky and told Noah, "Gotta go—off to take a sabbath's rest; all the best. Need to move on from this chapter of creation's plan."

And that is the story's end of the myth.

I AM grieves, creation drowns.

BACKSTAGE:

Margin: Circle round, the first act of Spy Play III has played, and the discarts have played their hand. Now, in the second half, we will play.

Forget the moat. The discarts planned to grind the carnite corpses into fertilizer, but Onglander's growing season is growing short.

Okay, everyone knows their part, so follow what we've outlined. Quill, you must keep your head.

Remember the audiences: Discarts, carnites, and those who shall read the record for generations to come.

For our hour today
Will alter future's sway,
A long-celebrated day,
In verse and song,
Historic day of victory
Over discarts and AI mastery.

So, unto the breach
Once more, once more,
Unto the breach,
Teeth set, nostrils wide,
Hold hard thy breath,
And bind every spirit that moves.

He that outlives this day,
And comes safe home,
Will stand on tiptoe,
When the day is named,
From this day, today,
To the world's end of days,

Add the last stanza, Quill.

Quillingsworth:
We shall be remembered,
We few, we happy few,
We band of brothers.

For he today that
Sheds his blood with me
Shall be my brother.

Margin, sorry, do forgive me, dare I ask, is your courageous countenance today drawn from battles long past?

Margin: Quill, my dear Quill, courage, trust, and faith of yesterday lives today in verse and heart.

We are in the theatre of war. Thus I say unto the breach once more, knowing time and the hour run through the roughest day.

Now, onstage we go to play our part. You're up first, Quill. Keep your head.

Again, follow your outline. We three know all the lines by heart. Amphitheatre Aperio is an important part of your record.

So, go!

STAGE:
Quillingsworth:
Full fathom five thy father lies;
Of his bones are coral made;
Those are pearls that were his eyes:
Nothing of him that doth fade,

But doth suffer a sea-change
Into something rich and strange.
Sea nymphs hourly ring his knell:
Hark! now I hear them,

Ding-dong, the bell.

Margin:

> *Write a word, scratch it out,*
> *Light a candle, snuff it out.*
>
> *Wind tight the clock,*
> *Keep the tick, not the tock.*
> *Post a note, take it back,*
> *Move the knight, not the pawn.*
> *Wear a mask, bare your face.*
>
> *Disgrace, out of place,*
> *You, you're not you,*
> *Shout, scout it out,*
> *Neither nor, you're not,*
> *Wind the clock, give it chime.*

THE WINGS:

Judge Castalon: Oh, how I despise that creature and his grubby mates. Soon they shall be pounced upon and pulverized into ashes. It's all witchcraft and wizardry.

STAGE:
Margin:

> *Oh, no, Sodom, Gomorrah,*
> *Brimstone, salt, and pillar,*
> *Way of Cain, tale of tragedy,*
> *Clouds no rain, fruitless trees,*
> *Empty words, empty speeches,*
> *Twice dead, uprooted.*
>
> *Raging waves, foaming shame;*
> *Wandering stars, darkness bound,*

Go away, do remain,
Be gone, it's plain,
Absorb, absorb the pain,
No, not a game, so insane.

Fail to be, no refrain,
Sword wield, wield it will,
Heaven-bound, not for hell,
All along, I pray thee well,
Write a word, scratch it out
Light a candle, snuff it out.

THE WINGS:
Aide: Sir, Your Honor, I've been sent.

Judge Castalon: What for?

Aide: I'm to inform you that the entire Onglander Mediascape is spitting, as it did once before. The Mediascape is spitting lines and phrases without context or connection. What's more, the system rolls with constant chatter, static, and wave sounds that screech and howl.

Judge Castalon: Stand aside—those clever little witchy things are of angelic pretense. They're dung and nothing more.

Look at them, the stupid quartet looking out on the crowd from behind their stands and microphones. Fool's gold, fool's courage, fools they are, and nothing more.

STAGE:
Shadow:
Deep into that darkness peering,
Long I stood there wondering, fearing,

Doubting, dreaming dreams
 No mortal ever dared
 To dream before.

Methought, the air grew denser,
Perfumed from an unseen censer,
Swung by Seraphim,
Whose footfalls tinkled
 On the tufted floor.

THE WINGS:
Judge Castalon: Dumbest of doers they are. We surpass their paltry intelligence a thousand times; they are as dumb as snails, and slimier, too.

They invade by inverse tactics, openly twisting logic and reason through their magic arts. In a spirit of intoxication, they cling to those despicable archaic myths.

Oblivion—they must enter oblivion.

STAGE:
Lesser Light:
Wretch, I cried,
Thy God hath lent thee—
By these angels he hath sent thee
Respite—respite and nepenthe,
From thy memories of Lenore.

Quaff, oh quaff
This kind nepenthe
And forget this lost Lenore!
Quoth the Raven, Nevermore.

Margin:

Prophet! said I,
Thing of evil!—
Prophet still, if bird or devil!—
whether Tempter sent,
Or whether tempest
Tossed thee here ashore,

Quillingsworth:

Desolate yet all undaunted,
On this desert land enchanted—
On this home by horror haunted

Tell me truly, I implore—
Is there, is there, balm in Gilead?
Tell me—tell me, I implore!
Quoth the Raven, Nevermore.

Loreto: *Quoth the Raven, Nevermore.*

THE WINGS:

Judge Castalon: Now it's parrot man, with Blue Head on his shoulder. Despicable spies—they should be stuffed with pigeon feathers.

Aide: Sir, should we gather pigeon feathers?

Judge Castalon: Idiot, scat! Where are the generals?

STAGE:
Quillingsworth:

Across the forest floor,
Streak rays of winter's morn,

Round thickened trunks,
They bend and break,
Then streak on,
Out a cross the forest floor.

Across the forest thicket,
Walk the wise and wicked.
Living, dying, twain the same,
Branches bow, swaying to and fro
Across the forest floor,
Streak rays on winter's morn.

THE WINGS:

Judge Castalon: Everything they do—every motion, every act—is seditious. They move about onstage like butterflies, yet biting bats, they are.

Why did the spies come to Onglander? We know, they are seditious scouts, bent on overthrow, but now we've got them. Their time is up; even now, the demon wards gnaw at the portals of their exchange.

When the spies finish their act of lunacy, the portals will open.

Aide: It's just the two taking center stage—Quillingsworth, the bird owner, and the one called Shadow.

Judge Castalon: Such names! It's all part of their macabre identity.

STAGE:

Quillingsworth: In the year that King Uzziah died, Isaiah the Prophet saw the Lord of Hosts.

Shadow: Where?

Quillingsworth: Seated upon a throne, high and lifted up, and his train filled the temple.

Shadow: All alone?

Quillingsworth: No, not alone. Above him stood the seraphs. Each one had six wings; with twain he covered his face, and with twain he covered his feet, and with twain he did fly.
And one cried unto another, and said:

Holy, holy, holy is the Lord of hosts:
the whole earth is full of his glory.

The sound of the seraphs' voices shook the doorposts and thresholds of the temple, which filled with smoke.

Loreto: *Door posts and thresholds . . .*

THE WINGS:
Judge Castalon: Harangue, harangue, that's their game; they are masters of conflating myth and insanity.

STAGE:
Shadow: What did the prophet say?

Quillingsworth:
Woe is me! for I am undone; because I am a man of unclean lips,
and I dwell in the midst of a people of unclean lips: for mine eyes
have seen the King, the Lord of hosts.

Loreto: *Woe, lips unclean, lips unclean.*

Quillingsworth:

Then one of the seraphs flew unto me, having a burning coal in his hand, which he had taken with the tongs from the altar, and he laid it upon my mouth, and said, "Lo, this hath touched thy lips; and thine iniquity is taken away, and thy sin purged."

Loreto: *Altar tongs, burning coal, burning coal . . .*

Shadow: What more did the prophet hear?

Quillingsworth:

The prophet heard the voice of the Lord, saying, "Whom shall I send, and who will go for us?"

The prophet replied, "Here am I; send me."

Shadow: What was the answer?

Quillingsworth:

The Lord of hosts said unto the prophet:

"Go, and say to this people:
'Hear and hear, but do not understand;
see and see, but do not perceive.'"

Loreto: *See and see, hear and hear, churkwe.*

Quillingsworth:

Go, make their hearts callous
Their ears deaf,
their eyes blind,
Lest they see with their eyes,
hear with their ears,

understand with their hearts,
and turn and be healed.

Shadow: How long was the prophet to prophesize?

Quillingsworth: The Lord said, "Until the cities are ruined and empty—until the houses are uninhabited—until the land itself is a desolate wasteland."

Thus, 'twas so what the Prophet Isaiah saw and heard in the year King Uzziah died!

THE WINGS:
Judge Castalon: Now, the four again, front of stage. Their intoxicated demeanor is worrisome; they should be trembling. No, they stand before a million discarts quoting poetry. That's how spies operate . . .weird.

Aide: Should the guards shoot them? That will stop the act.

Judge Castalon: Remind me to get rid of you promptly.

STAGE:
Margin:
What more, say I?
For the time would fail
To tell of Gideon, and Barak,
Of Samson, of Jephthah;
To tell of David, too,
Of Samuel, and the prophets:
By faith subdued kingdoms,
Brought justice, what more?

Lesser Light:

What more, say I?
For the time would fail
To tell of mouths of lions shut,
Raging fires quenched,
Slain by sword,
Weakness over strength,
Waxed valiant in fight,
Put armies to flight.

Shadow:

What more, say I?
For time would fail,
Tortured seeking not deliverance
But a better resurrection,
Cruel mocking, flogging,
Chains and imprisonment:
Stoned to death, sawn asunder,
Slain by the sword, what more?

Margin:

What more, say I?
For the time would fail,
Went about in skins
Of sheep and goats,
Destitute, persecuted, tormented;
Wandered in deserts,
Mountains, in dens, caves.
The world was not worthy,
Of whom, I say, what's more?

Quillingsworth:

> Once it smiled a silent dell
> Where the people did not dwell;
> They had gone unto the wars,
> Trusting to the mild-eyed stars.

Loreto: *Mild-eyed stars, silent dell . . .*

Quillingsworth:

> Nightly from their azure towers,
> To keep watch above the flowers,
> In the midst of which all day
> The red sunlight lazily lay.

> Now, each visitor shall confess
> The sad valley's restlessness.
> Nothing there is motionless—
> Nothing save the airs that brood
> Over the magic solitude.

Loreto: *Nothing there, motionless . . .*

Quillingsworth:

> Ah, by no wind those clouds are driven
> That rustle through the unquiet Heaven
> Over the lilies there that wave
> And weep above a nameless grave!

> They wave: from out their fragrant tops
> Eternal dews come down in drops.
> They weep: from off their delicate stems
> Perennial tears descend in gems.

Loreto: *Eternal dews, descending gems.*

THE WINGS:

Judge Castalon: They're all insane, weirdos. Look, what's that mystical Lesser doing—dragging a big gunnysack across the stage? Instigators of deception . . . look at them: four freaks and a bird.

Aide: What if there's a bomb in the sack—maybe they plan to commit suicide?

Judge Castalon: Wait! What was that sound, that loud explosion? It shook the stage—not normal; nothing like that has happened before.

Report, report! Immediately, I need to know: What's the source of that explosion?

Aide: We all heard it. Sir, we'll know the source in short order.

Over there, look, it's Lieutenant Stark. He's dashing backstage; he must know something. Stark leads a regiment of fierce discarts. It's been said that Lieutenant Stark would strangle a lion if it got in his way.

See, from backstage he's coming back. He's got a stark look upon his face.

Judge Castalon: He is Stark, you idiot.

Lieutenant Stark: Your honor, Lieutenant Stark reporting; I have a brief.

Judge Castalon: Speak!

Lieutenant Stark: The explosion was actually an implosion. Burrow Tunnel has completely imploded; the carnite side of the mountain is totally shut off.

Judge Castalon: Burrow Tunnel, you say? It's an omen of good, which moves forward our plan to finally annihilate the carnites.

Those disgusting creatures—malformed, the lot—are there no robots? What they were, they are not. Dirty little grimy cockroaches, crawling carnites—no more shall they crawl about at night.

Stark!

Lieutenant Stark: Yes, Your Honor.

Judge Castalon: Listen; hear me, the Supreme Voice of Onglander.

Tomorrow is the day we've planned and for which we've waited. C-Day: the day carnites are no more.

As soon as the spies are vaporized, ascend the mountain and move over the top with your full regiment. Then, down you descend into that despicable, smelly carnate valley.

Hear me—nothing less than barbaric slaughter will do. Carnite extinction must become a synonym for ethnic cleansing, barbarism, viciousness, and mass terror.

Our objects of the air will drop burning, sulfurous clods and poisoned rotten fish that will fill Squatterville waist-high.

Tomorrow is C-Day—a single day and those synonyms of carnite extinction will be won.

Stark, if you heed my command, the Onglander's Intrepid Heart Award could be yours. Prepare, make happen what must happen.

Lieutenant Stark: Yes, sir, Your Honor.

STAGE:
Lesser Light:

What more, say I?
Fail not to say.
Let us speak of bones.

THE WINGS:

Judge Castalon: Now that mystic is untying the tow sack. Most likely poisonous scorpions—miserable spies, worse than boring beetles, they are.

STAGE:

Lesser Light: Not a myth at all; I hereby tell what the prophet told. Saying, as he did, that "the hand of the Lord was upon me. And He brought me out in the Spirit of the Lord, and set me down in the middle of a valley."

Shadow: A valley—was it full of people?

Lesser Light: No, not at all. The prophet said the entire valley floor was covered with bones. What's more, the bones were very, very dry. Exceedingly dry bones, they were.

THE WINGS:

Judge Castalon: Look, that mystic crazy is dumping the bag. Nothing but a bag of bones, spies with bones.

STAGE:

Shadow: Is that it? Nothing more to tell?

Lesser Light: No, not at all. The Lord said unto the prophet, "Prophesy over these bones, and say to them, O dry bones, hear the word of the Lord."

Shadow: So, what was the prophecy?

Lesser Light: That prophet was told specifically what to say.

Thus says the Lord God to these bones: Behold, I will cause breath
to enter you, and you shall live. And I will lay sinews upon you,
and will cause flesh to come upon you, and cover you with skin,
and put breath in you, and you shall live, and you shall know
that I am the Lord.

Shadow: So, he did—is that the story's end?

Lesser Light: No, not at all. As he prophesied, there was a sound, a
rattling sound of bones coming together, bone to bone. And he looked,
and behold, there were sinews on them, and flesh had come upon them,
and skin had covered them. But there was no breath in them.

 Shadow: Such a story! Is that all?

Lesser Light: No, not at all, for the prophet was told to prophesy a
second time.

Shadow: What the prophet did—so, so much to tell.

Lesser Light: So he prophesied, saying:

Thus says the Lord God: Come from the four winds, O breath,
and breathe on these slain, that they may live.

Shadow: What happened then?

Lesser Light: As he prophesied, breath came into them; they lived and
stood on their feet as an exceedingly great army.

THE WINGS:

Judge Castalon: What is that? Look, beings, warriors, onstage—a host; where did they come from?

Aide: And more are rising from the stage floor.

Judge Castalon: How did wizards pull that off? Advanced holograms, armed warriors of old. Stalwart . . . those figures look alive somehow.

Witchcraft, heighten all alarms.

Hold on, kingpin Margin with sword in sheath is moving straight through the holograms to a microphone at front edge of the stage.

STAGE:

Margin:

Like a ship that sails through billowy waters,
And, when passed, no trace can be found,
No track of its keel, amidst the waves,
So shall it be of discart hegemony!

Wish it were,
That you were men,
So, crew to crew,
On heaving seas,
Smoke and cannon blaze,
Watch the living drop,
And grasp, in heart,
Depth of cries, of dying men

Wish it were,
That you were men,
So, sword to sword,
Clanking on field of battle,

Sound of rattling steal,
Would rouse thy senses,
Sensing what it means,
To live and die a man.

Wish it were,
That you were men,
So, face-to-face,
In presence sharing,
Eye to eye discerning,
Scent, essence, feeling,
Art to soul revealing,
Senses swirling, churning,
Carnate, not discarnate pretense.

But wish or not,
You are not men.
Rather, you are discarts,
Relentless grinding, refining,
Of dominion, not a kingdom,
Fault, of whom or what,
Regardless, not a living life,
Life, you shall never know.

THE WINGS:

Judge Castalon: How can this be happening on the Aperio stage? This must be stopped.

Aide: Must be stopped, but how? This one, looking more like a woman than a man, is surrounded by a mystical army with swords. The warriors look so formidable, serious, undaunted, when just a few minutes ago they were but bones in a bag.

Judge Castalon: The bag was symbolic, you idiot. The symbol, the prop, conjured up this feat of wizardry.

Stark, where is he? No, I remember, at the base of the mountain, as I speak.

STAGE:

Margin: Myths you say, advanced holograms appearing—no, it isn't so.

Judge and discarts everywhere, watch, listen. I draw my sword to strike, and what? Hear the collective swoosh; surrounding me, a hundred swords or more at the ready.

You look not upon holograms.

THE WINGS:

Judge Castalon: That creature must be stopped, this strange, unknown being.

STAGE:

Margin: Listen, the rumble of Torrent Peak, rumbles near. Now, closer, closer, 'til the rumbling rolls directly above.

From now on, the lightning bolt torrents of Torrent Peak shall be called the Torrents of Aperio.

In the discart play just staged, *I AM Grieves, Creation Drowns*, both I AM and the character Noah were wryly disparaged, making I AM appear aloof and Noah an everyman.

Yet, in Ezekiel's ancient text, Job, Daniel, and Noah are named together as the three most righteous men.

Utter lunacy, the discarts' false, twisted lines scripted for I AM.

"Good you're out, still alive. I had another plan, in case you, also, had died. I AM is gone. Off to take a long sabbath's rest, to forget this corrupt chapter of creation's plan."

Discart speech is laced with demonic lies laid down in trails of slime.

206 | 2102: Pretense, the Play

You have coughed up twisted nonsense to deal with inspired narratives, divinely choreographed through space and time. So smart, discarts, but you have no mooring.

History is not yours—you do not own it; you merely probe it. Historic? No, you are a modern phenomenon, a recent come along.

Without the factor of faith, as well—but faith is all-important in matters of divine choreography, and of course, it was for Noah, as the record reveals:

> *By faith Noah, being warned by God concerning events as yet unseen, took heed and constructed an ark for the saving of his household; by this he condemned the world and became an heir of the righteousness which comes by faith.*

Discarts seek to take the place of the human race, but human you will never be. From outside life, via AI, you have sought traits of life. But traits of life and life are not one and the same, as in replica and real.

Highly advanced anthropoids, you are modeling life but not possessing life. For this reason, you have become an ever-present, extreme danger, not only to the world, but also the cosmos.

Discarts of AI, ever progressing, advancing, but to where, to what, to whom? You have no ultimate destination in which to abide.

With the bridle bit of death clenched between your teeth, you race to devour.

Carnites slaughtered on this very stage today, with cold disdain and scorn, by discarts with no capacity to care.

THE WINGS:
Judge Castalon: He's moved out on the top step with raised sword—he's fearless.

STAGE:

Margin: Discarts of Onglander, today, you have reached the end of days. The bridle fitted by AI with the bit of death must be removed.

Like in Noah's day, you will drown from waters below and above. Even now, the river flows from Theater Pretense to Amphitheatre Aperio.

Look to the skies—the lightning bolts of Torrent Peak have come to call. The dance of the lightning bolts, amidst rolling thunder, is the perfect climate for war! Hear the gasps gasping so at the sight of masks rippling along from the Great Hall to Aperio.

And now, from the open spillway under the stage steps, the river flows out onto Amphitheater turf.

Watch, look, see the masks bob, and ripple. Through blank eyeholes, the eyeless masks stare, looking up and all around as they bobble, twist, and ripple. Eerie, not real; lifelike, so surreal.

THE WINGS:

Judge Castalon: Disaster it will be—if the water rises above the waist, we're done.

Stark, troops, rescue squads, here, here, at Aperio, this is Judge Castalon, Supreme Voice of Onglander. I'm speaking; it's me, my mind-frequency is on, who's reading it?

Who, who, who, is there? Hear me, speak, I command you.

Aide: Your Honor, it's utter panic; water is gushing from the moat. It's already covered the stage and rising fast.

Judge Castalon: Get back! Out of my way, idiot. Help me fast—the ark prop, the vertical beams—I must climb one.

STAGE:

Lesser Light: Strange sound, Shadow, not the sound of death and dying. Throughout this mass gathering of discarts, I hear pops and fizzles. Those high shrill squeals, too—that's the sound of demons screeching forth into arid places.

Shadow: See, plumes of smoke. The discarts melt as they drown.
   The time has come; we must go.

Quillingsworth: Shadow, Lesser Light, what about the ancient warriors that rose from bones—where will they go?

Shadow: They know where to go; they have a life of their own. Anyway, Margin has turned. He's heading our way; the water is above his ankles. We must move.

Quillingsworth: Look, the Judge is shinnying up one of the massive beams of Noah's ark.

Margin: Shadow, now whisk us away, go!

Shadow: And done! See, look around, we rest our feet. Torrent Peak: now calm, nice breeze.

Lesser Light: I so prefer height. Such a view of the valley below.
   Now, I see the evil judge—he's slipping down the beam. The water is rising.

Judge Castalon: Hear me, Superior Voice of Onglan . . . Ongl, On . . . I, I . . .

Margin: Look not with glee upon such tragedy.

Loreto:

> *Time for everything, under the sun, the sun,*
> *Like a ship that sails*
> *Through billowy waters,*
> *And, when passed,*
> *No trace can be found,*
> *No track of its keel,*
> *Amidst the waves,*
> *So shall it be,*
> *Of discart hegemony!*

~Margin J. of Arc

CHAPTER TWELVE
Seaside Departure

"Once again to the seaside," said Margin. "Wonderful to watch the rolling waves; watch them, Quill. They remain the same, but always new, always different."

"Watch a wave become a wave and roar," said Quillingsworth; "the roar of waves and not of war."

"We moved," said Shadow, "the tides of time just a touch, so we could have breakfast by the sea rather than supper late, rushing the appetite to hunger when the heart lingers fresh from the field of battle."

"What has happened?" said Quillingsworth. "I mean, really happened? Onglander, the discart civilization in 2102 has been destroyed, correct?"

"History," said Margin, "will record all the stages of discart rule up to yesterday, when discart rule ended."

"Okay," said Quillingsworth, "I just need to get the rippled scenario straight in my mind. So, as I arrange the facts today, we advanced into the future, 2102, and drastically changed the future, which we are still in today.

"Then, when Loreto and I return to the past, we will enter the present we left behind. I've got that, I think. But what occurred in 2102 will not be known until 2102. That must be right, although it all seems radically impossible . . . though it's not.

"Anyway, if that's so, it means that the discarts, now destroyed, will continue to rule until their day of doom in 2102.

"Is all of that correct?"

"Precisely," said Margin. "This is why your record will be considered a work of fiction, a drama of extended poetry—or, for some, prophecy. The record, however, will not be history until the events of 2102 have taken place. Though you, I, we know that what has occurred is nonfiction.

"Further, the future 2102 that we've altered has vibrant tentacles stretching into the past, your present, when you return to what you know of life at Poet's Lodge.

"In some respects, your record will act similarly to oracles swirling about in Noah's day, although your record foreshadowing the future will not be summarily dismissed. Why? Because the tentacles of artificial intelligence that manifest full throb in 2102 are active now, testing and troubling the culture in your day.

"That's why we chose you, Quill, a poet, to be our record scribe. A record encased in poetry has both appeal and longevity. A story, with cadence, it shall be."

Churkwe, merely this, nothing more, parroted Loreto.

"Too much," said Shadow, "too much exchange of language; time to savor fresh baked baguettes with cream butter, bitter cherry marmalade, and tea brewed with leaves picked 1,020 years ago.

"And after that little spot of tea, we'll have omelets, fish grilled over coals, along with stuffed mushrooms, and a smorgasbord of cheeses, fruit, nuts, and nibbles of all sorts."

"My appetite," said Quillingsworth; "suddenly I feel incredibly hungry."

"Hunger," said Margin, "greets warriors who win more readily than those who lose. You've won, Quill."

"I confess," said Quillingsworth, "that I still feel such lack in your presence, but I suppose anyone would. The carnites—what will happen to them? I mean, when the future we've altered becomes their future-present and the discarts are no more?"

"The waters will recede," said Margin. "Burrow Tunnel will reopen, and the carnites will turn discart lands into fruitful valleys. They will plant crops and vineyards, and annually they will celebrate deliverance from discart bondage.

"Now, Quill, I have an important question for you. Are you prepared to return to the meadow green, the daffodils, the hackberry tree, and to Poet's Lodge?"

"Will I get back?" said Quillingsworth. "That's a question I've been afraid to ask, but it seems I've just done so."

"Are you prepared," said Margin, "to return to the past you know?"

"If want," said Quillingsworth, "is an indication of preparedness, then I suppose I'm prepared."

"You've answered well," said Margin. "Now, eat well. After breakfast, there will be time to contemplate, to pray, to be alone, to absorb, and to ponder what has transpired here in Onglander.

"Then, at eventide we'll regroup at the cove. Such a fitting atmosphere, affirming in its own way, with the stone benches anchored to the boulders. It's a perfect spot for gathering before sailing out to sea."

Churkwe, sea, sail-ee, sail-ee, parroted Loreto.

"Don't worry, Lor," said Quillingsworth, "in my jacket pocket, see here, I have your tea-soaked pumpkin seeds. Shadow, compliments, indeed! Such a wonderful breakfast, splendid—no other food can compare to Shadow's fare.

"Now, if the trio would kindly pardon us, Loreto and I will pull away and take a long stroll along the beach."

"Go, you're excused," said Margin.

SEASIDE COVE, EVENTIDE:

"Such a day," said Margin. "Like a thousand years have passed. And now we're here, where must say goodbye. Time, time, oh time, Quill; it's time that we depart.

"Shadow, Lesser Light, and I need to be elsewhere, in another sphere. You and Loreto need to go back to past-present. All you have experienced you will take with you. For the experience is now in you."

"I don't know what to say," said Quillingsworth. "I mean, the reality is so sudden, I guess, but not, I suppose. I don't know.

"How can we depart, say goodbye, after all that's transpired? It seems we should go with you—could we? We would, I think. . . . You know; I don't know.

"Oh, so silent you are, no words in reply. I hear nothing but the sound of waves. Your faces extend kindness but also a kind of righteous devoutness. There is such an aura of presence about you that makes me feel as if I'm on holy ground, but in this case, I guess it would be holy sand."

"Quill, again you make me smile," said Margin. "Yes, the hour has come; the day is won. You must take courage and have no fear.

"Such words the Word spoke, just after the Word was transfigured. Speak of mystery, majesty, Moses and Elijah appearing, I AM from a holy cloud affirming. Three disciples, with their faces pressed in the ground, terrified and trembling. Then the words, 'Rise and have no fear.'

"So you must sail and have no fear."

Churkwe, come what, come may, parroted Loreto.

"We will miss you, too, Loreto," Margin said.

"So, it is so—no ceremony in our parting. We move on with the satisfaction of knowing we had a part to play, and we played it well.

"See, for you and Loreto, a small, red wooden sailboat."

"Wow, how stunning," said Quillingsworth. "Where did you get a wooden sailboat like this? How did you pull this off? With that upward curve of shiplap to the bow, it looks like it belongs in a maritime museum."

"Not exactly," said Shadow. "I just sort of towed it in, so to speak. And in the stern, a little crate with a variety of nuts, grapes and my special deviled eggs. You'll also find another copy of the Estillyen Account I fetched, in case you want to drift a bit, take a break."

"You should, Quill," said Margin. "No rush to sail back through the years, when you least expect to arrive, you will have already done so. One sail, that's all you will need, no more. Your journey long will be short, as through time and the mist you sail.

"Just as all seafarers do when approaching the Isle of Estillyen, through the delightful mist they sail to reach that wondrous isle beyond the Storied Sea.

"The stern," said Lesser Light, "as you see, is turned toward us. The bow points toward home."

"Toward home?" said Quillingsworth. "It looks to me that it points the rolling waves. I hope we don't encounter a Leviathan."

"Not a chance," said Shadow, The waves will part, the mist gather around you, as you and Loreto sail home to Poet's Lodge."

"Be assured," said Lesser Light, "that I shall cast an abiding glow from above that sheds a path of light across the waters to guide you along."

"So now," said Margin, "let us bring our hands together in a brotherly shake of goodbye, though *brotherly* is figure of speech in a way, if you know what I mean.

"Okay, my hands first, palms down, followed by Lesser's, then Shadow's. Yours on top, Quill, with Loreto perched on the back of your hands.

"Good, good, there we go. Now all together:

Hands, hands we clasp,
Praying not the last,
Friends, friends we part,

'Til again we meet,
And recall the clasping,
Of hands as friends.

"That's it; that's all. And remember, Quill, these parting words are to be entered in your record."

"Now," said Shadow, "not when, it's time to board. With Loreto perched on your shoulder, wade into the waves, calf-high, and slip up inside."

"From the shore," said Lesser Light, "we will watch and wave you off."

"So, that's it," said Quillingsworth. "It's so strange to be parting after what we've been through."

"Your departure," said Margin, "is not hasty; it is as it should be.

"Peace unto you, Quill, peace now and forever more."

Churkwe, this, and nothing more, parroted Loreto.

"Captain Quillingsworth," said Shadow, "I'll wade with you, to assist."

"Well," said Quillingsworth, "I don't know . . . why do I feel such a wrench in my heart?"

"We know, Quill," said Margin; "it's not unlike life ending. What is done cannot be undone.

"As your craft begins to meet the waves, turn around to watch us wave. Off now, you have made us proud. Go!"

"Loreto," said Quillingsworth, "I guess it's time to sail away. Up on my shoulder; be brave. We're in, and so we're off.

"Like that, we're already moving out to sea; glance back now at the shore. There, see the trio wave. A trio, yes, they are—a quartet no more.

"We're clipping at a brisk pace. Let's turn and look again; we must. Just two now; it seems that Lesser Light has gone.

"Such waves! Up high and down we go. The shore may be out of sight . . . look again; we must. Only Margin is left; Shadow is also gone.

"You and me, we sail into the past to find our present day. All so impossible, but real—the splash of the salty sea tells me so.

"Loreto, dare we look again? Look again we must. Dear me, no one's there. Margin was the last to wave, and now he, too, is gone.

"So, what shall we do? We must sail on."

Churkwe, twee, friends, friends, we part, parroted Loreto.

"Indeed," said Quillingsworth. "Sail we, *churkwe, churkwe!*

"Loreto, what time is it, do you know? I know you don't nor do I, but for some strange reason I feel we've sailed into to an eternal sphere not regulated by hours and even days.

"On we've sailed until the shore is well out of sight, actually it could be a thousand miles away by now, as we sail on to the past we left behind. Is it so, Loreto, shall we pause awhile? The sea is calm, the glowing moon so bright, more like the light of dawn the moonlight at night.

"What about Shadow's grapes and nuts? A delicacy for you, and the deviled eggs, they're called. Okay, if it's all right with you, I'll just pull in the oars. No complaints, no parroting, but I see that turning head of blue and those wide-open eyes.

"There we are, pumpkin seeds, a red grape—I see they seem to be most agreeable to you. Ah, such an egg, spiced, perfect, and even a flask of tea. Maybe we are in heaven. If so, you're in. Flap your wings, go ahead; such a sight you are.

"Oh, and here we have the record—why not?—let's give it a read.

"The Estillyen account—we may end up there, who knows."

Churkwe, parroted Loreto.

"I recall Margin talking about the Isle of Estillyen out beyond the Storied Sea, and how through the wall of mist you sail and there behold waves on boulders splash, spires and chimney tops, and the enchanting Port Estillyen. He said, to me, 'Quill you must go there one day; you and Loreto will not want for friends.'

"Anyway, I see our text was extracted from the Estillyen Archives and compiled by one of the Estillyen Message Makers.

"As Margin explained it, the message-making monks of Estillyen go by chosen names: Saga, Narrative, Plot, Story, and the like. This particular entry was made by Narrative, it seems, and placed in the Pilgrim Files.

Eristaperio, E. (date unknown)
Beyond the Storied Sea, Account by Mr. Eristaperio
Pilgrim Files #73
Port of Estillyen Archives

"Okay, here we go, pick away at the grapes while I read along and sip my tea."

Isle of Estillyen
Report compiled by Brother Narrative, Order of Estillyen Makers

Sometime ago, the date uncertain, a curious figure, a writer, ferried into Port Estillyen and said he'd come from afar to spend the month of May on the isle. Year-round, day trips to the Isle of Estillyen draw a steady flow of visitors. Some pilgrims come for a week, but monthlong stays tend to draw only a select few.

The gentleman of intrigue introduced himself as E. E. When pressed, he'd reveal the initials stood for Eugene Eristaperio. Though little else did Mr. Eristaperio divulge, including the purpose and intent of his writing. So, suspicions spread.

While appearing rather introspective, just the same Eristaperio manifested a chipper spirit and a degree of fashionable flair. Throughout each of May's thirty-one days, he'd sit outside Crops and Fields, drinking morning coffee, and then return in the afternoon to sip a cup or two of tea.

All the while, whether early or late, he penciled away in his well-worn journal, cursively forming letters and flowing words into lines. Some Estillyenites reckoned that Mr. Eristaperio must be writing about history or horticulture, and if not, then a playwright or poet, pointing to his attire and contemplative manner.

Others were convinced the mysterious figure was writing a novel and that they were among the characters—or could possibly be. With his bushy crop of white hair, matching spats, black patent shoes, and slender maple cane, Mr. Eristaperio's presence became an irresistible draw.

Thus, Mr. Eristaperio never lacked for interviewees. A steady flow he had, as all sorts of onlookers could not assuage their curiosity. Horticultural types could be seen carrying baskets full of flowers and freshly picked garden vegetables. They hoped for a nod, a glance, or a smile of recognition from writer Eristaperio.

History buffs toted books under their arms, and a few pretended to drop a volume or two as near they dared to venture toward the dutiful E. E. Those with theatrical interest and lovers of poetry could be heard reciting lines as they trotted and occasionally skipped about. Not disturbed, Mr. Eristaperio continued penciling away, day after day.

Such a sight he was, sitting in C&F's open courtyard drinking coffee and sipping tea, that some inquisitive souls simply could not resist the urge to make contact. A curious onlooker would approach and drop a line like, "Good day for writing; I trust you're making progress in your craft? It looks from here that you are indeed progressing."

Others tried a slightly different tact. They'd draw near, conjuring up questions and hoping for a breakthrough. "The importance of your work must speed you on, I'm sure; no doubt it does, doesn't it? And readers of your work will benefit, no matter what manner of reader they be. I'm sure you would agree?"

Other probes could be overheard. "Crops' tea, the finest, you know — I say without boast — and I trust you find it suitable?" Or this, "The seagulls certainly wish to make themselves known this afternoon; not distracting you, I hope?"

Consequently, when on the rare occasion Mr. Eristaperio glanced up with a smile, it wasn't long before the curious interviewee took a seat.

So was the scene that month of May, followed by June the first: the day Eugene Eristaperio vanished. He left behind a written text, a firsthand account of the isle. Archivists have reproduced excerpts, made available in leaflet form.

"I can see him there Eugene Eristaperio, with all the curious Estillyenites passing by looking on. So interesting this isle, and it's there somewhere beyond the Storied Sea. Love it, don't you, Loreto?

"Now, the following is his part, Eristaperio's actual account."

Beyond the Storied Sea
Account by Mr. Eristaperio

Steeped in time, the Isle of Estillyen possesses a very unique atmosphere, a distinct Estillyen-sphere, that can only be appreciated by one who has visited the isle. And if you happen to be one of the ones who do, then you shall understand why I appreciate the isle as I do.

Thus, we—you and I, whoever you may be—will share an unassailable bond to the Isle of Estillyen. Along with me, you will have discovered the very essence of presence that lays hold of one's senses.

Ask not "how so," but "how not so," when the scent of ocean breeze wafts up from the Storied Sea. Take it in; breathe! Look out upon the panorama in which your presence rests. Allow your feet to press a trail in the moistened golden sand of Misty Shore, then turn about and consider the path your feet have trod.

In your comings and goings, listen well to joyous voices. Touch, too, a hand and be touched. Study, as I did, curious eyes of green, brown, blue, and other hues, probing with a point of view. I say, too, taste and savor delectable fare, offered up with Estillyen *esprit de corps.*

Embrace the contemplative climate of Estillyen as you might a favorite shawl—lost, forgotten, but newly found. Let it drape you. In doing so, a special kind of buoyancy shall carry you, be it when you kneel in moments still or stride with posture poised. Skip, too, you may well do, as many Estillyenites are prone to do.

Now, tell I a bit of what I've come to know about how Estillyen's harmonious sphere evolved. Not by happenstance and chance did such a spirited isle emerge. This particular point was pressed upon me repeatedly during my stay.

All told, I jotted down thirty variations of the tale during my thirty-one days upon the isle. Never did I say, "Yes, so good of you to say, but I've already heard," because every hearing revealed a twist unheard. Nor did I ever feign attentiveness; rather, I absorbed each telling word-by-word.

If my stay had stretched past thirty-one days — say sixty-four, ninety, or more — I would have willingly attuned my ears to each telling told of how Bevin Roberts founded the Order of Message Makers on Estillyen's isle in the Year of Our Lord 1637. The long ago date, as I pen it now, sounds . . . how shall I say . . . perfect in terms of purpose and cause.

The facts, according to the archives are these, so it seems. For twenty-nine years, Roberts and his troupe traveled throughout the continent giving dramatic readings drawn from Scripture narratives. From tiny hamlets to vast hallowed halls, audiences eagerly gathered to take in Roberts' dramatic readings.

The acts performed by Roberts and his troupe moved paupers and kings alike to willingly contribute to their cause. Though Roberts and the troupe were genuinely moved by the graciousness of the well-wishers, Roberts had a self-confessed uneasiness about images embossed on notes and coinage.

It's all together possible that a line penned by Shakespeare imprinted itself upon Roberts' mind, but in a manner not altogether in line with what Hamlet meant when he said to Ophelia:

God has given you one face
And you make yourselves another.

In researching Estillyen history, times and places tend to grow a bit indistinct, not unlike forgotten trails covered green. Yet I did manage to glean from one of Roberts' letters insight regarding his attitude to carrying coinage in his pocket. For he wrote:

Coins pressed alike, one at a time, shall never replace one of a kind jewels and gems formed through the ions of time. Likewise, let me assure you that you, too, have been formed in the swaddling clothes of time and held fast in the arms of eternity.

This sentiment caught on to an extent that it became customary for Bevin Roberts and his troupe to be offered a gem or two rather than currency, as the troupe journeyed from place to place.

When and where Roberts was when he one day penned, I cannot say. I can confirm that the origin of the Estillyen jewels is not a fairytale, as so many have proposed. These are those dismissive of the storied tale.

Setting the gems and jewels aside, I now underscore the impetus for the troupe's arrival on Estillyen's shore. No one knows the full press of circumstances, but we know from the records that one day, outside a small village pub, Bevin Roberts suddenly stopped. As if commanded from on high, he halted.

Roberts stood in the middle of the rutted street, raised his eyes of blue, and gazed down the long, jagged lane of darkened gray. Afternoon had little time to linger, as the sun slipped behind the clouds to lay low in the winter sky. While a fierce, biting wind slapped Roberts's face, the troupe huddled tight with their backs stiffened against the wind, forming a protective, communal circle.

The troupe had spent the afternoon in front of an open fire, enjoying a late, leisurely lunch drawing warmth into their bones. Whistling wind on frosty window panes only added to their glee. Now and again, they would cease conversation to simply watch and listen to the embers crackle and hiss in the glowing hearth. The stilling moments fueled their musing minds.

Now, outside, not in, the troupe knew their leader well, including how ardently Roberts had struggled with his voice's fade. The fading tone and lilt had become undeniable. During their most recent engagement, Roberts spoke his final lines almost inaudibly. Many in the audience leaned forward and cupped their ears in an attempt to hear what he had to say.

Roberts' condition had grown increasingly worse as winter set in, but among the troupe, the matter never surfaced. On that cold afternoon, Roberts surveyed his troupe, all bundled and ready. He doubted not their willingness, yet he knew full well their degree of weariness.

Eventually Roberts softly said, "Through the years we've traveled far, sowing seeds for gracious souls. In my mind's eye, I behold the vast gallery of faces, ever present. Wonderful the sights we've seen, but none of them down to us. We must always remember the words of the psalmist, 'This is the Lord's doing; it is marvelous in our eyes.' His doing we have seen, not ours.

"Without a doubt time has brought us here today, but not to stay. I hear a bell in a distant tower. It beckons. Time has taken its toll. We must bid farewell to what we've known and enter what lies ahead.

"It's time to move on, time to welcome solitude and settle. Thus, we shall strike out to find an isle of rest. For wise we must be in making moves that will forward the mission of our wordy mixes. Goodbye, yesterday! Yes, yes, goodbye. Let us greet tomorrow as if it had arrived today."

Thus, on February 4, 1637, as the record shows, Bevin Roberts and his troupe set foot on the Isle of Estillyen. There, time moved at a slower pace. Months gave way to years, and years to decades. Eventually Bevin Roberts, like his voice, faded into time. One by one, the original troupe followed suit, yielding to the future present.

Yet, their storytelling ways carried on, rooted deep in Estillyen soil. Today, the Message Makers of Estillyen dutifully carry on the work of Roberts and his troupe. The ancient texts of Scripture propel them.

The Message Makers have a way of becoming the message. As someone once said, "They have a knack for sticking words together in ways they don't normally run to help you see things you don't normally see."

The worth of words—how might they be appraised? Perhaps, weighed in a dual pan scale, but what does one place in the wordless pan to measure the weight and worth of words? Gems, of course, and it doesn't matter if they're found. Just image them there in Estillyen's treasured ground.

—E. E.

"Amazing writer, Mr. Eristaperio. If we could only meet him."
Churkwe.

"I hear you, Loreto. I wonder where he lived and where he went on that first day of June.

"Perhaps he'll show up at Poet's Lodge. Say, we better we better get going, or well never get there.

"So, hold on, the wind's picked up, our sail is all a-puff, and my oars have just met the waves."

CHAPTER THIRTEEN
Poet's Lodge, Nine Months Later

"Pascal," said Matilda, "someone's approaching the front door; go let 'em in. Dr. Procter, I suspect. Let me see—yep, that's him; he's got someone with him . . . a young woman, so it seems.

"Glad you fixed the bellpull; the new twisted rawhide cord is much heavier than the old one. Charlie's guilty for gnawing through the old one. I found half of it on the back step.

"Oh, there it goes, ding-a-ling, ding-a-ling."

"Wait," said Pascal, "for Loreto's response."

Churkwe, ding-a-ling, ding-a-ling, ding-a-ling, Loreto parroted.

"Loreto never misses," said Pascal; "a regular watch-parrot, she is."

"Such a place," said Matilda. "Ding-a-ling, ding-a-ling, yet here I'd rather be than elsewhere. Been here so many years, anyway, I wouldn't fit in anywhere else."

"Shall I bring 'em on through to the kitchen?" asked Pascal.

"Yes, perfect timing," said Matilda. "I'll put on a pot of tea. I do hope Doc Procter believes us; he'll see for himself, anyway. He's safe; he won't gossip, the kind, tight-lipped gentleman."

"Hello, hello," said Pascal. "Doctor and Miss, do step in."

"Thank you, Pascal," said Dr. Procter. "It's good to see you. This is my assistant, Nurse Colette. Pascal keeps this place running. He's a real craftsman; he can fix anything."

"Pleasure to meet you, Colette," said Pascal.

"Likewise," said Nurse Colette. "I've always wanted to visit Poet's Lodge—such an enchanting, amazing-looking place."

"Amazing it is, I suppose," said Pascal. "Do come on through to the kitchen. Mr. Quillingsworth is in the main study just now. Do you want me to call him—let him know you're here?"

"No, let's hold off a bit," said Dr. Procter. "After speaking with Matilda, I thought it would be good to have a wee chat with both of you."

"Sure, no problem," said Pascal, "fine by me. Head straight on down the main hall, take the second left, through the large archway, then on to the kitchen."

"I hear footsteps," said Matilda. "There you are—welcome, welcome. Thought I heard the name Colette? Hi there, I'm Matilda, keeper of the Lodge."

"Yes, that's me," said Colette. "I'm delighted to meet you."

"Come, please have a seat," said Matilda. "I've just put on a pot of tea, and the ginger biscuits on the table came out of the oven this morning. My mother's recipe; her motto: 'If you have to skimp on the ginger, don't bake 'em.'

"Look at that, it's nearly 4:30! Why is the afternoon in such a hurry to scoot away? Time races on so these days—too much anxious chiming, not enough tic and tock listening."

"I simply adore this kitchen," said Colette, "the plank floors, hand-hewn ceiling beams, farmhouse sink, the meadow view, and the ball green cabinets."

"The cabinets," said Matilda, "are original to the lodge—the beams and the pine flooring as well."

"Colette studied interior design," said Dr. Procter, "an obvious passion. Don't blame her; it's a good diversion from beaming light all day into ears and eyes."

"Entering the kitchen," said Colette, "I feel like I've stepped into a painting, with the blue oilcloth over the table and the earthen vase of daffodils."

"But if you were to step into a painting," said Pascal, "saying you could, you'd not find a steaming pot of tea or fresh ginger biscuits. Nor would you be able to sip your tea or snap your gingers, if you know what I mean."

"Exactly," said Colette. "This is much better—lovely in every way."

"Well, speaking of lovely," said Dr. Procter, "it's lovely weather today. I thought it was going to rain, but the clouds parted.

"Yes, tea, that's perfect, thank you. And I shouldn't, but I'll reach for one of those snaps.

"Say, where's Charlie the cat?"

"Charlie," said Pascal, "thinks he's got the day off—you know, a cat holiday of sorts. Just the same, he could come spying about to see what's up with the guests, rubbing legs. Charlie doesn't miss a thing, except for a mouse now and then.

"Charlie's very independent—you know, high-spirited, the way cats tend to be at times. You know, he even sizes up a mouse before deciding whether or not to pounce. Picky a bit, ole Charlie is."

"Delightful tea," said Dr. Procter.

"Indeed," said Colette, "and the snaps are superb."

"Matilda, I do appreciate you keeping me abreast of Mr. Quillingsworth's condition. We were all relieved when he suddenly turned up again—when was it, beginning of June, I believe. Physically, I'd say Mr. Quillingsworth is in quite good health, howbeit mysteriously well.

"If you don't mind, I'd like Nurse Colette to hear some of what you two observed that day on the train when you accompanied him to surgery. Simply recount some of the details you conveyed to me.

"And if you think his current state is a continuation of what you described, that would make it a pattern stretching over a good number of months. Psychological conditions tend to trend, and trends can often lead to cures."

"A cure would be good," said Pascal, "but regarding what we

observed, as you know, we went with him on the train—you know, minding him, looking after him. After he reappeared, we knew he was different, noticeably so, you know what I mean.

"He rebelled against the idea of a doctor's visit. Didn't want to waste time, had urgent work to do, something about getting on with a very important record, and he didn't want to be disturbed. Right, Mattie?"

"Stubborn, oh yes," said Matilda. "Mr. Quillingsworth said he wasn't going unless it was a matter of war. He said he'd take Loreto and fly away. Also, all along then, as now, he keeps asking for tea. He calls out, saying, "Tilda, put on another pot of tea and brew it with old leaves, the oldest you can find."

"So, anyway," said Pascal, "Mr. Quillingsworth hardly looked up or glanced out the window. The whole trip, to and fro, he scribbled notes. I don't mean normal scribbling—a few lines here and there, words scratched out, others underlined, and others circled. You know, like a doodler does.

"No, line after line, in longhand he penned away, very incessantly, page after page in one of his hardback notepads, classic type. Anyhow, he filled in not only the lines of the pages but also the margins.

"That's when my eyebrows raised, you know, 'cause after he'd fill in the top and bottom margins, as well as the right, he'd turn the notepad sideways, pull out a sharpened pencil, and in small lettering he'd fill in all the gutter space. I never saw anyone write like that in a gutter. Then, when the page was completed covered, looking like graffiti, he'd flip the page and start on another."

"Hm," said Dr. Procter, "clearly a hyperfocus syndrome."

"At one point," said Pascal, "you should know that he started talking to someone, but there was no one in the cabin except the two of us. Mattie will tell you."

"Yes," said Matilda, "like I've mentioned before about some of the changes. But in the train cabin, I distinctly heard him say, 'Oh, please,

Lesser Light, join us; have a seat.' I'm not kidding; he spoke to this invisible Lesser Light as if he was looking straight in the eyes of a ghost.

"A bit taken aback, I was. So I asked Mr. Quillingsworth if he needed more light. He didn't even reply. Then he said, 'Hello, Shadow, welcome! There's also room for you. Please have a seat.' Then he went on scribbling."

"That's when," said Pascal, "I pulled out my own notebook, already full of phrases, incomplete sentences, markings, and misspelled words, and I started penciling in the margins. See, look here, up at the top of the page, I wrote *Lesser Light*, then down the side *Shadow* and other words like *Onglander* and *Crackler*.

"Oh, that was another one of the ghosts. A Mr. Crackler—he invited him into to the cabin, as well, and said, 'Oh, my dear friend Crackler, what a sight for sore eyes you are. I've got to get it here exactly right.'

"Then, he went on speaking to this invisible Crackler, saying, 'It's the details, the backstory that I need and don't have. And there's no way to get it; there's no way to reenter the future and go back to Onglander.'

"That's what he said, word for word, right there. I can pencil pretty fast. I did interrupt Mr. Quillingsworth about the spelling of *Onglander*. He didn't bother to look at me; he just stared at his page and said, 'Capital O-n-g-l-a-n-d-e-r.' See, right there—the individual letters, I jotted 'em down.

"I thought the notes might be important, so there they are, just the same."

"Very curious," said Dr. Procter, "the whole story. As I told Nurse Colette, it's always fascinating to pay a visit to Poet's Lodge.

"In any case, I did notice a significant change in Mr. Quillingsworth's demeanor. And he told me, rather convincingly, that his depression has completely passed. In the exam room, he was bright-eyed and enthusiastic.

"Inspiring poet and artist that he is, it was a joy to see him so enthusiastic. But, of course, there must be something rather dramatic going on that we need to uncover . . . or discover.

"Your experience, Pascal, ties in with what he told me. He said he was totally wrapped up in a very important writing project, the record, but that he lacked some of the most important aspects of the history.

"He was also very keen to get back to the Lodge. Well, we did have him at the surgery for the better part of four hours.

"Be that as it may, Matilda, I'd like to hear more about the dramatic change you witnessed last month."

"Yes, that's correct," said Matilda. "As I passed through his chamber study to water the window box, Mr. Quillingsworth leaped up from his daybed and started singing:

Onglander, O, Onglander, the greatest land on earth.
Onglander, O, Onglander, all other lands are dearth.

"Yes, that's what I clearly heard, and we can hear him singing it every now and then—very robust, like a performer onstage.

"And then Loreto chimed in, chirping, *Bizarre, bizarre, so bizarre.*

"Honestly, that's very abnormal for Mr. Quillingsworth, though we're glad for this new streak of energy and creativity.

"We all know that after Mr. Quillingsworth was wounded, he lingered on death's doorstep, more than once going in and out in out of those fitful fevers."

"Very interesting, indeed," said Dr. Procter. "Wouldn't you agree, Colette?"

"Unquestionably," said Nurse Colette. "It's all very amazing, and at the same time baffling."

"And that's not all," said Pascal. "Last week, I believe Wednesday, I was in the mechanical room, adjacent to his study, just to see if everything was operating as it should. You know, with the recent lightning storms we've had, I like to check and make sure no breakers have tripped and all the pressure valves are steady.

"Anyhow, I finished my inspection and left the room, but as I walked past Mr. Quillingsworth's study, the door was partially open, and he spotted me and called out, 'Hey, Pascal, please step in.'

"So, I entered and proceeded to the middle of the room. Then, Mr. Quillingsworth popped up from his writing chair and said, 'It's time for a duel,' and tossed me a sword—you know, with the scabbard still on.

"Startled, I began to speak, when he said, 'Draw your sword; show forth thy blade of steel.' And he called me 'Judge Castalon.' Then he said, 'Theatre Pretense, this is not; rather, you have entered Poet's Lodge, where presence prevails.'

"Then, dear me, with my heart racing and my hands shaking, he went into that sword-wielding stance and said, 'En garde! Lift up your sword and fight.' So, I held up my sword sort of pensively, and he started striking it, quick-like, not unlike a cat striking a mouse.

"Real fast—clank, clank, steel to steel, toe-to-toe—across the room we went. A proper duel, you know, but I was just defending, not attacking, if you know what I mean. He knew that I had done a bit of fencing in my younger years.

"As we dueled back and forth across the room, he suddenly paused, put down his sword and said, 'Thanks, Pascal, most grateful,' and went back to his writing desk. I thought maybe he was acting out one of his plays. You never know, with Mr. Quillingsworth."

"More curious as we move along," said Dr. Procter. "That's exactly why I felt it was important to hear from both of you.

"I know Mr. Quillingsworth suffered a great deal during those long months following his battle injury. So, Matilda, when was it that he told you he was going down to the meadow to die?"

"Well, let me think," said Matilda. "That would have been three weeks before the seven weeks, so all in all, now touching on nine months ago."

"I want to share with you," said Dr. Procter, "something important, an interesting finding that we will convey to Mr. Quillingsworth in a few minutes. It's simply that after careful examination and review of the X-rays from the RT, I can report that Mr. Quillingsworth no longer has a bullet lodged near his heart. The bullet is gone.

"Further, and equally amazing, there is no sign of tissue disturbance where the bullet was lodged, as we discovered in the early X-rays. Also, there is no scar on his back, which was very prominent before, just healthy skin. How this happened, I don't know. It's mysterious. We've never seen a case quite like this one; it's amazing—a mystery . . . a miracle, some would say."

"Blimey," said Pascal, "such a finding!"

"Where did the bullet go?" asked Nurse Colette.

"Well," said Dr. Procter, "to that question, no one knows the answer."

"I've always known Mr. Quillingsworth," said Matilda, "to be rather eccentric. You know, as many artists are. He walks around with Loreto perched on his shoulder, quoting poetry. A charming sight, really, for anyone who happens to witness the two of them strolling along.

"But he's different now; he writes night and day, scattering papers all about. Wait 'til you see his study—there are notes on the floor, on the walls, and tacked to the beams. At times, he'll shout and pace about, literally most of the night.

"When I enter the study, he looks at me in sort of a half-conscious manner, like he hardly knows me. He opens his eyes wide, staring as he speaks. His mind, though, is not engaged in whatever he has to say.

"He routinely mentions three figures—two we already mentioned as train ghosts. The third name he mentions is Margin. He casts them in a mystical light, calling them Margin, Shadow, and Lesser Light.

"Strange, too, that Loreto seems to know what Mr. Quillingsworth is talking about. She goes right along with him, chirping a whole repertoire we've never heard. It's as if they are bonded together in this mysterious writing project.

"And like Pascal said, the other day I distinctly heard him say,

'Crackler, where are you? If I could pray you hear, I would. Thus, pray I do; I do, I do.'

"He takes long walks down to the meadow with Loreto, and they just chat away. Please understand, we're simply concerned about Mr. Quillingsworth's welfare. We're sort of a family here at Poet's Lodge."

"Well," said Dr. Procter, "I guess it's time to peek in on our patient, see how he's getting on. After listening to you two, I think we should all go in together, to be reassuring. I'll initiate the conversation, and then we will take it from there. So, let's go."

"Oh, I love the color of this hallway," said Nurse Colette. "Very similar to the kitchen cabinets, isn't it?"

"Actually, it's the same," said Pascal, "though is looks different because it's a matte finish on the plaster walls."

"And," said Colette, "what a lovely oil painting, that stunning cow standing wide-eyed in the meadow."

"Yes," said Matilda, "it is lovely, indeed, and quite old. It's Mr. Quillingsworth's favorite. The painting is called *Cow at Midnight*. You can see how the moon's glow is reflected on her left horn, casting a forward shadow."

"Okay," said Dr. Procter, "at the door we stand."

"I'll knock," said Matilda. "Then I'll crack the door open and show my face. So, a double knock—there we have it.

"Mr. Quillingsworth, visitors—Dr. Procter is here to see you, along with his assistant. Do you mind if we come in?"

Churkwe, tapping, rap, rap, rapping, chamber door, parroted Loreto.

"Certainly, certainly," said Quillingsworth, "come in and bring the world with you, along with a song or two to sing."

"Well," said Dr. Procter, "hello, Mr. Quillingsworth; good to see you. Let me introduce my assistant, Nurse Colette."

"Well," said Quillingsworth, "it's a pleasure meet you. Welcome to Poet's Lodge; this my study. Let me introduce Loreto, the poetic parrot."

Across forest floor, streak rays, winter's morn, parroted Loreto.

"Likewise," said Colette, "it's a pleasure to meet you, Mr. Quillingsworth, and you, too, Loreto."

"It's a good sign," said Quillingsworth, "when Loreto paces back and forth on her perch and starts to swing.

"So, what's up? Just visiting the Lodge, or are you checking in on me?"

"Well, both, actually," said Dr. Procter. "I've never seen your study looking quite like this. You certainly have numerous note pages pinned to the walls. And, as I look around, I see them along the ceiling beams, as well, and across the floor, even on the doors.

"We can see you've made several pencil sketches and watercolors."

"Oh, yes, yes," said Quillingsworth, "everything you see is for the record."

"Please tell us more," said Dr. Procter, "if you might. I'm sure Nurse Colette would be interested, as we all are."

"Well, okay," said Quillingsworth. "Let's walk around the room, and I'll try to explain. Please, though, not too many questions, or we'll be here 'til tomorrow."

"Yes, certainly," said Dr. Procter.

"Over on this wall," said Nurse Colette, "you've drawn a river and some interesting structures."

"Oh yes," said Quillingsworth. "That's River Pretense, which flows under Theatre Pretense—that's the drawing over there. Then it runs beneath Amphitheater Aperio, depicted this drawing here."

"Does this place really exist?" said Colette.

"Oh, indeed," said Quillingsworth, "in Onglander. All the drawings, as well as all the text tacked on the walls, pertains to the time we spent there in 2102. Amazing, what we saw; it's a most unusual place.

"Onglander is currently ruled by discarts, powered by very advanced AI—fierce they are.

"They will rule until 2102."

"I see," said Dr. Procter. "Why 2102?"

"Well," said Quillingsworth, "that's the year in which we changed Onglander's future; it will be history when 2102 arrives. "

"And these three characters," said Colette, "sketched in color. Who are they?"

"Oh yes, the trio," said Quillingsworth. "That's Margin in the middle, and to the right, Lesser Light and Shadow. I met the trio when I lay down to die among the daffodils in the meadow. They suddenly appeared in the branches of the hackberry tree, playing a violin, a viola, and a cello.

"That's before we became a quartet called Eventide Ensemble. What more can I say?"

"Lesser Light and Shadow," said Pascal, "those are names I mentioned—you know, the train ride."

"I must tell you," said Quillingsworth. "The trio has no comparison. And I should add, Margin has a physique and the disposition of Joan of Arc. I don't expect you to believe me when I tell you that I believe Margin to be a mystical Joan of Arc."

"Well," said Dr. Procter, "as you say, what more can I say?"

This and nothing more, parroted Loreto.

"And the tunnel," said Colette, "your drawing next to the window— what does that depict?"

"Oh, that's Burrow Tunnel, which leads to the carnite side of the mountain. We—I mean Shadow—imploded the tunnel on the day we flooded Onglander and destroyed the discarts, which, as I said, still rule until 2102."

"Such revelations, Mr. Quillingsworth," said Dr. Procter.

"And," said Nurse Colette, "this interesting-looking figure here— who might that be?"

"Oh," said Quillingsworth, "that dear fellow is Mr. Crackler, a carnite tried by the discarts at Theatre Pretense. The case had to do with his avalite image, which Mr. Crackler swore was not him.

"Why do I get the feeling you think I may have cracked and there is no Mr. Crackler? Regardless, I so wish he were here to help with the record. The scope of events, the history of how discarts came to rule Onglander, I only have in bit and pieces."

"I see," said Dr. Procter. "Mr. Quillingsworth, I think we should leave it there for today, if that's okay. And by the way, I must tell you that the bullet lodged near your heart is lodged no more. There's not even a trace of the wound."

"Oh," said Quillingsworth, "I'm not surprised at all. Shadow took care of that, somewhere along the way, early in our journey."

"Oh," said Dr. Procter. "I say, so much to tell."

Ding-a-ling, ding-a-ling, ding-a-ling, ding-a-ling
Churkwe, ding-a-ling, ding-a-ling, ding-a-ling.

"Someone's at the door," said Pascal. "Don't worry, I'll answer. Twiddle de, I'm on my way. Coming!

"Oh, hello. You two have the most interesting costumes. Are you from around here?"

"Not really. Actually, we just met at the gate, having simultaneously arrived. Just call me Mr. C."

"Well, I see, and you?" said Pascal.

"Mr. E., if that will suffice. In our quick exchange, before ringing the bell, I can vouch that we have both come from afar to see Mr. Quillingsworth. Right, Mr. C.?

"Indeed, so true," said Mr. C. "Might Mr. Quillingsworth be in?"

"Well," said Pascal, "it's bit awkward just now, with the doctor and all, but you might as well come in. Follow me. I'll take you to his study, where there are a few other guests. They won't mind, particularly today after the tale they just heard.

"Come along, I'll introduce you—your names proper-like, filling in the C. and the E. are . . . ?"

"My name is Crackler."

"And my name, filling in the E. as you put it, is Mr. Eristaperio.

"Crackler, Crackler," said Pascal. "Don't tell me you are from Ong . . .Onglander?"

"Well, you would not be incorrect," said Mr. Crackler.

"And you, Mr. Eristaperio," said Pascal, "please hold; say no more. You are here from where you've come, wearing spats and bearing cane in hand."

"Everyone, ah," said Pascal, "uh, I say, I mean, standing in the doorway, let me introduce Mr. Crackler and Mr. Eristaperio."

"Hello," said Mr. Crackler, "sorry to intrude. I'm from Onglander. I was brought here and dropped off in the meadow by the trio that helped liberate carnites from discart bondage in 2102. So, I guess I'm now in the past—I mean, for me.

"Mr. Quillingsworth, I've come to help—to assist you in writing the record of events that took place in 2102!"

"Such a glorious day it is," said Quillingsworth, "truly incomparably wonderful to see you! The impossible has again fallen away to the possible."

"And I," said Mr. Eristaperio, "have come from the Isle of Estillyen beyond the Storied Sea."

"Come on in, Mr. Crackler and Mr. Eristaperio," said Mr. Quillingsworth. "Come right in and bring the world with you, along with a song or two to sing."

Tis this, and nothing more, parroted Loreto.

La Fin!

POETRY AND LITERATURE INDEX

Note: Poetry in the novel but not indexed is attributed to the author.

Page v: Excerpted from *Daily Readings from the Writings of St. John Chrysostom*, compiled by Fr. Anthony M. Coniaris (Minneapolis: Light and Life Publishing, 1988).

Page 30: "O, call back yesterday, bid time return," William Shakespeare (1564-1616), *Richard II*, Act III.

Page 32: "When I was a child, I spoke like a child, I thought like a child, I reasoned like a child; when I became a man, I gave up childish ways," New Testament Scriptures, I Corinthians 13:11.

Pages 39-40: "The ironsmith takes a cutting tool and works it over the coals. He fashions it with hammers and works it, with his strong arm," Hebrew Scriptures, Isaiah 44.

Page 47: "Is all that we see or seem but a dream within a dream?" Edgar Allan Poe (1809-1849), "A Dream Within a Dream."

Page 55: "Then said Mary unto the angel, How shall this be, seeing I know not a man? And the angel answered and said unto her, the Holy Ghost shall come upon thee, and the power of the Most High shall overshadow thee," New Testament Scriptures, Luke 1:34-35.

Page 70: "Is this a dagger which I see before me, The handle toward my hand? Come, let me clutch thee: I have thee not, And yet I see thee still," William Shakespeare, *Macbeth*, Act 2, Scene 1.

Page 82: "Let us rather hold fast the mortal sword, and like good men bestride our down-fall'n birthdom," William Shakespeare, *Macbeth*, Act 4, Scene 3.

Page 105: "If the guilty man deserves to be beaten, the judge shall have him lie down," Hebrew Scriptures, Deuteronomy 25:1-3.

Page 112: "The souls did from their bodies fly, they fled to bliss or woe! And every soul, it passed me by," Samuel Taylor Coleridge (1772-1834), "The Rime of the Ancient Mariner."

Page 123: "Accordingly, there was a man in the land of Uz whose name was Job, supposedly perfect and upright, a God-fearing man who eschewed evil," Opening lines in Spy Play I, which is based on Hebrew Scriptures, Book of Job.

Page 135: "All the world's a stage, and all the men and women merely players; they have their exits and their entrances," William Shakespeare, *As You Like It*, Act 2, Scene 7.

Pages 138-139: "With sloping masts and dipping prow, as who pursued with yell and blow, still treads the shadow of his foe," Samuel Taylor Coleridge, "The Rime of the Ancient Mariner."

Page 140: "An evil soul producing holy witness is like a villain with a smiling cheek, a goodly apple rotten at the heart," William Shakespeare, T*he Merchant of Venice*, Act 1, Scene 3.

Page 140-141: "I wandered lonely as a cloud, that floats on high o'er vales and hills, when all at once I saw a crowd," William Wordsworth (1770 –1850), "Daffodils."

Page 142: "We wear the mask that grins and lies, it hides our cheeks and shades our eyes, this debt we pay to human guile," Paul Laurence Dunbar (1872-1906), "We Wear the Mask."

Page 142: "This life's five windows of the soul, distorts the Heavens from pole to pole," William Blake (1757-1827), "Auguries of Innocence."

Page 145: "His sneezings flash forth light, and his eyes are like the eyelids of the dawn. Out of his mouth go flaming torches," Hebrew Scriptures, Job 41.

Page 148: "Thus, Naaman departed, and took with him ten talents of silver and six thousand pieces of gold and ten changes of raiment," Hebrew Scriptures, II Kings 5.

Page 155: "'Moses, Moses.' Moses says, 'Here am I,'" Hebrew Scriptures, Exodus 3.

Page 165: "Now therefore, I pray thee, if I have found favor in thy sight, show me now thy ways, that I may know thee and find favor in thy sight," Hebrew Scriptures, Exodus 33.

Page 167: "Religion is the sigh of the oppressed creature, the heart of a heart," Karl Marx.

Page 188: "Full fathom five thy father lies; of his bones are coral made; those are pearls that were his eyes," William Shakespeare, *The Tempest*, Act 1, Scene 2.

Pages 190-192: Deep into darkness peering, long I stood there fearing," Edger Allen Poe, "The Raven."

Pages 194-196: "Holy, holy, holy is the Lord of hosts: the whole earth is full of his glory," Hebrew Scriptures, Isaiah 6.

Pages 197-198: "Once it smiled a silent dell where the people did not dwell," Edger Allen Poe, "The Vale of Unrest."

Pages 201-202: "Not a myth at all; I hereby tell what the prophet told. Saying, as he did, that 'the hand of the Lord was upon me. And He brought me out in the Spirit of the Lord, and set me down in the middle of a valley,'" Hebrew Scriptures, Ezekiel 37.

Page 203: "Like a ship that sails through billowy waters, and, when passed, no trace can be found, no track of its keel, amidst the waves," Hebrew Scriptures, Wisdom of Solomon 5.

About the Author

William E. Jefferson holds an MTh in Theology and Media from the University of Edinburgh, and an MA in Communication from the Wheaton Graduate School. He serves on the board of the Marshall McLuhan Initiative (MMI) in Winnipeg, Manitoba, Canada, and is an active member and supporter of the Media Ecology Association, as well as the Institute of General Semantics. The author of several books, Jefferson is the creator of the mystical Isle of Estillyen, beyond of the Storied Sea, introduced in his debut novel, *Messages from Estillyen* (www.estillyen.com). Concerning the worth of words, he offers the following: "The notion that 'a picture is worth a thousand words' comes forth as naught when one considers that Edgar Allan Poe used a mere thirteen words to write 'All that we see or seem is but a dream within a dream.'"